A NEW SENSATION

"Why were you riding so hard and so far away from my village? Did you leave of your own choice, or from fear? Was I wrong to trust you? Did you come near my village because you were helping white men who would enjoy seeing me and my people dead? Did you leave my village to return to those men?"

Sheleen gasped.

She went pale at the accusation.

"No, I wasn't near your village to bring harm to your people," she blurted out. She reached up and wiped tears from her cheeks with the back of her hand. "And, no. I didn't leave your village of my own choosing. Your…Shaman…Moon Eagle…he encouraged it. He made it very clear that I wasn't wanted among your people."

Midnight Wolf was so stunned by what she'd said, he found it hard to speak.

His Shaman?

Moon Eagle?

How could his trusted Shaman do such a thing, knowing that his chief had powerful feelings for this woman?

It was proof of just how much Moon Eagle resented the woman—not only because her skin was white, but because she had stolen his chief's heart!

CASSIE EDWARDS

SAVAGE INTRIGUE

LEISURE BOOKS NEW YORK CITY

A LEISURE BOOK®

June 2007

Published by

Dorchester Publishing Co., Inc.
200 Madison Avenue
New York, NY 10016

ISBN-10: 0-8439-5536-8
ISBN-13: 978-0-8439-5536-1

The name "Leisure Books" and the stylized "L" with design are
trademarks of Dorchester Publishing Co., Inc.

Printed in the United States of America.

Visit us on the web at www.dorchesterpub.com.

O ye people, be ye healed;
Life anew I bring unto ye.
O ye people, be ye healed;
Life anew I bring unto ye.
Through the Father over all
Do I thus.
Life anew I bring unto ye.

—Good Eagle,
Dakota Holy Man

SAVAGE INTRIGUE

CHAPTER ONE

And now on the midnight sky I look,
And my heart grows full of weeping,
Each star is to me a sealed book,
Some tale of that loved one keeping.
—*Mrs. Crawford*

*Secret Lake, Wisconsin—1865; April, In the Moon of
the Grass Appearing*

Dawn had swept away the darkness; the stars now
rested until another night brought them forth to
shine and sparkle again against the midnight sky.
The sides of the tepee glowed warmly from within
as the flickering of the cedar fire in the fire pit
burned low. Midnight Wolf, a young chief of twenty-
five winters, stared into the dancing flames, deep in
thought.

He was a warrior, fine and tall, and strongly mus-

1

cled. His long, sleek black hair framed his bronzed, sculpted face, and hung down his back to his waist. He wore a breechclout and moccasins that were beautifully stitched with beadwork.

His midnight-dark eyes were filled with painful memories as he thought back three winters to the time when several of his Dakota brethren were hung by *washechu,* white men. The families of the hanged warriors had then been forced to leave beautiful Minnesota, their true homeland.

Afraid that his Dakota Wolf Band might be next, although Midnight Wolf ruled with a peaceful hand, he'd led his people away from the misery that had swept their homeland, taking them to a more peaceful place called Wisconsin.

Hiding their homes deep in a great forest wilderness, they had found a peaceful, loving sanctuary there.

Ho, yes, all of his people were content in this village of one hundred lodges that was surrounded by thick trees on three sides, a lake on the fourth.

They had established their homes beside the lake that Midnight Wolf had, himself, named Secret Lake. He hoped that it would remain a secret place known only by his people.

Thus far, since having arrived there, he and his Wolf Band had not been disturbed or harrassed by the white community.

Midnight Wolf continued to ponder what had happened three winters ago, when he had been a witness to what lengths the *washechu* would go in their efforts to annihilate people with red skin.

He knew that confrontation with whites was something he must keep from happening. Peace must be kept for the preservation of his race!

"My chief, might I have a word with you?"

The sound of a voice outside his lodge drew Midnight Wolf's thoughts back to the present.

He knew the voice.

It was Night Walker, his best friend and most trusted scout, who kept Midnight Wolf informed about news of the white community.

Midnight Wolf knew that some of his Dakota brethren had not fled Minnesota when they had been ordered to go to a reservation far away, but instead hid themselves in small groups throughout their homeland.

He knew that the white government would not give up until all the Dakota were gone from Minnesota. He feared the times when he heard that friends from other bands had died at the hands of the *washechu.*

Afraid that this might be one of those days, Midnight Wolf rose dispiritedly to his feet. He held back the entrance flap and nodded to Night Walker. "*Hun-hun-he,*" he said in greeting. "What news have you brought your chief?"

He already knew that the news was not good. He could see pain in the depths of his friend's dark eyes.

"The White Chief, Abraham Lincoln, was shot

and is dead," Night Walker said, his voice devoid of emotion as he stepped past Midnight Wolf into his chief's lodge. "It happened some days ago, but this was as soon as I could carry the news to you."

Midnight Wolf heard the words, but found them hard to believe. The White Chief had been so powerful, all he had to do was say the word and what he had asked was done.

"Who killed him? How was it done?" Midnight Wolf demanded. "Did the one who did this thing have white skin, black . . . or red?"

"It was a white man who shot him," Night Walker replied. His response surprised Midnight Wolf. Night Walker's eyes showed that he had felt the same shock as his chief when word had come that Abraham Lincoln had been killed.

"One of his own people?" Midnight Wolf asked incredulously. *Ho,* he *was* stunned to know that someone from the white community had hated their leader enough to kill him. He had thought the *washechu* almost worshipped the man, as the Dakota worshipped their *Wakan Tanka* or Big Holy, who was the maker of all things—earth, sky, and water.

Wakan Tanka breathed life and motion into all things, both visible and invisible. He was over all, through all, and in all. Great as was the sun, and good as was the earth, the greatness and goodness of the Big Holy were not surpassed by either.

The Dakota could look at nothing without seeing

4

Wakan Tanka; they could never, evade his presence, for it pervaded all things and filled all spaces.

All of the mysteries of birth, life, and death; all the wonders of lightning, thunder, wind, and rain, were but the evidence of his everlasting and encompassing power.

Midnight Wolf had thought that Abraham Lincoln was all those things to his people. He now knew that there was one main difference: no man could kill *Wakan Tanka!*

"*Ho*, a white man worked single-handedly to kill the *wasechu* leader." Night Walker lowered his eyes before telling the rest of his news.

"Night Walker, is there something else that must be said?" Midnight Wolf asked. He noticed how his scout had gone suddenly, strangely silent, and knew it was not out of grief over the death of the white leader.

No Dakota would grieve the loss of life of any white leader. To them, one *washechu* leader was as untrustworthy as another.

Night Walker lifted his eyes and gazed directly at Midnight Wolf. "*Ho*, there is more to tell you," he said thickly. "As before, the whites are searching for any Dakota people they can find, and hanging all the warriors."

His eyes narrowed angrily. "I just barely escaped with my own life after seeing one of our brethren killed by the hangman's noose, where he still hangs today, to teach the red people what will happen if we show ourselves in a white community," Night Walker said fiercely.

Midnight Wolf felt an anger inside his heart that made him almost feel sick to his stomach. The hangings were beginning all over again, just as he had feared when he fled Minnesota with his Wolf Band.

He slowly shook his head back and forth. "Will it ever stop?" he said, his voice drawn.

"Not until there are no more Dakota walking on Minnesota soil," Night Walker said. "I came today to tell you what I know so that you can warn our band to be even more cautious than before. I know that we have been safe where we now make our homes, and that the Wisconsin whites seem not to have the same hatred for our people as those who have taken our homeland from us. But one never knows. You must prepare our people well for what may come our way."

Midnight Wolf placed a gentle hand on his friend's bare shoulder. "*Pilamaye*, thank you, my friend, for coming to your chief with this warning," he said. "And it is best that you do not return to our homeland now, at least not until the lynching fever has again passed."

"Until now, I have managed well to avoid contact with *washechu*, except for those who are my secret, trusted friends," Night Walker said, nodding. "But I realize that for now it would be best to stay close to home. I will spend time now with my family."

6

"That is good," Midnight Wolf said, nodding. "Go now, though, and before you go to be with your family, spread the word from tepee to tepee and tell our warriors about a council that we must have to warn the others of what is happening in our homeland."

"I do not understand why their grief over their lost chief makes them kill our people," Night Walker said angrily.

"They need no true reason to go against our people," Midnight Wolf replied. "I just wish that all of those Dakota who stayed behind in our homeland had fled with us. Thus far, our new home has been untouched by the white man's evil and greed."

"Give more white people time to realize the beauty of this land where we now reside, and they will come and cut down the trees and clear the land for their own lodges," Night Walker said, his voice drawn and tight. "But first they will clear the land of us red people."

"Until that time, we must make the best of what we have and keep an eye out for interlopers on this land we have now claimed as ours," Midnight Wolf said, his eyes gleaming with anger. "If necessary, we will draw our weapons against those who do come. Although I am chief, a *wicasa okinihan*, an honorable and respected individual, who leads with the promise of peace, if I am pushed by the *washechu* again, as we were while we lived at our homeland, I will no longer be a man of peace. I will fight to the end to save what is ours."

His voice softened as he added, *Oyatenimk-tewacinyelo,* I want our people to live."

He lowered his hand from Night Walker's shoulder. "Go. Go now," he said. "Spread the word about our council. I will join you at the council house soon."

Night Walker nodded, then turned and left the tepee. He ran from lodge to lodge announcing the council, while Midnight Wolf stepped from his tepee and looked around the village.

Strings of smoke from cooking fires were twisting slowly into the air from the smoke holes of each lodge.

Although it was early on this new day, the children were outside their homes, playing and laughing. The boys were practicing their foot races, while the girls were playing with the dolls their mothers had made for them out of corn husks.

Some elderly warriors sat in little circles, moving their eagle wing fans slowly, the red willow bark in their pipes fragrant in the air.

Midnight Wolf walked around to the back of his tepee and sighed at the wonder and loveliness of the green forest. There were maples, birches, and tall and statuesque pine trees.

The forest was so peaceful, a paradise his people enjoyed in every way.

He turned and took in the peacefulness of their lake, where a few ducks had landed to enjoy the water. Most of them had gone farther, to a lake a short distance away, where no one lived close to bother them.

He then turned and gazed at the fields of corn where the summer's crops would grow and mature. The garden area was protected by a fence of bushes, and branches of trees that were skillfully woven together, and also by piles of dried corn roots and weed debris placed along the field edges over these past three years of their residence in Wisconsin.

He walked back around to the front of his tepee and watched as more of his people emerged from their lodges to begin their morning activities.

It was such a wondrous scene of peace and contentment. He vowed that he would do what he must to keep it that way.

His eyes followed one warrior after another as they walked toward the large council house that had been built at the far side of the village. He knew he must go soon and tell them about this newest disaster that had befallen their Dakota brethren.

It made his heart ache to know that white people thought nothing of hurting and killing the Dakota, as though they did not realize that his people had souls!

It was as though they saw red people as no more than a fly or gnat one swats to be rid of an annoyance.

"My chief! My chief!"

The voice of a young warrior brought Midnight

Wolf out of his reverie. He was glad of the interruption, because he did not like where his thoughts had taken him.

He smiled as a young brave of ten winters ran up to him, his dark eyes anxious, his right hand gripping a small bow of his own making.

"You have finished your bow, have you not?" Midnight Wolf said, reaching for the bow and taking it from the child.

He looked it over carefully, ran his fingers along the carvings on the wood, then tested the spring of the bowstring.

"Do you like it?" Gentle Bear asked, his eyes anxiously staring into Midnight Wolf's. "Do you approve? Do you think I will be able to bring home food with my bow and arrows for my mother's cook pot?"

Smiling broadly, glad to have this momentary reprieve from his duties as chief, Midnight Wolf placed the bow in Gentle Bear's hand again. "You did yourself proud," he said. He placed a hand on the young brave's bare shoulder. "I see much food in your mother's cook pot after your hunts."

"I am so glad you approve," Gentle Bear said. He proudly positioned his bow over his left shoulder and held it in place there with a hand. "I would like to go and try out my new bow today. My chief, I have seen many green-headed ducks headed toward the larger body of water, but only a few have landed in our lake. I would like to go where there are many and use my bow and arrows to bring back some of the fatter ones. Would it not be easy to down a duck even with a young brave's bow? Would these ducks not be a juicy feast on my mother's roasting fire?"

Knowing that he had no choice but to disappoint Gentle Bear this morning, Midnight Wolf slowly lowered his hand from the young brave's shoulder. It was not safe for Gentle Bear to go alone into the forest, not with the possibility of renewed trouble with whites, even this far from Minnesota land.

He hesitated to tell Gentle Bear his decision, for he understood the importance of learning the art of independence.

And this child meant so much to Midnight Wolf.

It was the custom among the Dakota that each warrior voluntarily adopt, as a special charge, some younger boy. The older one appointed himself as guardian and helpmate to the younger; the obligation lasted throughout life. Through war or peace, in times good or ill, the brotherhood was to exist.

The ties assumed were as strong as if they had been actual blood ties. This trust put in the older companion was never questioned, not even by parents, and a mother never worried when her son was with his caretaker.

Gentle Bear's *ahte*, father, had died in a panther's attack a moon ago, so Midnight Wolf's duties to this child were now twofold.

"My chief, you have not answered me," Gentle Bear said. He searched Midnight Wolf's eyes. "Why do you hesitate?"

11

"All I can tell you at this time is that I do not believe it wise for you to leave the village to hunt, especially by yourself," Midnight Wolf said. He saw the questioning and disappointment in Gentle Bear's wide eyes. "Troubling news has been brought to me today. I do not feel that you should go alone today, to hunt, even though I know how anxious you are to try out your new bow."

"What news?" Gentle Bear asked, his eyes widening. "What has happened that makes you so wary?"

"It is something a young brave should not worry himself about, so go and play with your friends until I tell you it is safe for you to go into the forest alone," Midnight Wolf said gently. "Show them your bow. Let them run their hands over the carvings that you worked in the wood, yourself. It is something to be proud of. Show it off so that others can see why you are so proud."

"I so badly wanted to try it out," Gentle Bear said solemnly; then he smiled. "But I know that if you thought it was safe for me to go into the forest to shoot my mother a duck for her cook pot, you would not keep me from doing it."

He looked over his shoulder at his friends, who were still practicing for an upcoming foot race, then again smiled up at Midnight Wolf. "I will go and show off my bow and then join the others to practice for the race," he said anxiously. "My *ina*, mother, will understand if I do not bring her a duck today."

12

"*Ho,* yes, she will," Midnight Wolf said. He smiled warmly at the young brave who made his chief so very proud of him. He was pleased by the boy's ability to take advice so well.

He watched Gentle Bear run over to his friends. He smiled proudly as he watched the young brave show off his new bow, and saw how each child took turns holding it and running his fingers across the carvings. Obviously the boys admired Gentle Bear's skills at bow making.

Then Midnight Wolf's eyes were drawn elsewhere as he noticed more of his warriors entering the council house. He walked toward it, himself, ready to talk business with his trusted warriors.

He was proud of them all; they were men of vision and humane ideals. There was great honesty and loyalty among his warriors, as well as a beautiful faith and humanity. But that was not so surprising; they came from an unselfish, devout people.

The philosophical ideal of his Dakota people was harmony, and their goal was peace.

But when forced to fight for a just and righteous cause, for the preservation of their race, *ho,* yes, they would fight! Today, however, he planned to speak of ways other than fighting that would still keep his people safe and happy at their Secret Lake.

He was their leader.

He must assure them of these things!

He hated thinking about those Dakota people

who had stayed behind on Minnesota land, They were being hunted like mad dogs, and he knew there was nothing he could do for them.

He had his own people's safety to secure! And . . . he . . . would!

Proud-shouldered, and with a tight, set jaw, he stepped inside the council house and found his faithful warriors sitting around a fire in a half circle, their eyes going to him trustingly.

He hated telling them what was transpiring elsewhere, but he must make them aware of the need to be even more cautious than before.

He looked from man to man, then began. "My warriors, Night Walker brought news today of the white chief's passing," he said, "killed by one of his own people."

He heard soft gasps from the warriors. They were as stunned as Midnight Wolf when he had first heard the news. Everyone had thought that the white leader was someone who would never die, especially not at the hands of one of his own kind.

He told his warriors all that he knew about how the fallen white leader had died. Then came the warnings.

"Everyone must be more careful than ever before since we arrived at our home at Secret Lake," Midnight Wolf said solemnly. "Keep your children close at hand, as well as your wives. If your wife needs to go and dig roots, or anything else that takes her from the village proper, then you must accompany her. If your children wish to run and play, they must do it in the circle of our village."

He continued telling them what was expected of them, then stopped and again looked at each man, one at a time.

"Do you all understand the danger we might be facing?" he then asked.

Everyone nodded and spoke up, confirming that what he had said had been heard and understood.

"It is with a sad heart that I say our lives might once again be threatened by the *washechu*. Some white men have taken the law into their own hands at the news of their leader's assassination," Midnight Wolf said tightly. "But what must be, must be. We will do what we must to protect our loved ones."

Again his warriors nodded.

Slowly they dispersed and went to their own lodges to share this latest news with their wives, while their children played trustingly outside their homes.

Midnight Wolf lived alone. He had never taken a wife because troubled times had not given him enough peace to search for the woman he would have children with.

With his mother and father already gone to the heavens, to walk amid the clouds, Midnight Wolf went alone to his own tepee.

Again he sat beside the fire, his mind going over all that he had told his warriors today, hoping that it was enough.

Then he thought of Gentle Bear and how disappointed he had been to have to curtail his activities because of the danger posed by white people.

"Some day, oh, some day, surely it will be different," Midnight Wolf whispered to himself.

He heard a strange sound, like a whisper, and then he was aware of the shuffling of his entrance flap, which hung loose and untied, as wind swept through it.

"*Ahte*, Father? *Ina*, Mother? Are you there?" Midnight Wolf whispered. He truly felt their presence, as he did so often when he was troubled.

CHAPTER TWO

The link of nature draw me: flesh of flesh,
Bone of my bone thou art, and from thy state
Mine never shall be parted, bliss or woe.
—*John Milton*

Attired in a pretty, flowing dress, her long black hair blowing in the wind behind her, eighteen-year-old Sheleen Hicks was eager to return home. Ever since the announcement of the death of President Lincoln, she had not felt safe riding out alone.

Sheleen snapped her reins and sent the horse and wagon at a faster clip down the long, narrow path that led to the cabin deep in the woods where she and her father lived. It had been built isolated from neighbors so that they would feel safe.

Until now, they *had* felt safe.

She and her physician father had fled St. Paul,

Minnesota, three years ago, immediately after hearing of the unrest in Mankato, where some Dakota Indians had rebelled against the white government over not being given the annuities promised them.

With starving families, the Dakotas had gone to the government begging for the supplies that had been promised them by treaties, only to be laughed at and told that if they were hungry, they should go and eat grass, or cow dung.

That had been the last straw for those Dakota warriors. They had rebelled.

Several white people had been killed.

When those warriors were finally stopped and rounded up, they were found guilty of their crimes by the government, and hanged.

Sheleen and her father, a kindhearted and gentle physician, had cared for the Dakota through the years, treating the sick and wounded. After the hangings, they got wind of some men saying it was time to lynch the traitor physician. Sheleen and her father had fled Minnesota and had found safe refuge in the woods of Wisconsin.

They had established their new home and had kept to themselves. They had felt safe enough until they'd heard of Lincoln's assassination and how it was causing renewed unrest in Minnesota.

There was a search for those Dakota who had not fled Minnesota three years ago. Lynching fever had grabbed hold of the lawless again, as it had three years earlier. People were taking advantage of the unrest in the country and were now hanging all of the Dakota people they could find.

Afraid those unruly men might go across the border between Minnesota and Wisconsin and renew the search for Sheleen's father and herself, she had encouraged her father to flee again.

He had agreed.

Sheleen had left home just long enough to gather supplies for their journey. She had gone to the nearest small town, where no one knew of her father's connection with the Dakota, or even that he was a physician.

Eager to be on her way, Sheleen had grabbed up what she needed at the General Store and was close now to her cabin built in the midst of a thick grove of trees.

The noonday sun was streaming down through the leaves overhead onto the worn path. Sheleen spotted the cabin a short distance away.

She sighed in relief to know that she would soon be with her father again. As soon as they possibly could, they would be on their way to a new home, and hopefully, continued safety and freedom.

Sheleen was proud to say that although she was of slender build, she was a self-sufficient young woman nonetheless. Her father had always said how pretty she was with her angular face, dark brown eyes, and her waist-length raven-black hair.

The physical traits that she had inherited from her father were her slight build, and her fair skin.

19

Other than that, she had taken after her mother, whose eyes had been dark and whose hair had been black.

At times like this, when Sheleen felt danger all around her, she missed not only her true mother, but her stepmother, as well. She knew that her father missed them, too.

In so many ways her stepmother and true mother had been different. Sheleen's stepmother had been tall and stately, with golden hair in a tight, demure bun atop her head. Her skin had been fair, and burned easily if she stayed in the sun for too long. Her delicate complexion had kept her from her favorite pastime of gardening, making it difficult to care for her beautiful red rose bushes.

Because of her stepmother's love of roses, Sheleen's father had tended to her garden for her. As long as the roses had been in bloom, one long-stemmed rose had always sat in the middle of their dining table.

Yes, this mother had been vastly different from Sheleen's first, true mother. Her stepmother, Dorthea, had been originally from Connecticut, and although she adapted to the Minnesota frontier way of life after traveling there with her family before she met and married Sheleen's father, she had retained a taste for Eastern fashion.

She followed the contemporary trends in both

clothing and culture, even subscribing to *Harper's Weekly* and *Mother's Magazine*.

Her wardrobe had included silk, cashmere, linen, and chenille dresses. Her favorite hat had been of green velvet, brimming with artificial flowers and colorful feathers. In the winter she wore kid and beaver gloves, otter muffs, and cuffs.

She had been the exact opposite of Sheleen's true mother, who had worn buckskin dresses and whose black hair fell long and loose to her waist.

But it had been the second wife who took full advantage of her husband's role of physician, as well as the prestige and wealth that went with it. She had loved everything about being a physician's wife, until the day those who resented her husband's past life among Indians followed and killed this woman, his second wife, with one gun blast to her belly.

Both of Sheleen's mothers had been dead now for some time and she and her father had grown used to being alone. Sheleen had to confess, though, that she missed a normal way of life. At her age, most women were married and had children. With her and her father's need to stay hidden from the world in order to survive, she had not had the opportunity to meet a man, much less fall in love and marry one!

Yes, she did miss that side of life. She doubted she would ever have a husband, for as long as there were men out there who hated the Dakota people, and Indians in general, they would also hate her and her father for their role in helping the Dakota.

Putting such things as marriage and children from her mind, Sheleen wiped tears of regret from her eyes. She knew her father also felt regret. He missed being able to help people by doctoring them.

Knowing it was not wise to linger on the sadness of her past, Sheleen forced her thoughts elsewhere. Her mind turned to a mystery that she often struggled to understand. For as far back as she could remember, she had had dreams of wolves. They were never threatening dreams, but instead left her filled with awe after awakening.

In her dreams, it was always the same. When she was smaller and did not yet have the skill to ride a horse, the wolves appeared in her dreams of being alone, running through fields of flowers.

There were always several wolves, all beautifully white, and with eyes so piercingly blue, it was as though the sky were reflected in them.

It was as though they were there to protect her, as though they knew it was dangerous for a young girl to be alone so far from her home.

Then when she was older, she would dream of riding her favorite horse, and traveling too far from the safety of her home before realizing it. Again, the wolves would appear in number. In the dream they would be running on both sides of her horse, their mystically blue eyes gazing intently into hers.

Never had she felt threatened by the wolves in

her dreams, and when she awakened and realized that she had dreamed about them again, she was not frightened but intrigued.

She had had the same dream last night, but this time the wolves had paced back and forth in front of her and her father's cabin. . . .

"It is as though they always came in my sleep to warn me about something," she whispered to herself.

Suddenly her thoughts were swept away as the rays of the sun flashed in her eyes through the trees, blinding her.

But as she rode onward, out of that slash of sunlight, she saw something that was so unreal, she did not understand how it could be!

She blinked her eyes, then gazed ahead again. She felt as though a knife were piercing her heart when she understood that what she saw was real enough.

In her absence, her father had been hanged!

From the limb of a tall, old oak, he gently swayed in the soft breeze.

Filled with a despair that she had felt before when she had lost loved ones, Sheleen drew a tight rein and stopped.

She stared unblinkingly at her father, too stunned by what she was seeing to even move, or to think. It was as though the world had come to a standstill.

Her father?

How could he be dead?

And who . . . ?

It suddenly came to her that whoever had killed her father might be waiting for her!

She slid her fingers around the small pearl-handled derringer that she had slid into her pocket this morning before leaving the cabin.

She was so remorseful. Her father had meant the world to her, a man who had taken more than one family of Dakotas into his home, to feed them before their flight from Minnesota.

Sheleen choked back a sob as she gazed at her father. His eyes stared straight ahead as the breeze rocked his body back and forth beneath the thick limb.

She knew that no matter how much she might be placing herself in danger by doing it, she would take her father down from that horrible place and remove the hideous rope from around his neck.

She pulled the wagon directly beneath her father and drew rein.

Her heart pounding, knowing that her father's assailant could even now be taking aim to kill her, Sheleen withdraw a knife from her supplies and cut the rope. Her father fell directly into the wagon.

She forced herself to hold back her tears. She had to keep her sanity at this moment in order to survive. But it had never been as hard as now to move onward. "Papa, oh, Papa, why?" she sobbed.

Knowing time was passing, time that she needed to escape the killer's wrath, she sat back on the seat and guided the horse and wagon into the barn.

Knowing that she had no time to bury her father, she did the next best thing. She laid him inside the barn, then spread straw over his body as thick as she could. She knelt beside the makeshift grave and said a silent prayer.

She hurried to her feet, her hand on the derringer in her pocket. She stood perfectly still for a moment, just listening.

Thus far she had heard nothing threatening, not even a horse that could belong to someone else.

She stepped slowly outside.

Again she saw nothing that seemed out of place.

Her breathing shallow, her pulse racing, she crept into the back door of the cabin, through the kitchen, toward her bedroom, then stopped in horror when a man stepped from her bedroom. He stood directly in front of her, holding a rifle that was aimed straight at her belly.

He was a grizzly looking man, whiskered, burly, and large, with piercing green eyes.

He was someone she did not know.

But she was sure this was the man who had hanged her father.

He laughed and said, "Gotcha! First your pa, and now you."

His gaze raked slowly over her and then he looked directly into her eyes. "But you know what?" he said, his eyes gleaming with evil intent. "I'm gonna get way more from you than I did your pa. I'm going to rape you before I kill you."

"Is that why you allowed me time to take my father down from the tree?" Sheleen demanded, feeling foolish for having stepped right into a trap.

She was very aware of the cold steel against the palm of her hand as she tightened her fingers around the pistol in her pocket.

Now she had to find the right opportunity to use it, or she was most certainly as doomed as her father.

Just as the man took a step toward Sheleen, a movement behind him, a sound, a cat's sudden meow, caused him to flinch. He looked away from Sheleen just long enough for her to grab her pistol from her pocket and shoot the man's rifle from his hand.

He let out a cry of pain as he looked down and saw what else Sheleen had done.

Not only had she removed the rifle from his hand, but she had also shot off his trigger finger!

He stared, mortified, at the bloody finger that lay on a braided rug at his feet, and then at the blood dripping from his hand where the finger had just been.

He glared at Sheleen. "Bitch!" he growled.

And then he changed his tune as a look of desperation came into his eyes. "You've gotta help me," he said, his voice quivering. "I'm losing a lot of blood. I'm gonna bleed to death if you don't help me stop it!"

"Well, now, you should have thought of such possibilities when you hanged my father and then waited to ambush and rape me," Sheleen said, standing her ground, her pistol now aimed at the man's gut. "I should finish the job and kill you, but I doubt you'll be any more trouble for me, or anyone, so I won't waste another bullet on you."

She nodded toward the front door. "Get out!" she screamed, furious that she couldn't murder anyone in cold blood, even though this man had killed her father.

"Please help me," the man begged. "You can see that I'm losing too much blood. Your pa was a doctor. Surely you know what to do to help me. I promise if you do, I'll never cause you any more trouble."

Sheleen nodded toward the door. "Go to where you've hidden your horse and get out of here," she said, doubting that he would get far because he was losing so much blood.

Holding his injured hand with the other, the man stumbled from the cabin, looking pale and faint.

Sheleen stiffened and listened for him to ride away. When she heard hoofbeats, she was overwhelmed by relief that he was gone and then sorrow at the loss of her father. Weak-kneed at coming so close to losing her own life, she crumpled to the floor and held her face in her hands, and cried.

Her white cat, Fluffy, came and climbed on Sheleen's lap, purring.

Sheleen cuddled her close. "Thank you for saving

27

my life," she sobbed. "If you hadn't made a noise, drawing the murderer's attention from me, I'd probably be dead right now."

Realizing that the man might get as far as someone's house, and lie about her, saying that she had attacked him, she realized time was of the essence. She had to flee. Sheleen placed Fluffy on the floor, stood up, and hurried around the cabin.

She stuffed what supplies she could carry on her horse into her saddlebag, and started to leave, then stopped.

She looked down at what she was wearing.

She would be a target if she traveled in anything other than men's clothes, for it was not normal for a woman to travel alone.

She went to her father's bedroom and hurriedly pulled on some of his clothes: a pair of breeches and a shirt. She was glad at this moment that he had been of such a slight build that she could wear his clothes. Her father had grown gaunt after having lost two wives, and also his freedom to help people who were in need.

Sheleen coiled her hair beneath the crown of one of her father's hats, then again started to leave, but stopped and looked at two things . . . her father's satchel filled with medical supplies, and her cat.

She would take them both.

She took her saddlebag and her father's satchel outside, chose their faster horse, a black mustang, and readied it for travel, leaving the saddlebag open, so she could slide Fluffy into it atop her clothes.

Then she freed the other horse, went back inside, and grabbed a rifle and her cat.

She stopped and took a long look at the severed finger that lay on the rug at her feet, shivered, then hurried outside again.

After getting everything secured on her horse, she turned and took one last look at the barn where her father was resting peacefully beneath the soft, sweet-smelling straw.

Sobbing hard, she mounted her horse and left.

She knew that if that whiskered man had anything to say about it, and could find a way to come after her, she might not live to see many more sunsets. Tears filled her eyes again as she recalled the times when she and her father had sat on the front porch of their cabin in their wicker rocking chairs as the setting sun splashed the sky with glorious orange.

Those times were gone now, forever.

"It's just the two of us now," Sheleen said, reaching over and stroking her cat's thick fur, so glad Fluffy was content at the moment to rest comfortably in the saddlebag.

While looking into her cat's unusual blue eyes, she was suddenly reminded of the dream that she had had last night.

The wolves!

She now understood.

They had appeared to her in her dream, to warn

her about the danger that had faced her and her father today!

She was stunned to know that her dream of wolves did have a meaning. Oh, if she had only been able to interpret it soon enough, her father might still be alive.

CHAPTER THREE

> Where thoughts serenely sweet express
> How pure, how dear their dwelling place.
> —*George Gordon, Lord Byron*

Gentle Bear couldn't be more proud as he walked through the forest beside Midnight Wolf.

Although he had not been able to go hunt the green-headed ducks with his new bow the day before, his chief had come early this morning to take him hunting. This was even better than his original plan.

He was especially happy because today's expedition was his chief's idea, not Gentle Bear's.

That meant that his chief also wanted this hunt with Gentle Bear.

Midnight Wolf gazed at Gentle Bear, noting how the child walked with a lifted, proud chin, as his eyes scanned the woodlands for any sign of a rabbit, their chosen prey today instead of duck.

Knowing how he had disappointed Gentle Bear the day before, and realizing just how eager a young warrior can be once he did make a bow for himself, Midnight Wolf had decided to take Gentle Bear on a hunt today. This was not only to satisfy his young charge's need to use his new bow, but also to make Gentle Bear feel at ease with the world after hearing the horrible news of hangings back on land where they had once made their home.

Midnight Wolf had first thought not to tell the women and children about the threat, planning to leave the responsibility for their safety in the hands of their husbands and fathers.

But he had changed his mind. He preferred to be open with all of his people about things.

He decided that it was best if they all shared in the responsibility of knowing not only the good that happened in their daily lives, but also the evil.

If the women knew about the hangings, they would keep their children close at hand, and not allow them to go too far from their homes, unless they were accompanied by their warrior fathers.

Even the women were not allowed to leave the village now, not even to dig for roots for their cook pots, or anything else that might draw them far from the village. There was enough wood for their cooking fires close by in the forest, as well as water in the nearby lake.

For now, that was all they needed to sustain them other than what their warrior husbands brought home for their cook pots.

"You are not disappointed that we are not going to hunt for ducks today, are you?" Midnight Wolf asked Gentle Bear, drawing the young brave's eyes to him. "It is much safer to stay closer to our home right now and limit your hunt to rabbits. Will you not be proud to show off the rabbit's fluffy tail? Are you not eager to have rabbit's feet to hang on a string of leather for your good-luck charm?"

"*Gah-ween,* no, I am not disappointed," Gentle Bear said. He smiled broadly up at his chief. "It is good to be alone with you wherever you choose to take me. I am proud to be your charge, my chief."

"I am proud that you are," Midnight Wolf said.

He reached over and placed a gentle hand on the young brave's bare shoulder as he gazed at what his charge wore today. Like Midnight Wolf, Gentle Bear wore a brief breechclout and moccasins.

And like Midnight Wolf, the young brave wore a headband that held his long black hair back from his eyes.

But only Midnight Wolf wore a single eagle feather in a loop of his hair; it was a sign that proud chiefs always wore to prove they were the leader of their people.

Like Gentle Bear, Midnight Wolf carried his own bow, and on his back was a quiver of arrows.

"If we do return home with rabbits, I plan to dye

the tails pretty colors for my mother to wear as hair ornaments," Gentle Bear said. "I will also save some strips of fur to make my mother a neck ornament."

"You are a good son to your *ina*," Midnight Wolf said, pride in his eyes as he gazed down at the child. "Both your mother and I are very proud of you."

"I hope never to disappoint," Gentle Bear said.

Then he jumped with alarm when a rabbit hopped suddenly from the bushes at their left side. It appeared so quickly that Gentle Bear was caught off guard, unable to notch his bow with an arrow fast enough to shoot it.

"He is gone so quickly," Gentle Bear said, disappointment in his eyes and voice as he lowered his bow to his side.

"*Hi-yupo*, come. Where there is one, there are more," Midnight Wolf said, putting a hand out before Gentle Bear to stop him. "A good hunter watches all animals, for one often betrays the presence of another, just as this rabbit has betrayed those who are hiding in those bushes at your left side."

"There are more rabbits?" Gentle Bear asked. His eyes were wide as he slowly drew an arrow from his quiver, notching it to his bowstring.

"*Ahpe*, wait. Just watch, do not move, and scarcely breathe," Midnight Wolf said.

Gentle Bear held his armed bow ready to fire as he watched the bushes whence the first rabbit had come.

As his chief had suggested, he barely breathed, and watched everything around him. He had hunted with his chief before and Midnight Wolf had taught him the signs to watch for while he was on the hunt—bits of hair, grass, broken sticks, bark of trees, footprints, and overturned stones.

But most of all Gentle Bear had been told to depend on his sense of smell. The most noticeable scents were of the porcupine, badger, bear, and skunk. He had been told that a beaver dam could be smelled for some distance.

Suddenly there was a flurry of feet and fur as more than one rabbit leaped from hiding in the bushes, scattering in several directions.

Gentle Bear adjusted the position of his bow, keeping his aim on one of the rabbits in particular. Midnight Wolf realized that Gentle Bear hated taking the life of something so tiny and sweet, but that the boy was trying to prove his worth as a hunter to his chief and would not disappoint him.

Gentle Bear released the arrow from the string and watched it take down the rabbit, while another rabbit beside him fell, too, killed by an arrow in its side.

After both rabbits fell and were still, Gentle Bear

looked over at his chief. "Both of our aims were accurate," he said, smiling broadly.

Midnight Wolf had not planned to actually participate in the hunt until he saw that his charge was only going to be able to kill one of the rabbits.

Knowing that Gentle Bear had wanted more than one, from which to make his gifts for his mother, Midnight Wolf had made a quick decision to take down one rabbit, himself, then give it to Gentle Bear.

"*Ho,* your aim, as well as mine, was accurate today," Midnight Wolf said. "But since the rabbits are for gifts you will make your mother, besides the meat that she will cook in her cook pot, I will leave the skinning of the animals to you."

Gentle Bear's smile faded. "You will?" he gulped out, his eyes wide. "You . . . have always before . . . skinned what I killed."

"That was because I did not think you old enough to handle a knife. Now I feel that you are," Midnight Wolf said.

He walked with Gentle Bear over to the rabbits.

They stood over the carcasses for a moment, then Midnight Wolf took his knife from the sheath at his right side and handed it toward Gentle Bear.

Gentle Bear stared for a moment at the large, sharp knife, swallowed hard, then took it.

He gazed up into his chief's eyes, then laid his bow aside and knelt beside the rabbits.

"You have seen me clean many animals, so you should know what to do," Midnight Wolf said. He moved to his haunches beside the young brave. "But be very aware of the sharpness of the knife. We do not want to add one of your fingers to your mother's cook pot."

That comment made Gentle Bear turn pale; then he laughed. "*Gah-ween,* no, it would not taste very good," he said.

As Midnight Wolf watched Gentle Bear skin the rabbits, his mind wandered. He could not help thinking about the evil being done to the Dakota people. A part of him wanted to go and help those who were being sought by the washechu, yet he knew that to do this would be to bring doom to his own band of people, and he was the one who was supposed to keep them safe.

"Do you see?" Gentle Bear said. He smiled proudly up at Midnight Wolf. "I have skinned them both."

"That is good, very good," Midnight Wolf said, smiling down at his charge. "Your chief is proud."

Gentle Bear blushed shyly. "*Pilamaye,* thank you," he said, then held a rabbit tail in each of his hands. "See how fluffy they are? *Ina* will wear them proudly once I dye them pretty colors."

"*Ho,* she will wear them proudly," Midnight Wolf said. He patted the child's head. "Now let us return home. Your chief has many tasks waiting to be done."

"*Pilamaye,* thank you, for taking time from your

duties to hunt with me today," Gentle Bear said. He gathered up the skinned rabbits and slid them into a bag made of the skin of a mink, tanned with the hair on, which all men carried while hunting.

This bag was his chief's, but one day Gentle Bear would have his own, for he had proved today that he was a skilled hunter.

With the rabbits inside the bag, the tails tucked into the waistband of his breechclout, Gentle Bear walked proudly beside his chief toward home.

He could hardly wait to show off his kill to his friends, and especially to his mother.

She was his truest, best friend of all . . . next to his chief!

CHAPTER FOUR

Who walks with beauty has no need of fear;
The sun and moon and stars keep pace with him.
—*David Morton*

Sheleen had traveled until she reached a thick grove of rustling trees, where the limbs of tall cottonwoods hung low over a creek.

The sun was setting in an orange haze along the horizon, giving off just enough light for Sheleen to build a fire beside the water.

She had traveled as far as daylight allowed, and except for the company of her cat, this would be her first night alone beneath the stars.

She laughed to herself as Fluffy scampered away, chasing a field mouse.

"It's good you found yourself some supper," Sheleen said, spreading a blanket beside the fire. "I don't think you would like sharing mine."

She had not taken the time to bring food from her kitchen. A crack shot with a rifle, she knew that she would never be without food over her evening fires.

But this evening was different. She was exhausted, and not just from her long day on horseback. It was the realization that she would never see her father again, or be held in his loving arms, that left her so dispirited.

Because of one madman, her father was dead. She abhorred violence, but she did not regret what she had done to that madman.

"Yes, even if you live after losing so much blood, you'll never fire a gun again, unless . . ."

The thought of his learning how to shoot with his left hand caused Sheleen to glower into the softly burning campfire.

But that would take time, more time than he would have before she got far, far away from this part of the country.

While he healed up, if he survived, and then learned to shoot all over again, she would be settling into a new life somewhere new.

She forced herself not to think more about the hideous events of the day. She focused, instead, on her beautiful cat.

Fluffy had romped back to her and settled near the blanket, the mouse she had scampered after clasped gingerly between her teeth.

Then her cat dropped the mouse and allowed it to get a few inches from her, leapt on it, and again had it in her mouth.

"Fluffy, stop teasing the poor thing," Sheleen scolded. "Either let it go, or . . . or . . ."

She didn't have to say any more. The cat took the mouse away and began truly enjoying its catch by eating it, making Sheleen turn her head quickly away.

She hated seeing anything suffer, or die. She was a woman of much warmth, compassion, love, and emotion. The way life was these days, however, something had to die in order for something else to live.

"But not tonight as far as I'm concerned," she murmured, having eyed the tall brush a few feet from the creek. There were several berry bushes twined together with grape vines. On those vines were huge, round grapes just waiting to be picked and enjoyed. After today's traumatic experiences, all Sheleen felt she could eat was fruit. Anything else would lie too heavily on her stomach.

She rose and went to the bushes, plucked a handful of the grapes, then sat back down and stared into the slowly burning flames of the campfire.

Again her father came to her mind; she could not banish the image of him hanging in the tree. Tears filled her eyes and a shiver down her spine. She knew that she would live with that sight for the rest of her life.

She also hated the way she'd had to leave him, without a proper burial. But had she taken the time to dig a grave, the grizzly man would have more than likely come upon her as she was doing it and she would have been at his mercy.

She knew that she had done all she could for her father. She knew that he would have wanted what was safe for her and would have understood.

"I love you, Papa," she whispered, almost choking on the grape she was in the midst of swallowing.

"I've got to stop thinking about it," Sheleen whispered, as the sky darkened above her and stars twinkled down.

The moon was hidden momentarily by clouds, and then was bright and full again, giving the land around Sheleen a lovely, white sheen.

Somehow that made her feel safer.

Weary, bone-tired, and wanting to find solace in sleep, Sheleen reached for Fluffy and snuggled down on the blankets with the cat. Fluffy meowed, snuggled even closer, and both were soon fast asleep.

But it seemed only moments later that Sheleen was suddenly awakened by the shrill screeching cry of a panther in the distance.

Fluffy had been awakened by it, too. She stood up, snarling and baring her teeth as Sheleen quickly added wood to the fire, which she hoped would keep the panther at bay.

"Come on, Fluffy, things are okay now," Sheleen said, taking the cat in her arms once more.

Again she settled down on the blanket beside the fire. This time she pulled another blanket atop her and Fluffy as her cat again snuggled against her.

"Fluffy, one night, when I was a little girl and I was frightened by the dark, my father came to my bedroom and sat down on my bed and told me that whatever one fears in the dark is also afraid of you. Remember that, Fluffy, for Father was the smartest man on the earth."

Yes, she had always thought that no one could be as smart as her father, and had always remembered what he had told her that night whenever she was frightened by something.

But even as she hugged her father's words to her, she doubted that what he had said was true about a panther!

After a while, she finally drifted off into a sweet, peaceful sleep again.

CHAPTER FIVE

Is there one link within the past
That holds thy spirit yet?
—*Adelaide Anne Procter*

Raymond Hauser groaned as he waited for someone to come to the door.

He was dizzy with pain. He was not sure how much longer he could stand there, waiting for someone to come and, he hoped, treat him with a measure of kindness.

The thought of that wench shooting off his finger still seemed too hard to believe. No woman, ever, had bested Raymond Hauser.

But this time one had, and in the worst way. She had taken his trigger finger from him, a finger very valuable to a man like him, for he had no friends, only enemies. To protect himself from such enemies, a man had to be able to shoot his firearm.

His thoughts were interrupted when the door finally opened.

Raymond stiffened when he found a man standing there with a shotgun in his hand, the glow of a kerosene lamp inside defining the firearm very distinctly. Trembling, Raymond took an unsteady step away from the man.

"What are you doin' here this time of night, disturbing me and my wife's sleep?" the man said, his dark eyes glaring at Raymond.

"Sir, I mean you no harm," Raymond said, clutching his hand, which he had wrapped with some material from the tail end of his shirt.

Redness stained it, where his wound continued to seep blood.

"I beg you for help," Raymond said, his voice breaking. "I . . . I . . . was accosted by a highwayman. He wanted my horse and what I had in my saddlebag. After shooting me, he thought he had left me dead. But as you see, I wasn't. Then I . . . I . . . succeeded in getting this far, still alive."

He held the bloody bandage out to the man. "As you can see, I'm in quite a bit of trouble with my hand," he gulped out. "One of my fingers was shot off. Immediately it began bleeding profusely. That's why the man didn't finish me off. He thought I was a dead man walking. He took my horse and my belongings. I . . . I . . . managed to walk this far."

He swallowed hard. "Please have mercy on me,"

he said, his eyes pleading with the man. "Please, I beg you, take me in and see to my wound. Everything I owned was taken from me when the highwayman took my horse and saddlebag, so I have no way to pay you for your kindness. But surely you wouldn't turn an injured man away just because he has no way to pay, would you?"

A woman's voice came from the darkness within the cabin. "Frank, who's there?" a woman asked, slowly stepping into view as she held a robe tightly around her.

Her golden hair hung down to her waist. Her blue eyes were wide in wonder as Raymond slowly assessed her with squinted eyes.

"It's a man in trouble, Molly" Frank said. "Do you think we should see to his wound or send him away?"

"Why, Frank, you know that God would frown upon us if we did not see to a man in need, so ask him in. We'll do what we can for him," Molly said, stepping aside as Frank nodded for Raymond to come into their cabin.

"My father was a doctor," Frank said. "I know pretty much what to do about anything, especially gunshot wounds. Go and lie down on the rug beside the fire. I'll see to you as best as I can with what I have available."

Molly disappeared into another room. Seemingly understanding the wickedness of the man who was now in her cabin, she stayed hidden while her husband took care of the wound.

Once the hand was doctored, Raymond felt that he had already worn out his welcome, mainly because the woman had made herself scarce. He got shakily to his feet.

"I won't bother you any more tonight," he said, holding his injured hand with the other. "But can I ask one more thing of you?"

"And what's that?" Frank asked as he walked Raymond to the door, realizing this was a man he didn't want to spend any more time with. He had seen how the man looked at his Molly. He had to get the grizzly-looking stranger far from his beloved Molly, or he might live to regret the day he'd offered this man help.

"I know it's askin' a lot of you, since I'm only a stranger in the night, but I need to get to St. Paul, and it's too far for walkin'," Raymond said, his eyes narrowing as he stared into Frank's.

He cursed his own horse, which had run off when Raymond had stopped to take a drink from a creek. He had tried to secure his horse's reins to a low tree limb, to keep him from running off. But without the use of one hand, he'd been unable to tie a proper knot. The minute Raymond had fallen to his knees beside the creek, his horse had fled into the night, leaving Raymond even more helpless than before.

"I don't know how easy it's gonna be for me to

48

ride a horse with this injured hand and all, but I do need one," Raymond said solemnly. "I don't think I'd last long walkin' that long ways, now do you?"

Frank hesitated.

"I'll return it to you as soon as I'm well enough," Raymond hurried out. "Do you have a horse to spare?"

"I guess so," Frank said, ushering Raymond outside. He nodded at the barn. "Go and take the white one. She's a mare, and somewhat slow, but she'll get you where you need to go. And don't bother bringin' her back. She's of no use to me anymore. In fact, I was going to be shootin' her sometime soon."

Raymond's eyes widened. "Shoot a horse?" he said, finding it incredulous that anyone would shoot a horse only because it had lost its usefulness.

It was one thing to take a useless man's life, but another to take an animal's!

"Take 'er or leave 'er," Frank said, idly shrugging.

"I'll gladly take 'er off your hands," Raymond said, frowning. "And thank you, kind sir, for all you've done for this stranger tonight."

"Think nothin' of it," Frank said, turning and hurrying inside his cabin.

Raymond smiled ruefully when he heard Frank quickly latch the door.

He smiled even more widely when the back door was latched as well.

"By jove, that man don't trust me at all," he said,

walking toward the barn. "Now I wonder what I did to cause him not to trust me?"

Finding no saddle anywhere, and guessing that they were kept safe in the house, Raymond finally managed to haul himself on the mare, bareback. It would be hard traveling that way, but he was determined to get to St. Paul.

He was going to go to Fort Snelling, to encite the anger of the colonel against Sheleen. Surely the colonel would help him track her down once Raymond was well enough to travel on.

Yep, he just knew that Colonel George Robertson would be glad to help search out Sheleen, especially when Raymond told the colonel whose daughter she was.

Everyone in the military hated her father. They saw him as a traitor to his country because of his alliances with savages. Raymond was sure they must hate Sheleen just as much, for everyone knew she was her father's ally in crime, an Injun lover herself!

Now if only he could make it to St. Paul alive. That was his main concern. He was feeling weaker by the minute.

But when he was determined to do something, by jove, he got it done!

No matter that he had lost a lot of blood because that woman was such a crack shot; he would succeed at finding her!

"You'll pay for what you did to me," he whispered to himself as the white mare traveled onward beneath the bright light of the moon. "Yep, you'll get your comeuppance and get it soon."

CHAPTER SIX

I break all slighter bonds,
Nor feel a shadow of regret.
—*Adelaide Anne Procter*

Gentle Bear was standing outside his lodge, watching his mother. She was hard at work doing her daily chores, focusing today on the communal garden, and helping the other women prepare it for planting.

Gentle Bear felt guilty. Yesterday he had helped her a little by bringing the two rabbits home for her cook pot. But that was nothing compared to what he could have brought home for her.

Duck meat!

Lots of it!

He longed to put more food in her cook pot, for the rabbit meat was quickly consumed and today was another day!

Even though Midnight Wolf provided for them now that Gentle Bear's father was dead, Gentle Bear wanted to be the man of his mother's lodge.

Even if he did have only a small bow, he still wanted to prove his worth to his mother.

Ho, he still carried a boy's bow, but it was not the size of the bow that indicated one's strength and ability to hunt like a real man.

It was the power that Gentle Bear held in his heart that measured his true worth!

Ho, today he wanted a serious hunt.

He could not prevent himself from killing some of those green-headed ducks since he knew that many were still in the area.

The excursion yesterday had not been as much of a serious hunt as it had been a chance for camaraderie with his chief.

His jaw tight with determination, he decided, that he would go on another hunt today. But this time, he would go by himself.

He was man enough not to have to be escorted here and there, even though he understood the warnings of his chief about the unrest in the white community. But that white community was far, far away from where he would be hunting.

And no *washechu* had ever been seen this close to his people's village. The lake, where the ducks swam in such abundance, was not that far away.

Even though his chief had said that it was too far for a young brave to venture, he was going.

He would make his mother proud by bringing home much meat for her cook pot today!

Guilt pressing in on his heart that he was doing something his chief had warned him against, Gentle Bear hurried into his tepee and watched from the entranceway for his chief. After a little while, he saw Midnight Wolf go into the council house, where he usually stayed for some time with his warriors.

Gentle Bear's mother was still on her knees in the garden with sweat on her brow, working too intently to see her son leave their lodge. This was his best chance to leave the village without being noticed.

His heart pounding, he secured his quiver of arrows on his back, grabbed up his new bow with the designs carved on it, then crept again to the entranceway.

Again he held the flap aside and stared outside. No one was paying him any heed. This was the perfect time to go.

Breathing hard, he had a premonition that he should not be doing this thing.

But oh, he wanted to hunt so badly. He wanted to assure his mother of food in her pot for several days. Holding his bow in a tight grip, he rushed from the entranceway.

He fled around quickly to the back, where no one could see him, then ran hard toward the thick cover of trees. Once he reached the forest, he would run onward until he reached the lake where there were many, many green-headed ducks.

Some would be floating in the water.

Some would be resting on the embankment.

He knew they chose that lake over his people's Secret Lake because no humans lived near it. Up until now, the ducks had come and gone as they pleased without fear of someone suddenly killing them.

"But today things will change for the ducks," Gentle Bear whispered to himself as he continued to run through the shadowy forest, where the thickness of the leaves overhead kept the sun from penetrating.

Gentle Bear fought off gnawing feelings of anxiety that he was doing what his chief had absolutely forbidden him to undertake.

Gentle Bear could only hope that when Midnight Wolf found out that his charge had disobeyed his orders, Gentle Bear would have so many ducks for his mother's cook pot, his chief would not remain angry for long.

A movement at his right side caused Gentle Bear to stop abruptly, his heart pounding. Once again he recalled what his chief had warned him about. White men hanging people with red skin!

Had some of those men traveled so far from their own community in their search for red-skinned people?

Had they heard about the Dakota tribe who had fled Minnesota and now made their homes beside a lake their chief had named?

Those thoughts made Gentle Bear feel sick to his stomach. When his chief had explained to him about the true evil of the whites who hated people like himself, who would go so far as to place a noose around a red man's neck and hang him, Gentle Bear had not been able envision any man, white or red-skinned, evil enough to kill innocent people in such a horrible way.

But he knew that it had happened in Minnesota three winters ago. That was why his chief had led his people to safety on Wisconsin land!

And Gentle Bear had felt safe, until now, when his chief had told him that evil white men were hanging his people again!

He listened intently for any more movement.

His eyes darted from place to place to see if anyone was there, lying in wait to shoot him, or grab him and place a noose around *his* neck.

When a deer leapt from behind some bushes, Gentle Bear sighed deeply with relief. Now he felt foolish for having allowed himself to be so frightened that he could hardly breathe, much less notch an arrow on his bowstring for protection.

He turned quickly and looked back in the direction of his home. Like a coward, or a child, should he return where he knew he would be safe?

Or should he resume his journey toward the larger lake, where he would find so many ducks he would have only to aim and he would have one, and then two, and even more?

He felt foolish for having allowed the rustling of a deer to fill him with such dreadful fear.

Wanting to prove to himself now that he was brave enough to do anything he aspired to do, he turned back in the direction of the lake and broke into a lope.

Surely if whites were near, he told himself, his people's scouts would have came with a warning to their village. He tried to convince himself that he was absolutely safe to continue onward.

But the quicker he could get this behind him, the better, for no matter how much he fought this fear that had come into his heart moments ago, it was still there.

A flapping sound overhead caused Gentle Bear's eyes to dart quickly upward.

The trees had thinned out and he could see the blue sky. Silhouetted against it were many of the beautiful green-headed ducks that he so badly wanted.

They were moving gracefully through the air, the sun on the green of their heads making the feathers shine, almost mystically.

He admired the birds' loveliness, wondering if he *could* actually kill one if he got the chance?

He remembered how hard it had been to shoot an arrow into the furry little rabbit.

Would it not be doubly hard to kill one of these beautiful ducks?

The thought of cleaning a duck of its feathers, with blood on them, made him feel nauseous.

But he knew that was wrong!

He was trying to prove his worth as a hunter, as a young brave aspiring to be a powerful warrior, perhaps even an admired chief one day for his people, and there he was thinking like a baby, and worse yet, a coward!

To prove one's worth, a young brave must be skilled at hunting, no matter what the target was, beautiful or ugly!

"And I will," he whispered to himself, running onward and no longer watching the flight of the ducks overhead. "I must, and I will, kill some ducks today!"

CHAPTER SEVEN

Wake and seize the little hour,
Give me welcome, or farewell!
—*Edward Rowland Sill*

Raymond Hauser rode the white mare through the wide open gates of Fort Snelling. His hand throbbed so badly, he could hardly think straight, and he was weak from having lost so much blood before the kind gentleman had doctored and bandaged his hand.

As he rode onward, toward the main building of the fort, soldiers stopped and stared at him.

Some who knew him threw him a salute, yet in their eyes he saw puzzlement as to why he had been injured, and how, and by whom.

The only one who was going to learn that information was Colonel George Robertson. Raymond was not proud of what had happened, and he would admit to no one else that a woman had bested him and had actually shot off his most important finger.

His trigger finger!

He was going to have to learn all over again how to use a firearm. His left hand was going to have to perform all the deeds of life now, especially defending himself.

When he finally reached the headquarters cabin, he almost fell from the steed. His rump was sore, yet strangely numb, from having no saddle to cushion it while riding the long journey from Wisconsin.

Just as he reached the steps, Colonel Robertson stepped from the door and eyed him questioningly.

Raymond could only smile weakly at him, for he knew that he had no choice but to tell the man that a lady had gotten the best of ol' Raymond Hauser!

"What brings you here this early morn?" Colonel Robertson asked, taking a thick cigar from between his lips and flicking ashes from it onto the porch. "And on a mangy mare? Where's your own horse, Raymond? Tuckered out on you, did it?"

The colonel's thick, red, bushy eyebrows lifted as he stared at the bandaged hand. "And what do we have here? An injury?" He moved his brownish-green eyes up and stared into Raymond's. "Who did this to you, Raymond? How'd you allow it to happen? You are one of the best gunmen I've ever known. I'd have been glad to have you work beside me as my right-hand man, but, no, you wanted nothing to do with the army. Now I bet you wished you had accepted my offer."

The shiny brass buttons on the colonel's blue uniform cast flashes of sunshine into Raymond's eyes, almost mockingly.

The colonel's bright red hair was groomed down to his stiff collar, and medals shone like fire on one side of his jacket, proving his worth to the United States of America.

Raymond wondered just how many Injuns the colonel'd shot to earn himself those medals. But now wasn't the time to think about the colonel's luck or how he'd been honored by the government for the deeds he'd done for his country.

Now was the time to ignore the colonel's sarcasm and ask for help. Raymond needed it more now than at any other time in his life, not only because he was so weakened by the loss of blood, but because he felt driven by the need to find and silence the woman who'd robbed him of his finger.

"I'm plumb tuckered out, George," Raymond sighed. "Can we go inside and talk? Might you even have coffee brewin'? It'd feel mighty good to this parched mouth of mine."

The colonel shrugged a shoulder toward the open door. "Certainly to both your requests," he said, standing aside for Raymond to stagger slowly past him. "I've missed our little chats. Come on in and I'll have a cup of coffee with you."

Raymond nodded, smiled weakly, then went on

into an office that was familiar from other visits with his friend.

It was a room lined with shelf after shelf of gold-embossed, leather-bound books of all kinds. A huge oak desk stood in the center of the room. A fireplace roared with a huge, flaming fire. More logs had just been added to the flames.

"Sit," George said. He motioned with a hand toward a thick cushioned leather chair that sat opposite the desk. He, himself, sat behind it in an even plusher chair.

He reached for the pot of coffee that he had just set on a thick pad before hearing the arrival of Raymond's horse.

He slid a cup closer to the pot and poured coffee in it, then pushed it over to Raymond, who clumsily took it with his left hand.

The colonel rose from the chair, poured his own cold coffee into a basin, then went back and refilled it. He was soon sipping hot coffee from his cup as he eyed Raymond.

"Well? What've you to say for yourself?" the colonel demanded, slowly setting his cup on the desk beside a ledger where he had been adding figures before Raymond's arrival had interrupted him. "How'd you get injured? Was it a savage that did it? I guess you know about the unrest in the country because of Lincoln's assassination. Although most know no savage shot the president, his death just seems to be an excuse for those who hate redskins to search out the poor souls again and hang them without question."

"Yep, I know about that," Raymond said, then smiled wickedly at the colonel as he set his own cup aside.

Raymond leaned forward so that he was looking directly into the colonel's eyes. "George, redskins ain't all that's been placed at the end of a hangman's noose," he said, his eyes filled suddenly with a wicked glee.

"What do you mean?" the colonel asked, raising an eyebrow. "What sort of meanness have you been up to, Raymond? What . . . or who . . . caused you to get your hand injured? Who'd you hang? Who shot you for havin' done it?"

"I searched and found the doctor everyone was after three years ago when the government hanged those thirty-eight Injuns for having rebelled and killed so many whites," Raymond said, his eyes gleaming.

"You did what?" the colonel gasped, staring incredulously back at Raymond. "You found Harold Hicks? I'm almost afraid to ask what you've done. And how about that pretty daughter of his? Did you find Sheleen as well?"

The colonel paused, stiffened his jaw, then glared at Raymond. "You didn't kill them, did you?" he asked. "I know how much you wanted to do the dirty deed three years ago when there was a search for them. What . . . happened?"

"The female side of the two got lucky," Raymond growled. He relaxed again against the back of the plush chair. "But her pa wasn't that lucky. While Sheleen was away somewhere, I found her pa alone and finally rid the earth of the sonofagun."

"Are you saying what I think you're saying?" the colonel asked, his eyes narrowing.

"Yep, I placed a noose around his scrawny neck and watched him die as he hung from the limb of a big ol' oak tree. Must say, it did seem the right place for the Injun lover to find his end."

"You took it upon yourself to . . . hang . . . Doctor Hicks?" the colonel said in a deceptively bland tone. Colonel Robertson then slammed a fist on the desk top. "You fool!" he shouted. "You stupid ass fool!"

He stood up and leaned over the desk, his eyes holding Raymond's steadily. "And the woman . . . his daughter?" he growled. "You didn't say what you did to her. You said she wasn't there with her pa, but I'm sure she returned home before you left. You waited for her, didn't you? What . . . did . . . you do to her, Raymond? What?"

"You're right. She wasn't there while I was getting rid of her pa," Raymond said. He shrugged nonchalantly. "So . . . I waited for her."

He frowned. "I was about to get the best of her, too, but . . . but . . . her damn cat suddenly came meowing all over the place, drawing my attention from what I was doin'," he growled. "That's when Sheleen got a draw on me and shot off my trigger finger while blastin' my rifle from my hand."

Colonel Robertson smiled slyly, then slowly sat back down in his chair. "And so you let a woman best you, did you?" he said, chuckling. "Well, that's what you get for taking the law in your own hands like the others who are going around hanging Indians as they find them."

"I thought you'd be pleased to hear that Doctor Hicks won't interfere any more in the business of the government," Raymond said, truly puzzled by the colonel's attitude.

"Doctor Hicks hasn't caused anyone any trouble for three years now," Colonel Robertson grumbled. "And if you want to know, I've admired that man for quite some time, since way before he left his practice to care for down-and-out redskins. Certainly, I was among those who wanted to stop him from helping the Indians, but I'd never have placed a noose around his neck. He was a kind soul who never hurt anyone. And his daughter, who was at his side, always helping him, was the prettiest thing I think I ever saw, except for my own daughter, who is just as tiny and pretty. I'd never have allowed any harm to come her way."

He leaned forward, his eyes again peering into Raymond's. "Did you harm her after she shot you?" he asked.

"No, and damn it, I am lucky to be alive," Raymond said, resting his injured hand in the other. "Had she aimed for my gut, I'd not be sitting here today, George. I'd be damned dead."

"So she had mercy on your soul even after you hanged her pa, did she?" the colonel said. He chuckled softly. "You just don't know how lucky you are, do you? I happen to know that this young lady is a crack shot. Her father taught her when she was only a tiny girl. Even then he was mixed up with Injuns one way or the other." He frowned. "She was, too."

"And you still think it's all right that she is out there, a crack shot, firing at anyone she takes a notion to kill?" Raymond growled.

"She didn't kill you, did she?" the colonel said, again chuckling. "I think you are one mighty lucky sonofagun, Raymond. You're a very fortunate fella."

His eyes narrowed again. "And how is it that she let you go after learning you killed her pa?" he demanded.

"Well, after shootin' my finger off, she saw that I was losing a lot of blood and all. Blood was flowing from my finger like water comes from a well. She didn't expect me to live long, so she let me go on my way," he mumbled. "And as for her? I have no idea where she is now. I'm certain she ran for cover after I left."

Raymond's eyes narrowed. "But that's why I'm

here," he said harshly. "I want help searchin' her out. She was as much to blame for helping redskins as her pa was. She deserves no less punishment from we who love our country."

Raymond leaned closer, so that he could look the colonel directly in the eye. "I've come to ask for your help," he said flatly. "Can you spare some soldiers to go with me after I've rested up and got my strength back? Friend to friend, will you help me? Sheleen's a traitor to our country, George. Cain't you see that? She is no better than her traitor pa was."

"You won't be in any shape to go anywhere for quite a spell," the colonel pointed out. "So why not just forget it? Let the young lady go where she likes. She won't cause any more trouble. Without her father, she is nothing but a pretty thing who needs a husband to care for her. That's what she'll do now that her father is dead. She'll search for a fine young man who'll give her a comfortable life and babies."

"Babies?" Raymond shouted, scurrying to his feet. "If she has babies, she'll raise them talkin' against our government. She'll probably even raise the children like savages raise their kids. She's lived with the savages. Did you know that? Some time ago she lived with the Dakota Injuns."

George was taken aback by that. He stared dumbfoundedly at Raymond, then hurried to his feet. He motioned with a hand toward the door.

"Get out of here, Raymond," he shouted. "I've

heard enough hogwash from you. I don't want to hear any more."

"Hogwash, you call it? You just don't want to hear the truth," Raymond said sourly. "You keep comparin' Sheleen with your daughter and can't see farther than her pretty face."

He doubled his good hand into a tight fist at his side. "Listen to me," he growled. "You're gonna live to regret not helpin' me find and do away with that troublemaking wench. She'll be a thorn in your side one day. Mark my words, George. You'll wish you'd helped me find and kill her."

"I haven't ever seen the likes of you, hating a mere woman so much," Colonel Robertson said, walking from behind his desk and standing directly in front of Raymond. "And she's just that, Raymond. I can't see her as a problem. She is just a woman. Without her father, what harm can she do?"

"This!" Raymond cried, shoving his bandaged hand into the colonel's face. "This, damn it. Don't you see that she's proven herself to be heartless by having done this to me?"

"How can you say that?" the colonel asked. He took Raymond by an elbow and slowly ushered him toward the door. "Weren't you the man who had just hanged her father? Under similar circumstances, don't you think you'd be . . . heartless . . . if that's the word you want to use to describe the anger and hurt she had to be feeling after seeing her father hanging from a tree?"

He took Raymond to the door and then shoved him out onto the porch. "Let it go, Raymond," he said. He placed his fists on his hips. "Let *her* go. Let your need of vengeance go. There are other more important issues to take care of now that the President is dead. The whole country is in mourning. That's how you should be behaving, not going around mouthing off about a woman needing to be killed. Mourn the President, Raymond. Go home and let your hand heal."

"It can never heal the way it should," Raymond said, his voice breaking. "How can it, when one of my fingers is missin'?"

Knowing he was wasting time standing there with the colonel, Raymond gave Robertson one last look, then turned and walked slowly down the stairs.

He mounted the white mare and rode toward the gate, then stopped when he saw someone very familiar to him.

He turned his mount in the direction of Big Bear Moon, a Dakota Indian who had left his people some time ago to live in the white community and work with the military as a scout.

Big Bear Moon stopped and waited for Raymond after seeing him headed his way.

Raymond drew a tight rein beside Big Bear Moon and smiled slyly. "Mornin', scout," he said, sliding from the mare's back. He stood as steady as he could beside the scout, for he was getting more lightheaded by the minute. "How are things?"

"Get to the point," Big Bear Moon said dryly, his midnight dark eyes narrowing as he gazed directly into Raymond's.

"I'll pay you better than the military ever has if you'll help me find and kill a woman," Raymond blurted out. "How's about it? Are you ready to make some big, fat greenbacks? I'm good to pay you, you know."

"What woman needs to be killed?" Big Bear Moon asked, resting a hand on a huge knife sheathed at his right side.

Raymond noticed where the scout had placed his right hand and was uneasy over it. He had heard just how skilled this big Indian was with a knife. Indeed, with any weapon. He certainly did not want to get on the scout's bad side!

Raymond held up his bandaged right hand and showed it to the scout. "Do you see this? The woman did it," he said, before mentioning Sheleen's name. He was sure the scout knew her, as well as her role in helping down-and-out Dakota Injuns.

"What is her name?" the scout asked.

Raymond had always wondered how much of Big Bear Moon was still Dakota?

Could he truly trust the Injun not to stick him with that knife while they were resting some night beside a campfire?

Well, he'd have to take that chance, for he knew this scout was surely the only man on this earth who would have the skills to find Sheleen.

"Her name?" Raymond said cautiously.

"*Ho*, her name," Big Bear Moon repeated, his use of an Indian word unnerving Raymond.

Again Raymond could not help wondering just how much of this redskin was still . . . redskin?

"Sheleen," Raymond blurted out. "Sheleen Hicks."

He studied the scout's dark eyes and saw nothing change in them at the mention of Sheleen's name, but he knew the scout was very familiar with her reputation.

Everyone who had anything to do with the military knew!

"She is the one who injured you?" Big Bear Moon said tightly as he gazed at the bandaged hand.

"The very one," Raymond said, nodding. "Damn her, she shot off my trigger finger."

"And why would she do that?" Big Bear Moon asked, again holding Raymond's gaze.

"Well, that's the part I am not going to brag about too often, since I know there might be some who would call me an out-and-out murderer," Raymond said. "But Doctor Hicks was no good. He allied himself with Injuns when those Injuns had killed many white people. He deserved to be hanged, since that was the fate of those thirty-eight Injuns three years ago."

"You placed a noose around the doctor's neck and hanged him until he was dead just because you had the notion to do it," Big Bear Moon said, still emotionless as he stared into Raymond's eyes.

"Yep, because I had the opportunity to do it," Raymond agreed. He was growing a little uneasy at the way this Indian scout showed no emotion about anything! Damned if he wasn't as stoic as they came!

"So?" Raymond persisted. "Will you help me find his daughter? I need to find her now for more than just one reason. I want to make her pay for allying herself with redskins, and I want to take vengeance on her having shot off my finger!"

"You do not look like you are able to go searching for anyone," Big Bear Moon said, his gaze moving slowly to the bandaged hand, then again looking directly, unblinkingly, into Raymond's eyes.

"I plan to take some time to rest before heading out again to search for her," Raymond said. "But if you agree to ride with me, I will leave tomorrow. I just need one good night's rest and that should do it."

He leaned into the scout's face. "Will you go with me?" he asked, searching Big Bear Moon's eyes for any sign of emotion, and again seeing none.

"*Ho*, I will ride with you," Big Bear Moon said. "If you can promise much payment for it."

"I already did promise you," Raymond said, wincing when a sharp jolt of pain shot through his hand. Suddenly feeling dizzy, he reached out and grabbed hold of Big Bear Moon's arm, realizing that the Indian flinched at his touch.

Raymond wasn't sure he had made a good decision by asking a Dakota Indian to help him, especially since the person he would be searching for had allied herself with the Dakota.

But . . . it was true that this Dakota Indian had thrown in his lot with whites; why would he change his allegiance now?

"I will go with you," Big Bear Moon said, slowly sliding Raymond's hand from his arm. "But only if you pay me in advance."

"Pay you even before you earn the greenbacks?" Raymond asked, his eyes wide.

"Pay me before we leave to search for the woman, or you go by yourself," Big Bear Moon said matter-of-factly.

"Oh, all right. But first, help me to my cabin," Raymond said, again searching the scout's eyes. "I'll pay you there, just before we head out for the hunt. For now, I need my bed. I . . . I . . . suddenly don't feel so good."

"Your cabin is where?" Big Bear Moon asked, reaching out and steadying Raymond. The only reason he would help him was because he was going to be paid handsomely. Big Bear Moon loathed the whiskered man with a passion. He had known Raymond Hauser for some time now, and knew the complete worthlessness of the man.

"About a mile down the road, just outside of St. Paul," Raymond said, welcoming the scout's help to mount his horse.

"I will follow alongside you," Big Bear Moon said,

walking quickly to his own steed and vaulting onto it.

"Thank you," Raymond said, then rode with the scout from the fort.

When they arrived at Raymond's cabin, he welcomed Big Bear Moon's strong hands as the scout helped him from the horse into his cabin. The Dakota even took over building a fire in the fireplace as Raymond almost fell, exhausted, onto his bed.

After Raymond crawled in bed, Big Bear Moon slid a chair close to the bed. "Give me the greenbacks now," he said abruptly.

"So you can run off while I'm asleep?" Raymond said. He chuckled. "How stupid do you think I am?"

"Pay me now, or I leave," Big Bear Moon persisted.

"I shouldn't, but what the hell," Raymond said, too desperate to go to sleep to worry about this red man swindling him. Surely Big Bear Moon knew better than to swindle Raymond Hauser. He'd live to regret it!

He scooted from his bed and went to a dresser, where he yanked a drawer open. Hidden beneath his socks was a pile of money.

He counted out what he felt the redskin was worth, then went and shoved it in the scout's hand.

"And what's left had better still be in my drawer when I wake up," Raymond warned, turning and slamming the drawer shut.

"I don't take what is not mine," Big Bear Moon said, slowly counting the money.

Again Raymond went and stretched out exhaustedly on his bed while Big Bear Moon sat beside it.

After Raymond was asleep, Big Bear Moon glared at the sleeping white man, truly hating him. He was reminded again of what had started the Dakota's rebellion those three winters ago . . . when the Dakota warriors had been denied the annuities promised them by treaty, while the warriors' families were starving.

When the man in charge of handing out food to the Dakota had said, "If you are hungry, go eat grass or cow dung," the Dakota felt that they had no choice but to retalliate.

"*Washechu,* I believe you should eat grass when you awaken," Big Bear Moon grumbled, then smiled ruefully and went to Raymond's food supplies. He found two cans of beans.

He opened them and emptied the beans into a pot, which he hung on a tripod over the fire.

"But when you awaken, I will not force grass down your throat," Big Bear Moon whispered as he sat on the floor in front of the fireplace. "I have much more important and better plans to take care of first. . . ."

He looked over his shoulder when Raymond groaned in his sleep, while spittle rolled from one corner of his mouth. The sight was so disgusting to Big Bear Moon, he shivered and looked quickly away.

In his mind's eye he was remembering Sheleen. It

was oh, so many moons ago when their paths had last crossed, when he had left to ally himself with the white eyes, but only to trick them when they thought he was helping them.

He smiled at those times when he had proudly bested the *washechu,* leaving them completely ignorant of why they'd been defeated.

He never told anyone, red- or white-skinned, of his victories, for he was not one to brag . . . only do!

CHAPTER EIGHT

Constant love is moderate ever,
And it will through life persever.
—*Anonymous*

After a restless night, Sheleen had traveled onward and was now riding through a forest of beautiful hardwood trees.

It was so peaceful, with birds and squirrels everywhere, and she was just now seeing the shine of water up ahead.

Needing to refresh herself and wash the dust of travel from her face, she pressed her knees against the sides of her horse and rode toward what she surmised was a lake.

As she drew closer to the lake, she saw many green-headed ducks. Some were swimming peacefully in the water, while others rested along the embankment.

When she rode still closer, she noticed just how plump they were. She had not eaten meat since she had left her home. She was mainly existing on mushrooms and berries, so a nourishing meal of duck meat would make her stronger for the long road that lay ahead of her.

She was still not sure what her final destination was. It was just important to get as far as she could from those who might harm her because of her past alliance with the Dakota people.

The farther she got from the Minnesota border, the safer she would be. Surely no one would realize who she was if she were far enough from St. Paul.

No matter where she was going, though, she knew that she would face much loneliness. Without her father's love and companionship, she wasn't sure how she was going to exist. She had hardly spent a day away from her father from as far back as she could remember.

She fought back tears that threatened to spill from her eyes; she knew that from here on out, she had to be strong. She had no one else to depend on, only herself.

She was strong-willed and knew that she would get through this all right.

If she didn't, she knew that her father would be disappointed in her. And even though he was dead, she didn't want to disappoint him!

He had taught her well the need of being strong and capable of facing up to anything that might come her way. Well, she was most certainly facing up to new challenges now. "And I will survive it all," she whispered to herself.

Her belly was growling from hunger. She drew rein and stopped her horse. The thought of a fast supper of duck was too tempting to resist.

After dismounting, she checked on Fluffy, finding her cat fast asleep in her home in the saddlebag. Sheleen smiled, knowing that Fluffy would enjoy the change in food for today's meal, too. She would not have to find a mouse to play with, then eat.

Sheleen turned and again gazed at the ducks, which were now in a large group alongside the lake. One shot would be all that was required to get her a duck for dinner.

She didn't want to have to fire more than one shot, for even firing a single bullet could draw attention to herself.

She had no idea where she was, or who might be living in this forest. But to have meat for at least one meal was worth the chance she would take by firing her rifle.

She grabbed her gun from its boot at the side of her horse. Then she hunkered down, low, and moved stealthily away from her horse, her eyes never leaving the ducks.

She wanted to be close enough to take only one shot. The sound of rifle fire would frighten and scatter the ducks in all directions.

She moved quietly onward, making sure she was

hidden behind bushes so that the ducks would not be aware of her stalking them. But she was aware that the bushes rustled as she walked past them and she hoped the noise wouldn't alert the ducks to her presence.

She was already tasting the delicious flavor of roast duck in her mouth, and how it would feel so good in her belly.

As soon as she killed one duck, she would build herself a fire, and then remove the feathers.

Again she noticed just how lovely the ducks' feathers were. Any other time, she might take some of the feathers to make a fan as she knew the Dakota were wont to do, especially the old men who loved sitting and talking and cooling themselves with feather fans.

Suddenly she heard something.

It was a whizzing sound. . . .

She cried out in pain and dropped her rifle when an arrow pierced her breeches, going into her leg just below her right knee.

She crumpled to the ground, then noticed that it was an unusually small arrow that was protruding from her leg.

Thank the Lord, it was much smaller than most, or it would have done much more damage. It was a child's arrow.

She was torn between pain and fear, for surely the child who'd shot it was with an adult, more than likely his father. The child and father must be Indians, and were probably not far from their village.

She knew that any white person coming near an Indian village could be a target of hatred after all that had been done to Indians by the United States Government.

Suddenly through a break in the trees she saw a young Indian brave. He was holding a small bow, with a child-sized quiver of arrows secured at his back.

This had to be the one who had shot her. As he stared back at her, she saw that his eyes were wide with a mixture of stunned fear and guilt.

Because of his bewildered look, she wondered if she had been his target, or if he had shot her by accident?

Could he have been after the same ducks that she had been about to kill? Had he shot her by mistake when he'd seen her movement?

She was sure that he was alone, or the father would have made himself known to her.

Filled with pain, she held her leg, crying.

Through her tears she saw the child turn and run away. She was not sure whether she should be relieved or fearful that he had left her alone and injured.

Then another thought came to her.

Surely the child would return home and tell his parents, or even his chief, what he had done.

They would come for her.

If they hated whites and would not believe that she and her father had fought always for the rights of the red man, she would become their captive . . . or worse yet, be killed.

But those fears must be put at the back of her mind. She had her injury to see to. She had to remove the arrow, then medicate the wound.

Finding a courage she wasn't sure that she had, she broke the arrow in half, leaving the smaller portion imbedded in her leg.

Sweating from the pain and effort, she crawled back to her horse and managed to get her father's medical bag.

She was glad that Fluffy was still sleeping contentedly in the bag on the horse, unaware of the danger they were in.

Although the pain was excrutiating, Sheleen managed to crawl back to the lake. The sun was now covered by thick, ominous clouds, with sudden streaks of lightning racing across the heavens, followed by one boom of thunder after another. The ducks scattered when they were suddenly aware of a human's presence.

Panting, her pulse racing, she ripped her pants leg up to where the arrow was still imbedded in her skin.

Opening her father's bag, she removed a surgical tool used to cut through flesh. Crying and trembling, she cut into her leg, deep enough to remove the rest of the arrow.

Once the arrow was finally out of her leg, she

threaded a surgical needle and sobbed hard as she first washed the wound with water, splashed medicine into it, then stitched it together. She was glad she had gotten practice by helping her father tend to injured Indians.

Just as she got the wound bandaged, the rain began falling in torrents, quickly soaking her. Panic soon grabbed hold of her, for she knew that she must find shelter.

Injured as she was, exposure to the weather was more of an enemy even than Indians.

Dragging the closed satchel, and her leg, she went back to where she had left her horse.

To her horror, it and the cat were gone.

Surely the lightning and thunder had frightened the horse away. She hadn't secured the reins.

It had not been necessary until now.

The horse had been trained to stay where Sheleen left him.

But nothing could prepare a horse to combat its fear of lightning and thunder, especially such a fierce storm as today.

Or . . . had the young brave circled around and stolen her horse, and along with it, her beloved cat?

The rain still fell hard as Sheleen looked desperately for shelter, finding nothing.

She stretched out on the ground, then moved into a fetal position, her body shaking from fear and cold.

She sobbed out her father's name, then passed out.

CHAPTER NINE

> The winds of heaven mix forever,
> With a sweet emotion.
> —*Percy Bysshe Shelley*

Gentle Bear had arrived home just before the storm hit, and now he sat with his mother in the warm comfort of their home, as rain pounded the outside of their tepee.

He flinched when he saw the flash of lightning through the buckskin fabric of their tepee covering; a loud clap of thunder quickly followed.

But although he had reacted to the lightning and thunder, he knew that the lightning would do him no harm. Before his mother had heard the first clap of thunder, she had placed cedar leaves on the coals of their lodge fire, knowing their magic would keep the danger of a lightning strike away from their home.

Gentle Bear looked over at his mother. She was too involved in beading new moccasins to notice his nervousness and guilt over what he had done. He had not only gone against his chief's and his mother's orders, but had also accidentally shot a small white man with one of his arrows.

Although it was smaller than a warrior's, the arrow could still do damage, and it had. He remembered seeing the blood on the leg of the man's breeches where the arrow was imbedded in the man's leg.

When the storm warriors continued to throw their lightning sticks to the earth, shaking his lodge, and the rain seemed to be hitting the skin of the lodge harder, Gentle Bear's guilt increased. He knew the man he had shot was surely being pelted by the rain, too injured to move to shelter.

Oh, it was so hard not to tell someone what he had done! But he was too afraid to let anyone know just how far his disobedience had gone.

He most certainly had not brought home duck meat for his beloved mother!

All that he had brought home was guilt and regret!

He recalled the instant he had seen the small man in the big hat, the gruesome sight of the arrow in his leg, and then how the man had cried in pain.

He had never seen a man cry before, so surely the pain his arrow had caused was unbearable! He was mortified to know that he had caused such agony. And all because he had disobeyed his chief and his mother.

But he still couldn't get the courage to tell his mother that he had shot a white man.

No. He could not tell. He was already in too much trouble.

And he feared the wrath of his chief.

He knew what a disappointment he was going to be to his chief once Midnight Wolf discovered what Gentle Bear had done!

His chief might even decide to turn his back on Gentle Bear and choose another brave more worthy of being his charge. . . !

He hung his head in woe. His mother was watching him now, puzzled to see her son acting so withdrawn and strange and sad.

But she did not ask him what was bothering him. He knew that she was there to listen to him whenever he wanted to share things with her. He was growing up into a man and she did not want to make him think she saw him still as a child.

She focused again on the beads she was threading on a string, only occasionally looking over at Gentle Bear. She was sure something was wrong with him and hoped that he would soon open up to her and tell her what was troubling him this rainy afternoon.

CHAPTER TEN

With tongues all sweet and low,
Like a pleasant rhyme,
They tell how much I owe
To thee and time!
—*Barry Cornwall*

"My chief, a stray horse has arrived at our village, but no one is in the saddle."

Night Walker's voice awakened Midnight Wolf with a start. He leaned up on an elbow and gazed up and through his smoke hole. It was another day and the rain had finally stopped.

What was this about a riderless horse having arrived in his village . . . a horse that was still saddled?

This news gave him a keen feeling of apprehension.

Did the animal belong to someone who was a part of a larger group? If so, where was the rider?

And if there were a large group of men close to his village, where were they?

Could they have sent this riderless horse into his village as a tease? It might have been meant as a way to tell his people that where there was one horse, there were usually many, but those horses that had not yet arrived would have armed men in their saddles!

He quickly unfastened the ties at his entranceway, then stepped outside where Night Walker awaited him.

He did not have to ask where the horse was, for it stood beside Night Walker, who held the reins in his hand.

His jaw tight, his eyes wary, Midnight Wolf took the black stallion's reins. He led the horse around in a small circle, all the while studying it, admiring it.

Ho, it was a muscled beauty! It was a lively, fine stepping animal—a warrior's delight!

But it was not this warrior's horse. It most certainly belonged to someone else.

To whom?

He stopped the horse, dropped the reins, then stepped up to the saddlebag.

Strange how it was open. He noticed short, white hairs inside the bag on the possessions it held.

This was the fur of an animal, though he did not recognize it.

But he knew that it must have been a small animal in order for it to have fit in the bag.

He searched for signs of blood, finding none. Had the animal that had been in the bag been alive?

That possibility puzzled him, for who would travel with a small animal in their saddlebag?

He brushed the hairs aside, then slowly took one garment from the bag. His eyebrows rose when he found it to be a dress such as was worn by white women. He gave this over to Night Walker, then took another garment from the saddlebag.

It was a woman's shawl, with lace around the edges.

All the while that his chief was studying the horse and what lay inside the saddlebag, Gentle Bear stood at his entranceway, trembling with fear.

He knew whom the horse belonged to.

And because this horse had arrived at his village, he felt trapped, for his chief would eventually discover who the horse's master was and what had happened to the rider!

His chief was an expert tracker, as was Night Walker. Together they would find the man and the damage that Gentle Bear's arrow had inflicted.

Gentle Bear gazed up at the sky, relieved that the rain had stopped. He had not been able to sleep the entire night for thinking about the wounded man who must be lying in the rain and cold, perhaps even dying from exposure.

But what puzzled Gentle Bear were the clothes that his chief had taken from the little man's saddlebag. They were not clothes of a man, but . . . but . . . instead a woman!

That surely meant that this man was hunting for food for a wife when he was stopped by Gentle Bear. Now he had wronged not only one person, but two.

And . . . where . . . was the *mitawin,* the woman?

Had Gentle Bear caused her to be stranded in the rain, too? Was she as cold as her husband?

Or had she gone to him and helped him to a place hidden away from the rain?

Oh, this was all too confusing to Gentle Bear, and the guilt that was weighing on his heart was now almost too much to bear!

Gah-ween, no! He could not keep this to himself any longer!

He must tell his chief about how his trusted charge had disobeyed him.

And not only that.

His charge had wrongly shot a man with his arrow, not . . . a . . . juicy duck!

"My chief!" Gentle Bear cried as he fled from his tepee, his feet flying over the ground in his need to confess. He just hoped that telling what he had done would help ease his guilt. For he had been riddled by guilt the long night through.

He was not a liar. He had been taught better. But playing a game of deceit such as he was playing was the same as lying.

All eyes were on him as he stepped up to Midnight Wolf, panting.

Breathlessly, he confessed what he had done, how he had left the village alone, to hunt, even though he had been told not to, and how he had accidentally shot a small man with his arrow, instead of the duck that he had hoped to take back to his mother for dinner.

He hung his head. "I . . . I . . . saw movement and . . . and . . . loosed my arrow from my bowstring before thinking," he said.

He swallowed hard, then slowly looked up into the eyes of his chief, hoping that he would not see hatred there instead of love.

Midnight Wolf was momentarily stunned speechless. He had taken his charge hunting only two days before, so that Midnight Bear could use the new bow he was so proud of.

That outing had seemed enough for Gentle Bear at the time, even though Midnight Wolf knew that his charge had initially wanted to hunt for ducks, not rabbits, and he had wanted to go alone to prove his worth as a hunter.

But after Midnight Wolf had explained to Gentle Bear the danger of hunting alone at this time, the boy had seemed satisfied with the arrangement. He had seemed happy to walk side by side with his chief, carrying his new bow. Had Gentle Bear already been planning to leave on his own hunt all along?

Midnight Wolf understood the need of a young brave to prove his worth with a successful hunt. But that simply was not possible at this time.

"My chief, I know what I did was bad, that it was wrong, but . . . but . . . do you not see?" Gentle Bear blurted out, his eyes searching Midnight Wolf's. "I probably shot someone who was a threat to our people. He was close to our homes. He was probably coming to kill the Dakota people!"

"I doubt that," Midnight Wolf said, finally finding his voice again. "This man was traveling with a woman, because what I found in the saddlebag are mainly a woman's clothes. Normally, when a man and wife travel together, it is not to harm anyone. They were more than likely on their way to settle in a new place. Perhaps they do not approve of what is happening in their world; the hangings, the threats of more hangings. Like our Wolf Band of Dakota, who needed to find a place where we could live in peace, perhaps that man and woman were seeking the same sort of peace . . . a sanctuary."

Midnight Wolf shoved the clothes he had taken from the bag back inside it, then turned to his charge again.

He placed gentle hands on the child's bare shoulders and gazed intently into his eyes.

"You have spoken of having seen a man, the one you shot with your arrow, but did you not also see a woman?" he asked, searching Gentle Bear's wavering eyes. "The clothes speak of a woman. There is surely another horse with another saddlebag, in which are the man's clothes."

"*Gah-ween*, no, I saw no one else but . . . but . . . the man I downed with my arrow," Gentle Bear gulped out. "As soon as I saw what I had done, I hurried home."

Again Gentle Bear hung his head. "I stayed there," he said. "While it rained, and the winds blew cold and brisk outside my mother's tepee, I thought of that wounded man. Yet I still could not admit to what I had done."

He raised his head quickly. "I know that I was wrong," he cried. "And . . . and . . . if there are women's clothes in the bag, surely she was hiding when I shot her husband. Surely she is crying even now over what I did."

Midnight Wolf stared at Gentle Bear for a moment longer, still finding it hard to believe that his charge could have done such a thing.

But hearing that someone had been wounded by an arrow—even though it was a small one—he knew he must find the injured party and offer help.

Midnight Wolf stepped away from Gentle Bear. He noticed that their conversation and the strange horse that had arrived in the village had drawn his people from their lodges.

Midnight Wolf's warriors were standing together, their eyes questioning him as they awaited his command as to what should be done about this situation.

"You each have heard what has happened," Midnight Wolf said, raising his voice to be heard. "The man and woman must be found. The one that is wounded must be brought to our village and seen to by our shaman. The wounded man and his woman will be allowed to stay among us until the man is ready to travel again. If by then I feel sure they are people of peace, who meant us Dakota no harm, I shall pay them in horses for the harm done them by Gentle Bear. I hope that will be enough to keep them from reporting to the white government what was done to them. We are happy here in our forest home beside our lake. We must do everything to secure that happiness . . . to ensure our continued safety."

Midnight Wolf chose the warriors who would ride with him, and those who would stay and protect their village.

He turned to Gentle Bear, then looked over at Gentle Bear's mother. He gestured with a hand for her to come to him.

Rosy Dawn did as her chief bade her, then stood, trembling, as she gazed up into her chief's eyes.

"You have heard what your son has done," Midnight Wolf said. "He must come with me and my warriors. He will lead us to the wounded man and his wife."

Rosy Dawn nodded, then gave her son a look that made Gentle Bear want to crawl into the ground and stay there. He had rarely seen that expression on his mother's face . . . the look of someone who is ashamed.

It tore at his heart to know that he had caused his mother to feel ashamed of him.

He hoped in time he could prove his worth to her again. He was so glad when she fell to her knees and pulled him into her arms to give him a hard hug.

Yet it pained him terribly to hear the sobs she was trying to stifle, sobs created by a son who had disappointed her. "I am sorry, Mother," he said, fighting back the urge to cry, himself.

He had already done enough damage. He could not allow himself to cry and have his mother and chief see his weaker side, too.

"My son, you go and help our chief. We will discuss what you have done when you return home," Rosy Dawn said, standing.

She smoothed Gentle Bear's hair back from his eyes, patted him on the shoulder, then stepped back from him as he ran off to get his pony.

"I believe he has learned a hard lesson and will not give us cause to be disappointed in him again," Midnight Wolf said, gently drawing Rosy Dawn into his comforting embrace. "Do not be ashamed of your son. And do not fear that I will no longer want him as my charge. Lessons are learned in many ways. Your son has learned one in the hardest way."

"But what he did . . ." Rosy Dawn said, her eyes wavering.

"When we return, I will discuss with Gentle Bear the wrong he did, and explain the shame he has brought into your lodge," Midnight Wolf said compassionately. "I will be gentle and firm with your son. But now is not the time."

Rosy Dawn nodded, then stepped away from Midnight Wolf and watched her son leave on his pony beside their chief. The warriors followed close behind them on their own beautiful steeds.

"Hold your chin high," Midnight Wolf said as he glanced over at Gentle Bear. "Never show your shame visibly. And remember this . . . one learns from mistakes. I believe you have learned a very valuable lesson today."

Gentle Bear smiled weakly at him. "I have, and I have also learned that my chief is a forgiving man," he said softly. "I thank you, Chief Midnight Wolf, for understanding my faults. I shall never disappoint you or my mother again."

"Never say never," Midnight Wolf said. "But I trust that you will be earnest in your attempts to do better from now on."

"*Ho,* I will," Gentle Bear said anxiously, then rode

onward with his chin held high, proud to be ac-
knowledged by a chief whose heart was so good.

But Gentle Bear knew that if what he had done
brought the white pony soldiers into their village,
no one would forgive Gentle Bear, not even his forgiving chief.

He prayed that this catastrophe would not happen!

CHAPTER ELEVEN

When the praise thou meetest
To thine ear is sweetest. . . .
—*Thomas Moore*

Sheleen moaned as she awakened.

Her leg throbbed, as did her head, and she was aware of being feverish. She was chilled through and through from having slept in the rain the entire night.

She was very aware of just how weak she was as she tried to sit up, then fell back down onto her side when dizziness claimed her.

She was so glad when Fluffy came and snuggled next to her. Her cat had found her way back to her, but her horse seemed lost forever after fleeing during the storm.

She blamed the lightning and thunder for her loss, and the rain for making her even more ill than she would have been otherwise. It was one thing to have a wound that throbbed unmercifully, but another thing to have been wet and cold for so long. If she didn't get pneumonia, she would be surprised.

Too weak to move, she snuggled Fluffy even closer, taking what warmth she could from the cat. Pulling her hat off, she ran her fingers through hair that was thankfully dry.

She looked heavenward. "Oh, please, Lord, send somebody my way, or . . . or . . . I might not make it," she whispered. "But please send someone besides Indians to help me."

Tears fell from her eyes as she whispered, "And where were you, my wolves, to warn me of this danger? You did not come to me in any dream!"

She was also surprised that the young brave who had shot her had not brought some of his people's warriors to her. Surely they would want to know why she was there, so close to their village. They would also want to know if more white people were in the area.

She would have thought they would be searching the area all around her for any signs of other whites being there. It puzzled her that the young brave had not led any warriors to her. Surely he saw her as an enemy.

If she could only get the chance to tell them who her father was, his name would be quickly recognized. She hoped they would remember him as the one who roamed Minnesota land before the hangings of three years ago, helping Indians in need.

But not all Indians knew her father's name, nor his goodness toward them.

She would just have to wait and see if the young brave did lead his people's warriors to her, and what they would do when they found her.

Feverish and chilled, she fell into another restless sleep.

CHAPTER TWELVE

Her face it bloomed like a sweet flower
And stole my heart away complete.
—*John Clare*

As Gentle Bear led Midnight Wolf and the other warriors onward, Midnight Wolf felt even more disappointed in his charge than before. He was just now realizing that Gentle Bear had gone quite a distance from the village. He had gone way too far, considering that he had known the dangers facing his people.

"We are almost there," Gentle Bear suddenly said, looking quickly at Midnight Wolf. Ahead could be seen the shine of the lake through the trees. The sight of many ducks resting around it, made Gentle Bear feel guilty all over again for what he had done.

Midnight Wolf thought it best not to arrive on horses, for that would cause the ducks to scatter, alerting the injured party that someone was near. He would assume that the one who'd shot him was coming back to the scene of the crime. His female companion would ready her firearm and shoot without stopping to ask questions.

He nodded at his warriors as he drew rein. His warriors and Gentle Bear followed his lead, stopping their horses behind him.

"We will go the rest of the way on foot," Midnight Wolf said as he dismounted. He turned to Gentle Bear. "*Hiyupo,* come forward. You will lead. We will follow."

Gentle Bear gulped hard, nodded, then dismounted and led the warriors stealthily beneath the shadow of the thick trees.

He kept gazing from side to side, wondering if they were being watched. Were they even now the targets of whoever might have been traveling with the injured man? If this person had expected Gentle Bear's return, she might be aiming directly at Gentle Bear's gut.

Not wanting to think about those possibilities, Gentle Bear studied the forest ahead of him.

He now saw things that were familiar to him. He saw thick berry bushes. He smelled wild flowers that were abloom in the damp soil beneath the trees. He was keenly aware of honeysuckle that was twining its way up a tree.

There was one tree in particular that he remembered very well. It was a tree that had been struck sometime in the past by lightning. He could actually see the zigzag of where the lightning had hit, as though the lightning strike had become imbedded in the trunk of the old oak tree.

His heart pounded because he knew that this tree was where he had stopped and taken aim when he had seen movement among the brush yesterday.

"*Ahpe*, wait!" he said quickly. "This is where I loosed my arrow from my bowstring." A shiver raced across his flesh. "Look ahead, by that break in the trees, and you will see where the tiny man fell after my arrow pieced his flesh."

Much taller than Gentle Bear, and able to see farther than the young brave could see, Midnight Wolf sought and found a slight figure asleep on the ground.

Noting that the breeches leg of the sleeper was torn up to where a wound had been bandaged, he knew that they had just found the person Gentle Bear had shot.

But what truly puzzled him was why his charge would lie about having shot a man, when it was so obvious that, although this person wore a man's clothes, the injured party was a *woman*.

From this vantage point he could see long, black hair framing the delicate face of a woman, not a man!

Midnight Wolf again gazed at the wounded leg, and then at a white cat that snuggled against the woman. Surely that was the animal that had been traveling in the saddlebag on the black steed, for

109

the cat's fur was white like the hairs he had seen in the saddlebag.

A cat was a rare sight. Even whites did not seem to favor this animal, for rarely had he seen cats among them. The few times he'd seen a tiny replica of a panther like this, he'd asked what sort of animal it was.

His eyes were drawn back to the woman's face.

She had beautiful features, but he recognized the flush of fever on her cheeks. He also noticed that she was shivering.

He guessed that the fever was caused by her wound, or from having lain helpless through the night in the rain. Her clothes looked as though they were still wet.

"That is a *mitawin*, a woman," Gentle Bear gasped. He was stunned that he had actually shot a woman. And because this was a woman, his guilt was twofold.

He turned to Midnight Wolf. "When I saw this stranger, the hair was hidden beneath a man's hat," he blurted out. "That is why I thought I had shot a man with my arrow, not a *mitawin*."

He gazed again at Sheleen. "And I have never seen a white woman wear men's clothes before," he said, his voice breaking.

He turned pleading eyes up to his chief. "You do see how I could have made the mistake, do you not?" he said, almost pleadingly.

Midnight Wolf searched for a hat, relieved when he saw one lying not far from where the woman was asleep on the ground. At least he knew that his charge was innocent of lying about whom he had downed with his arrow.

He started to tell Gentle Bear not to worry any more about what had happened here, that a serious talk would come later, but stopped when the fluffy white cat sensed they were there. The animal came up to him and started rubbing herself back and forth against one of Midnight Wolf's legs.

Taken by the loveliness of the cat, Gentle Bear bent to his knees and gathered the animal into his arms.

He was captivated by the purring sounds the cat was making as he stroked her beautiful white fur.

When he had seen this sort of animal with white people, he had always hungered to touch one.

Midnight Wolf directed his attention once again only to the woman. As he studied her, his eyes narrowed with suspicion. "This woman might be a spy, sent to infiltrate our village," he said tightly. "How cowardly for the white people to use a woman, and especially one made to look like a man. Perhaps they realized that a woman traveling alone in woman's clothes would draw much suspicion her way."

And he was certain now that there was no man with her. The clothes in the saddlebag attested to that. It would be easy to get answers from her once she was well enough to speak.

But her welfare came first. He must take her to his village and make her comfortable and warm. He would have his shaman medicate her wound.

Answers would come later.

111

His gaze shifted to where her rifle lay so close to her. He must get it before she awakened!

He gathered his warriors around him, giving them instructions about his plans for the woman, and telling them to quietly move into a circle around her as he took possession of her rifle.

Gentle Bear stood back away from them, holding the cat, and stayed there as the warriors and his chief surrounded the woman. Still she slept, unaware that she was no longer alone with only her cat.

Quiet as a panther, Midnight Wolf approached the woman and plucked up her rifle. He handed it to a warrior, then knelt down beside her.

Before he awakened her, Midnight Wolf studied her face and hair. She had the hair of an Indian, coal black, somewhat coarse, and very long, yet her skin was the palest of pale.

So, no.

She could not be Indian.

She was a white woman who had no doubt come to cause his people trouble. Why else would she be so close to his village, alone?

Sheleen stirred in her sleep, then shivered from the fever reaching into her unconsciousness.

Slowly she began to awaken.

Her eyes flew open wide when she saw an Indian warrior kneeling beside her, and then she became aware of many others as they stepped closer.

When Gentle Bear came up to where she lay, still holding Fluffy, Sheleen gazed at him. Even through the cloudiness of her fever, she recognized the young brave.

He was the one who had shot her.

She silently prayed that the young brave had brought the warriors of his village to help her, not to finish what he had begun.

She gasped when she realized what he was holding.

Her cat!

Oh, surely they weren't planning to kill her cat! She tried to reach out for Fluffy, but she was so weak, her arms fell back to the ground.

Her only hope was that one among those who were there might recognize her to be the daughter of the man who had always looked after Indians in their time of trouble. Could these warriors even be among those her father knew?

Were they Dakota?

So weary, so tired, so feverish, Sheleen tried to fight off unconsciousness, for she knew she must stay awake, at least long enough to talk with the one who seemed in charge.

But before she could get one word spoken, she fell back into the black void of unconsciousness.

Panic grabbed at Midnight Wolf's heart when he saw the woman fall into another feverish sleep. Then he realized just how much seeing her collapse had startled him. It was as though something had grabbed at the pit of his stomach. Even his heart seemed affected, for it was now pounding hard from fear that this woman might not survive.

Why should he be affected in such a way by a mere white woman? She was no better than the men who so heartlessly took the lives of red men and women . . . and sometimes even children.

In truth, she was probably just like them . . . surely as ruthless and heartless!

But now was not the time to wonder about his attitude toward the woman. He must get her to his village so that she could be treated by his shaman.

And her clothes, the clothes of a man which had caused so much trouble, were still wet and a further threat to her health.

"We will take this woman to our village, where she can have warm, dry clothes, food, and medicine from our shaman," Midnight Wolf announced.

He looked from man to man and recognized a mixture of feelings among them.

He could tell that some of his warriors disapproved of his chief's decision to take the woman to their village, yet they did not voice this concern aloud. Their chief had already decided what would become of the woman and no one questioned his wisdom, for he had never led them down the wrong path.

He had been loyal to them all, keeping them safely hidden away from white people.

While some did not want the woman taken to their village, Midnight Wolf could tell that others saw her as an innocent, ailing woman, a victim of circumstances beyond her control. These openly agreed that she should go to their village, where she could be cared for.

"Come," Midnight Wolf said as he bent to his knees and slowly and carefully swept the woman into his arms. "We leave now for our home."

He carried her back to his horse and then, after getting her situated on his lap once he had mounted his steed, he started his horse toward home.

As he rode onward at a slow lope, he made certain to travel slowly, for he did not want to cause any more pain in the woman's injured leg.

She lay there against him, her cheek resting against his bare chest, and Midnight Wolf could not help but be taken anew by her loveliness, her petiteness.

He would never forget her eyes . . . so dark as they looked up at him. Again, he wondered about her heritage, then scoffed at his wonder. She was a white woman, no doubt with every other white person's hatred for the red man.

Yes, he would see to her health, get her well enough to question her, and then decide what to do with her.

He understood the danger of keeping her at his village as a captive, and it was not his practice to take captives. To do so would only bring trouble to his people, might in the end cause his people's freedom to be taken away.

Ho, he did have a big decision to make.

But not now.

This decision must be made later. It all depended on the woman, and the answers she gave him when he questioned her.

But first, he must get the woman to talk, so that she could explain why she was so close to his village, alone, and dressed like a man.

CHAPTER THIRTEEN

When she is absent, I no more
Delight in all that pleased before.
—*George Lyttelton*

Raymond had awoken feeling much better, and now he and Big Bear Moon had just arrived at Sheleen's cabin. They searched the cabin, making certain she was not there, then went outside again.

Big Bear Moon was an expert at tracking. He studied the land, searching for a horse's hoofprints. And when he found what he was looking for, Raymond rode beside him as the scout began following the tracks that led away from Sheleen's cabin.

Raymond smiled wickedly as Big Bear Moon continued to follow the tracks. He was depending on the redskin for everything, for Raymond's hand was still too sore to do much with it, and he most definitely had not yet learned how to shoot with his left hand.

But there was a certain benefit from having the throbbing wound; it kept him focused. He was determined to find the woman who had robbed him of his trigger finger, and when he did find her, he would make her sorry that she ever existed!

"Big Bear Moon, you do think we'll find her, don't you?" Raymond asked, wincing as the savage scout turned cold, dark eyes to him.

That look was not the one he'd expected.

It made his blood run cold, the iciness of the scout's stare was intensely unfriendly.

"What's wrong with you?" Raymond asked, his voice betraying the uneasiness he had felt more than once since he had started on this search with the Injun scout. "Why do you give me those . . . those . . . damn cold looks? I'm your friend, remember, not your enemy."

"Because I am helping you find the woman, that does not make me your friend, nor do I want your friendship," Big Bear Moon said coldly. "I am with you only because of the money you have paid me for a job you want done. Friendship does not go with the job. Greenbacks are all that I am interested in."

"You're some strange savage, you are," Raymond said, flinching when that word "savage" seemed to cause Big Bear Moon's eyes to narrow in fury.

"I take it back," Raymond gulped out. "You ain't

no savage. I . . . I . . . just have a habit of seeing all redskins as murdering savages. That's all."

"If you ever refer to me being a savage again, you will see just how savage this red man can be," Big Bear Moon said, his eyes gleaming like fire. "Now keep your thoughts and words to yourself and let me do my job. The sooner I get this behind me, the sooner I will no longer have to smell the stink of your white flesh."

Raymond paled even more at that comment. This was the sort of redskin who would just as soon use his huge, sharp knife to scalp a white man as to look at one.

Wanting to end their association as soon as possible, Raymond now looked for the tracks as well. But he was unskilled at tracking, and did not see a one.

He had no idea how the savage was seeing tracks that to Raymond did not even seem to exist!

He eyed Big Bear Moon suspiciously. Was the savage playing a game of hide and seek with him?

Was he not really seeing tracks, only pretending to? If so . . . why . . . ?

CHAPTER FOURTEEN

With longing eyes I wait,
Expectant of her.
—*William Makepeace Thackeray*

As Midnight Wolf rode into his village with the woman still sleeping on his lap, her cheek pressed against his chest, he was keenly aware of how his people came from their lodges and watched the stranger being brought among them.

Midnight Wolf could see much apprehension and questioning in his people's eyes, and he understood. They understood his feelings about taking anyone captive.

On those occasions when they had no choice but to take a prisoner, the captive had been treated with respect.

Most times the prisoner became a friend of the

Wolf Band because of how respectfully he was treated.

Their prisoners were never harmed. They were given comfortable lodging and fed until they placed a hand before them, saying they had already had enough food, thank you.

Because of this kind treatment, prisoners developed respect for the Wolf Band. They were then released to go on their way, but not clothed as they had been when they had arrived. When they left the Dakota village, they wore the best clothes of the Wolf Band!

As Midnight Wolf rode onward toward his shaman's lodge, he registered the concern in his people's eyes. They were worried that he had brought a stranger among them, and not just any stranger, but a person with white skin.

But he knew that none of his people would question him about his decision to bring this woman to their village.

They trusted his judgment in all things, and the woman's frailness was plain to all. They would not condemn him for aiding her.

His people were of kind hearts; he felt sure they would feel compassion for her, too.

They could see her injured leg and knew how the injury had happened. He noticed that many of his people were no longer looking at the woman, but instead at Gentle Bear as he rode on his pony beside Midnight Wolf. In Midnight Wolf's absence, his people had no doubt discussed the wrong Gentle Bear had done this woman.

Midnight Wolf and Gentle Bear halted their horses in front of the shaman's lodge, while the warriors who had accompanied Midnight Wolf on this mission went their own way, to rejoin their families.

Gentle Bear's mother soon appeared, tears in her eyes as she stood back and waited for her chief to either excuse her son, or continue to include him in what he was doing.

Moon Eagle, the village shaman, stepped from his tepee.

Midnight Wolf observed his shaman's reaction to what he saw. The woman still slept snuggled against Midnight Wolf's chest.

He read a mixture of emotions in his shaman's eyes and understood. Moon Eagle saw how frail this woman was, just as he must see the feverish flush to her cheeks. It was clear that she needed immediate attention, or she might die.

"Come inside," Moon Eagle said, holding aside his entrance flap.

Gentle Bear quickly dismounted and stood by quietly as his chief left his own horse, carrying the woman in his powerfully muscled arms.

"May I go with you?" Gentle Bear blurted out just as Midnight Wolf stepped up to the opened entrance flap.

Midnight Wolf turned to Gentle Bear, then gazed at the cat that had just leaped from where it had been sleeping inside Midnight Wolf's travel bag.

He shifted his eyes back to the child. "You go to your mother and give her a hug, then care for the animal," he said quietly. He saw that several children had come to look at the cat. On their faces he could see their eagerness to pet the beautiful animal.

He again gazed into his charge's dark eyes. "We will talk later," he said tightly.

Gentle Bear nodded, then ran to his mother and gave her a tight hug. He looked up into her tearful eyes. "I am sorry if I embarrassed and disappointed you," he said, his voice breaking. "I will never disappoint you again."

"That is a hard promise to make, but I will welcome it if you can manage to keep it," Rosy Dawn said, gently patting Gentle Bear on his head. She glanced over at the children, who were circled around the cat, bent to their knees as they took turns petting it.

"The animal," she said, looking back at her son. "Where did you get it?"

"It was the woman's," Gentle Bear said, humbly lowering his eyes, then looking up at his mother again. "Mother, I shot a woman, not a man. Are you even more ashamed of me, now that you know I did this to a helpless woman?" '

"Helpless?" Rosy Dawn said, then laughed softly.

"*Ho,* all men, even young braves wishing they were men, do not give women credit for much other than keeping house, making clothes, planting food, and cooking it, so I do not take offense when my own son makes the mistake. I forgive you that, my son."

She tousled his hair with a hand. "Go," she urged. "Play with the children and the lovely little animal."

Gentle Bear ran over to the children who were already playing with Fluffy.

Satisfied that Gentle Bear was occupied for the moment, and knowing that he would soon have a more serious talk with his charge about what he had done, Midnight Wolf stepped inside the shaman's lodge.

Moon Eagle gestured with a hand toward a thick pallet of furs and blankets that lay close to the lodge fire.

Midnight Wolf nodded and gently placed the woman on the pallet.

He then turned to his shaman. "The woman's clothes are wet, and so is the bandage she wrapped around her wound," he said. "I do not know what she used to medicate her wound. I have not even removed the bandage to examine it. I thought it best to leave that to you."

Moon Eagle nodded, then knelt beside the woman.

He placed a hand on her brow, then gazed up at Midnight Wolf. "She is very feverish," he said. "I will

125

see to her welfare. If you have other things to attend to, there is no need for you to wait here. What I must do for the woman will take time."

Midnight Wolf did, indeed, have something he needed to tend to: Gentle Bear. He had not yet had the time to talk to Gentle Bear about the consequences of disobeying his chief's orders.

"*Ho*, I do have things that I must see to," Midnight Wolf said. He placed a gentle hand on his shaman's shoulder. "I will return later to see how the woman is faring."

Moon Eagle nodded, then rose and went to the back of his lodge for the supplies that he would need to care for the woman. The first thing he would do was to wrap her in blankets until she was warmed through and through.

Midnight Wolf stood just outside the shaman's lodge, his eyes following the movements of Gentle Bear, who was proud to be the one that all the children were clamoring around. The cat also seemed to be enjoying the attention; it would prance, then suddenly flop on the ground on its back, rolling around in the thick grass that was like a carpet in the village, kept lush and green by the attention of the Wolf Band.

Midnight Wolf hated to disrupt the happy group, but he needed to speak with Gentle Bear. Midnight Wolf went to the children and placed a hand on Gentle Bear's shoulder.

When his charge turned wondering eyes up at

him, Midnight Wolf smiled. "*Hi-yupo,* come," he said. "We have something important to discuss."

He could see that the child swallowed hard as he rose to his feet, the cat no longer on his mind, but instead, his fear of disapproval that might last a lifetime.

Gentle Bear might have thought that he had gotten off easy with what he had done. Now he obviously realized that his chief had just postponed the reckoning until they had the time to discuss his wrongdoing more seriously.

Gentle Bear glanced over at his mother, who was sitting outside her lodge, sewing a new pair of moccasins. He smiled wanly at her, then went to Midnight Wolf's tepee with him.

As was normal, the chief's fire was kept burning at all times. The women took turns doing this for him, as well as bringing him nourishing food.

Midnight Wolf gestured with a hand toward a blanket that was spread beside his fire. "Sit and we shall have a serious talk about what you have done. You have displeased me as well as your mother," he said, watching the child as Gentle Bear nervously sat down on the blanket beside Midnight Wolf.

"All Dakota children yearn for wisdom and look for experience," Gentle Bear suddenly blurted out. "That . . . that . . . is why I went alone to hunt. I believe that if I grow wiser by doing, my people will honor me. If I become a good hunter, it will please

127

my mother. I could not just dream and think about learning to hunt alone. I had to do it."

Midnight Wolf was momentarily stunned that Gentle Bear should speak so openly of his feelings without first being asked to.

He did not want to add another disappointment to his list of disappointments concerning Gentle Bear, so he tried not to think about it, or scold the child for impulsiveness.

This was a time to talk, to teach, and for his young charge to learn. It was also time for Gentle Bear to listen, not talk.

Midnight Wolf crossed his legs at his ankles, placed his hands on his knees, then gazed at Gentle Bear again. "Do you see that going behind your chief's back to do what you were told not to do is the same as a lie?" he asked.

"My chief, I do not want to believe that it was," Gentle Bear said softly, his eyes now wavering beneath his chief's steady, almost accusing, stare.

"Young brave, a Dakota may lie once, but if he continues to do so, no one will believe him," Midnight Wolf said. "All Dakota despise lying above all things, and for the liar, they have no toleration. Truth is power, and dishonesty of any sort is bad."

Now knowing the true depth of disappointment that he had caused his chief to feel, Gentle Bear lowered his eyes. He was near tears. "My chief, I did not think about anything but wanting to be the man of the house, a brave capable of putting food on my mother's table," he said softly. "I did not see that as a lie, but I apologize if it was."

He then blurted out, "I did not believe killing a rabbit was enough to prove my skills as a hunter. I . . . I . . . wanted my mother to have duck in her cook pot."

Seeing how truly distraught the child was, and loving him as though he were his very own son, Midnight Wolf reached over and placed his arms around the child, drawing him into his embrace.

"I forgive you this one bad judgment, but do not make the same mistake a second time, for I will not be as generous again to you," Midnight Wolf said.

To himself, Midnight Wolf was thinking that, in a sense, Gentle Bear had done Midnight Wolf a favor. He had led him to an interloper on their land who might pose a threat to his people, even if the stranger was a woman!

"Thank you, oh, thank you, my chief," Gentle Bear said, giving Midnight Wolf a long hug.

Then Gentle Bear straightened away from Midnight Wolf and gazed at him. "How is the woman?" he blurted out.

"It is too early to say," Midnight Wolf said, rising. He placed a caring hand on Gentle Bear's shoulder. "Go home to your mother. But remember well what I have said to you today, and learn from it."

"I shall," Gentle Bear said. He scrambled to his

feet. He grew serious again. "What about the woman's cat? Can I have the cat, to care for it, while the woman gets strong and well again?"

"If your mother does not mind, yes, for now, the cat can be your responsibility," Midnight Wolf said, walking to the entranceway with Gentle Bear. "Go. Enjoy the animal, and share the cat with your friends. I saw how they also enjoyed petting and playing with it."

"I shall," Gentle Bear said.

He started to leave, but Midnight Wolf reached out and stopped him. "Wait," he said. "I have something for you."

Gentle Bear's eyes widened and his heart raced as he watched Midnight Wolf go to where he stored things of importance to himself.

His eyes widened farther when Midnight Wolf chose a small buckskin bag from his treasures, then turned and returned to Gentle Bear.

Gentle Bear was immediately aware of a strong odor wafting from the bag and understood what caused it. Horses had a strong odor that was carried in the small vestigial toe on the fetlock. For this reason the Dakota scaled off a small bit of this toe and put it in his medicine bag. This odor reminded an individual that he had his medicine bag with him to keep him from harm; it was also a reminder to pray often to the Great Mystery.

"I made this medicine bag for you," Midnight Wolf said as he handed it over to the child. "You add what is sacred and special to you. You will keep the bag with you when you are outside the safety of our village. When you are in our village, store it among your possessions and keep it safe."

"This is mine, to keep forever?" Gentle Bear asked, staring incredulously at the bag resting in the palm of his hand.

Then he turned slow eyes up to his chief. "Truly mine?" he said, curling his fingers around the bag.

"*Ho*, yours, and remember how to use it, and when," Midnight Wolf said. "Now you can go."

Gentle Bear smiled widely and hugged the bag to his chest. "*Pilamaye,* thank you, my chief," he said humbly. "I shall cherish it always."

Gentle Bear hurried from the tepee as Midnight Wolf held the flap aside for him. He ran to his tepee. His mother wasn't there to see his special gift, but he would show it to her later.

He placed the bag among his own stored treasures, in a box that he had made from an old oak branch.

He stared at the box before sliding it beneath a covering of blankets, still finding it hard to believe that his chief had given the bag to him, right after Gentle Bear had disappointed him.

That meant everything to Gentle Bear. That meant that his chief still loved and trusted him.

Feeling proud, Gentle Bear left his tepee and went back to the group of children. He knelt down among them, his hand reaching out to pet the white animal as others joined him. Yet even as he did so, his mind was still full of his chief and the gift that Midnight Wolf had given him.

Midnight Wolf's mind was full of the white woman and the mysterious way she seemed to have come into his people's lives. He gazed at his shaman's closed entrance flap.

He could not stop thinking about the woman's lovely, innocent face. Until now, all enemy whites had features repulsive to him; they seemed ungainly and awkward in manner.

But this woman was none of those things. She was beautiful, ah, *ho*, she seemed so innocent.

But she was also . . . *washechu!*

Needing guidance in prayer, Midnight Wolf left his lodge and ran into the forest. He ran until he came to a clearing where a knob of rock rose from the ground.

He went to its tallest height, where he could see over the treetops, and watch the slow spirals of smoke reaching up into the heavens from the women's cook fires.

He fell to his knees onto soft moss that grew over the hard rock, then lifted his eyes to the sky. His arms held above his head, his hands reaching heavenward, he began to pray softly to *Wakan Tanka*, the grandfather of all Dakota.

He prayed for guidance and knowledge, knowing that he was his people's leader and that the wellbeing of his people depended on him.

132

The woman's loveliness flashed into his mind's eye, but he forced it away, for this was not the time or place to let her enter his thoughts, or his heart. Perhaps there would never be a time, for he did not yet know her reason for being so close to his village.

Nor could he allow himself to forget that she was from the white community.

Until he knew her true purpose for being so close to his village, he could not see her as anything but his . . . enemy!

CHAPTER FIFTEEN

> Let thy loveliness fade as it will,
> And around the dear ruin each wish of my heart
> Would entwine itself verdantly still.
> —*Thomas Moore*

Sheleen slowly awakened. When she saw an elderly Indian sitting beside her, separating one plant from another, and placing them in small buckskin bags, she could not help being afraid. Clearly, she was among many Indians, in the midst of their village.

She knew that this Indian must be a shaman, for he seemed very familiar with medicinal plants. Her father had pointed out to her herbs such as the old man was sorting through, in case she were ever away from him and his medicines.

She recognized a purple cone plant, a single-stalked plant called *icahpe-hu*.

It had a long and slender black root that, when

chewed and applied to an injury, eased pain. It was known to almost magically cure cuts.

She believed that this particular plant had been applied to her wound while she slept. The wound where she had cut her leg open in order to remove the arrow seemed to throb less than before.

She tried now to concentrate on what had brought her to this time and place but it was hard for her to remember anything past the moment when she had fallen asleep in the rain, feeling as though she might never wake up again.

She did recall that she had been shot with an arrow!

She had removed the arrow from her leg with one of her father's surgical tools. The fact that she had remembered enough of his teaching to do it, still amazed her.

She was feeling less pain in her leg than before, but she was afraid to move, to see how the wound was faring.

All she knew was that her clothes had been removed and that she was warm in a blanket wrapped snugly around her, the close-by fire adding to her comfort.

She could not remember how she happened to be in this Indian's lodge. Flashes of that day, when the child had shot her with the arrow, came to her mind. But so much else was gone from her memory.

She didn't want the old Indian to see that she was awake, not now, anyhow, so she closed her eyes. She wanted more time to think through and remember the events leading up to her present circumstances.

She had thought that she was in control of her own destiny after fleeing the whiskered man who had killed her father.

But now?

She had no idea what lay before her.

She took it as a good sign that those who had brought her to this place were seeing to her welfare. Surely that meant they had accepted her into their fold, instead of casting her aside to possibly die a slow death.

She knew enough about wounds to realize that if she had been left alone, she would not have been able to travel for some time, or search for food.

Both she and her cat would have perished.

Her cat!

The thought of Fluffy caused her eyes to fly open. She found the old Indian gazing at her.

Surely he *was* a shaman, for he had all the signs of being an Indian doctor and holy man.

"You are awake," Moon Eagle said, yet not smiling at her as he reached a hand out to touch her brow. "And your fever has left you."

He drew his hand back and folded his hands on his lap. "You will live," he then said, matter-of-factly.

"*Pilamaye,* thank you for helping me," she murmured, seeing how her use of the Dakota language made his eyes widen in wonder.

She quickly asked him a question, for she did not

want to explain to him why she knew the Dakota language.

"My cat," she blurted out. "When I was brought here, was my cat brought with me?"

"Your cat is in the village," Moon Eagle said, slowly nodding. "The animal is being cared for by the young brave who led my chief and warriors to you."

Sheleen stiffened, for she could only surmise the young brave this shaman was speaking of was none other than the one who had shot her with one of his arrows.

Knowing that Fluffy was in the care of this particular brave made her wonder if her cat was in the best of hands. She did not trust a child who would shoot her with an arrow.

There were so many questions she wanted to ask this elderly man, but she was afraid that he, in turn, would want many answers from her.

Until she knew what these people's plans were for her, she did not want to offer any information to any of them, not even a shaman who was the most trusted man in any village second to the chief.

She purposely pretended to fall asleep. Until she remembered more of what had happened to her, and knew which Indians had taken her into their village and whether or not they were trustworthy, she would pretend to be asleep as often as she could.

She hoped that, soon she would be able to open

up and tell them all what had happened to her these past days, especially how she had lost a beloved father in such a horrible way.

But until she knew whether or not they held deep resentment toward all white people, she would not offer any more information about herself.

She hoped that the chief would make an appearance soon so she could look into his eyes and see whether he was a friend or a foe.

She had been taught such skills by her father who, although he had no Indian blood running through his veins, knew enough about Indian culture to have taught her many things.

CHAPTER SIXTEEN

> My lady comes at last,
> Timid and stepping fast
> And hastening hither,
> With modest eyes downcast.
> —*William Makepeace Thackeray*

Raymond and Big Bear Moon had traveled relentlessly onward, stopping only long enough to eat and sleep.

Raymond was proud that his scout was so skilled at tracking. Big Bear Moon spotted tracks along the way that other people surely could not see, for Raymond himself had not been able to see any of them.

Raymond had complete faith in the tracking ability of this Dakota Indian scout!

They had just spent a full night beneath a makeshift shelter that Big Bear Moon had made of flexible willow branches. It was morning now and they had already eaten and were again on their way.

Raymond would never give up on finding the woman who had shot off his finger! She would pay.

Ah, yes, he knew of many ways to make her wish that she had never used that tiny firearm on him.

The fact that she had managed to do such damage with such a miniscule weapon made him even angrier; yet he was also apprehensive about this woman's unusual skill with firearms.

Perhaps it was just luck that had allowed her to get the best of him. Well, he would make sure that nothing was left to luck once he found the hellion!

"Just how far can a woman travel by herself?" Raymond said, drawing Big Bear Moon's eyes to him. "Lord, Big Bear Moon, are you certain you're following the right tracks?"

"Do not question what I do," Big Bear Moon growled. "Just be quiet. When you are tired of searching for the woman, I will be glad to go on my way, as you go on yours."

"You won't get paid a red cent if you don't find her," Raymond said, his eyes narrowing angrily.

"You seem to forget that you have already paid me for my services," Big Bear Moon said, smiling slyly. "And just try getting me to hand the money back over to you."

"You'd better not be foolin' with me or you might not wake up to see another sunrise the next time we stop for the night," Raymond said.

He swallowed hard and wished he hadn't said that when the Indian scout placed a hand on his sheathed knife and gave Raymond a look that made chills ride his spine.

"I didn't mean it," Raymond blurted out. "Just go on and do your job. I'll follow and be silent while doin' it."

"You will live longer that way," Big Bear Moon said, easing his hand from his knife.

Raymond watched Big Bear Moon again search for tracks that to Raymond did not seem to be there. He had no choice but to believe the scout knew what he was doing and wasn't playing some sort of evil game with Raymond.

But Raymond would never know, not until he learned whether or not he was being led to Sheleen.

He sighed and rode onward, glancing up at the sun, which was beating down on him mercilessly.

He wiped his dry mouth with his right shirt sleeve, then winced when pain shot through his injured hand all over again. It was a constant reminder of why he was with the scout in the first place.

The pain.

Oh, Lord, the pain!

He glanced down at the rifle that he had placed in a gun boot at the left side of his horse, instead of the usual right side.

Even if he needed to use the firearm to protect

143

himself, he knew that he couldn't even grab the rifle from the gun boot without fumbling awkwardly.

He felt helpless, utterly helpless. . . .

"I saw you glance at your rifle," Big Bear Moon said, giving Raymond a hard glare.

"Do you have eyes in the back of your head?" Raymond growled. "And what if I was looking at my rifle? That doesn't mean I was plannin' to use it on you."

"If I get one more hint that you plan to ambush me by any means, I will not hesitate to use my knife on you and go my own way, happy to be rid of you," Big Bear Moon said flatly.

Raymond returned the glare, yet inside himself, his belly felt like a puddle of soft jelly!

CHAPTER SEVENTEEN

> I ne'er was struck before that hour
> With love so sudden and so sweet.
> —*John Clare*

The laughter of children outside of Moon Eagle's te-pee awakened Sheleen.

She looked slowly around her, perfectly aware now of where she was.

A fragrant mixture of sage and cedar filled the te-pee, as Sheleen gazed at Moon Eagle, who sat on the opposite side of the fire from her, his eyes closed while he prayed. She had become keenly aware of the shaman's coldness toward her these past two days.

Even though Moon Eagle had seen to her welfare since she had arrived at the village, it was quite evident that he resented her being there among his people, especially in his own personal lodge.

But his chief had not offered to take Sheleen anywhere else, and each day she remained, the shaman seemed to resent her even more.

She looked toward the closed entrance flap, wondering when the chief would come again. He had come to visit her every day.

Even through the foggy haze of her fever, which was fortunately gone now, she had been aware that the chief had been there sitting beside her.

While he sat there, he and his shaman had discussed things, thinking she couldn't hear or understand. She had discovered that the warrior, who seemed truly interested in her welfare, was these people's chief.

The shaman had addressed his chief more than once as Midnight Wolf. She had learned that she was among the Dakota people, and she also knew now that the young brave who had shot her was named Gentle Bear.

She was so relieved to have discovered that she was among the Dakota people. Her father had mainly helped them over other Indian tribes, and there was a reason for that . . . a reason that she soon hoped to be able to share with the handsome chief. She wanted him to know that he had not been wrong to offer her help, or bring her among his people.

When she was stronger, and there was trust between her and the chief, she would tell him everything . . . even more than she had shared with most people.

She would tell him things that only her father knew about her!

She felt that being completely open with the chief was necessary, for deep down, where she felt her lonesomeness so much, she preferred staying with these people to moving onward, where no one would truly welcome her.

She was a person without a family, a home, or love.

When she had listened to this chief's voice as he spoke with his shaman, she had learned much about him, for she was good at judging a person's true worth just by listening to what he or she said.

She had been taught this skill long ago by someone she had loved very much, and whom she had lost far too early in life. . . .

Before Sheleen could turn her eyes away, and pretend she was asleep again, as she always did when the young and handsome chief came to sit beside her as he visited with his shaman, Midnight Wolf was suddenly there. The entrance flap was drawn aside so quickly, Sheleen could only gape at it. Standing there was the young chief she found so heavenly handsome.

Yes, those times when he had stood to leave and was not paying attention to her, Sheleen had been able to catch a glimpse or two of him.

The first time she had seen his full facial features something warm had filled her heart, a reaction very new to her when seeing a man.

But she knew now that this was not just any ordinary man. He was good, through and through, and he was so handsome she felt feelings for him that no man had ever caused.

She knew now that what she was feeling was not only infatuation, but perhaps even love.

She had heard that there was such a thing as love at first sight. She had always scoffed at such a thing, calling it hogwash and nonsense. But it had now happened to her and she was not quite sure what to do about it.

She knew that if Midnight Wolf talked with her for long, he would be able to see how she felt, for she did not see how she could possibly hide it.

And she did not believe it was wrong to suddenly love this man, an Indian. She knew enough about him to know that even her father would approve of him. If he were alive, he would realize that his daughter had fallen in love for the first time in her life.

He would even give her his blessing, for he had had a special place in his heart for all people with red skin, as did Sheleen.

"I see that you are awake," Midnight Wolf began as he came farther into the tepee, drawing the shaman's eyes open, and interrupting his prayers.

"Yes, I am awake," Sheleen said, her voice sounding foreign to her because of the feelings surging through her.

As he came closer and gazed down at her, she

saw how bright and steady his gaze was, and how his midnight black eyes revealed strength and power.

Everything about him appealed to her: his quiet, dignified manner, his smooth copper skin, his sculpted features, his fur-wrapped braids that hung long over a plain buckskin shirt, the way his muscled legs fit into his fringed, buckskin breeches. Sheleen found it was difficult to keep her composure.

She knew that she must be blushing, for her cheeks were hot. But neither the chief, nor the shaman would know why. They would believe that she still had a touch of fever.

Just as Midnight Wolf took a step closer to her, he was stopped by frantic screams outside. With a quick turn, he was gone from the tepee again.

Sheleen leaned up on an elbow when the shaman left the tepee right behind him.

She gazed at the closed entrance flap and listened to a woman's frantic voice just outside the lodge, telling her chief that her daughter, Pretty Wing, only four winters old, had been bitten by a shiny black spider with a strange red design on its body.

Sheleen was almost certain that the child had been bitten by a black widow spider. When the woman described the red design on the body of the spider, Sheleen got a cold feeling around her heart, for she knew that the child's bite might be a lethal one.

Apparently the child was now unconscious and the woman was pleading with Moon Eagle to take her daughter inside his lodge and see to the bite.

Sheleen's eyes widened and she looked quickly around her. There was no space for another ill person in this tepee. Sheleen surely would be moved to make room for the child.

And if so, where would she be taken . . . ?

She heard Moon Eagle tell Midnight Wolf that the white woman must be moved, that Pretty Wing must take her place in the bed the white woman had been occupying. The child needed all the attention of the village shaman.

There was a moment of silence.

Sheleen could almost read Midnight Wolf's thoughts as he was faced with this dilemma. If Sheleen had to be moved, where should she be taken?

She was fairly certain he would not leave her alone in a tepee. He would expect her to try to flee.

Midnight Wolf came back into the lodge and knelt down beside her. "A child has taken ill from a spider bite," he softly explained. "My shaman feels it is best that she be here in his lodge so he can care for her, as he has so dutifully cared for you."

Even as Midnight Wolf was speaking, he was searching his mind for the best course of action. He was not certain where to take the white woman. All the tepees in his village were occupied, and he could not leave their captive alone.

Surely once she was stronger, she would try to leave as soon as she found an opportunity. He could not allow her to go.

He felt he had to learn more about this mysterious woman who was so tiny and vulnerable, yet had set out on her own in a world where all kinds of danger awaited a woman alone.

Ho, he needed more time to know her better.

"I will take you to my lodge," Midnight Wolf said. It was the only logical place. When he could not be there, he would assign someone to sit with her and care for her, if care were still needed.

He reached down and swept her into his arms.

With the blankets thrown aside, revealing the dress she now wore—one Gentle Bear's mother had generously given her—Midnight Wolf paused for a moment, just to look at her. The dress looked so right on her.

Then realizing how questioningly she was looking into his eyes, he rose with her snuggled in his arms, and walked to the entrance flap.

Sheleen clung to him. She had fallen willingly into his gentle embrace as he lifted her from the bed of blankets and furs, for to her this was the perfect plan.

She needed to be away from one man who despised her—the shaman's cold, unfriendly eyes attested to his dislike—and she longed to be with the other man, the handsome chief. She would feel much safer with him.

Just as Midnight Wolf left the tepee with Sheleen,

the sick child was carried inside by her father. Her mother, wailing and crying, followed after them. Sheleen sympathized with the anguish the mother was feeling for her child.

"How badly ill is she?" Sheleen asked, only now realizing how weak her voice was. She was not as well, or as strong, as she had thought she was. "I heard her mother describe the spider. I am afraid it is a black widow spider and if so, the bite can be deadly if it is not seen to quickly enough."

"I am aware of such spiders, and also of the wickedness of their bites," Midnight Wolf said as he carried her away from the shaman's lodge, and through the village.

Sheleen noticed that the tepees surrounded a carpet of green turf, not the stamped-down earth that was common in so many Indian villges. Evidently these people were diligent in caring for their village.

"My shaman knows many cures," Midnight Wolf said. "He has a cure for such a spider bite as this."

Sheleen had seen her father tend to numerous spider bites. She wanted to offer her knowledge to these people. But she guessed that the shaman would not welcome her advice, nor even allow it, so she didn't say anything.

Sheleen was deeply affected by the child's plight. Should the little girl die, she would feel the loss, herself, deep inside her heart, for some time ago, she had lost a two-year-old sister from the same sort of bite.

Midnight Wolf seemed to ignore the stares of his people as they watched him carrying Sheleen.

Inside his tepee, she saw how large it was, and how comfortable the blankets and pelts looked, especially those that lay beside the softly burning flames in the fire pit.

Hanging against the brown walls of the tepee were painted bags and clothes containers decorated with brightly hued quillwork.

She could tell that clean, sweet grass had been gathered recently and spread on the floor. Rugs of rawhide were placed neatly across the grass. She knew of such rugs. They were stiff and kept their place on the floor, their softer hair side up.

At the far back of the lodge, across from the central fire and entrance, blankets were spread over a bed. Several soft buckskin pillows, were, she knew, filled with soft cottonwood floss. Painted rawhide boxes would hold stored dried meat.

Although his lodge had many things to make life comfortable, there were no signs of a woman.

Sheleen found it hard to believe that a man such as Midnight Wolf would not have taken a wife, yet she knew of some Dakota leaders who put all of their efforts into leadership, ignoring their other needs, such as women!

Surely Midnight Wolf was that sort of leader, and did not allow himself the pleasures of the flesh. His people must be of prime importance to him.

She realized that since he lived in Wisconsin with

his people now, he was among those who had successfully fled the hangings in Minnesota three years earlier. His village was too well established to have only recently been settled.

Midnight Wolf took Sheleen to his bed of rich pelts and gently laid her there, then knelt beside her. His eyes revealed to her that although he might have planned to keep his focus one hundred percent on his people's needs, at this moment in time, he had found a woman he desired!

"Your belongings will be brought to you soon," Midnight Wolf said, trying to fight off his feelings of desire for this woman, yet finding it hard. She affected him so differently from the way other women did. He was finding it hard not to want this woman, and sensed that she felt the same.

She had the look of desire, of need, in her own dark eyes. He wondered if a white woman such as she could allow herself to have feelings for a red man, whom most whites saw as savages?

Seeing so much in his eyes, and having heard a trace of huskiness in his voice, Sheleen believed that Midnight Wolf did have feelings for her.

She looked quickly away from him, for she did not want him to know that she felt the same desire he did.

Then it came to her what he had just said about her belongings. All that she had had with her when he'd found her was her father's medicine bag. Her other bag had been left on her horse.

"By belongings, do you mean the one black bag?" she asked cautiously.

"That and the saddlebag with your clothes in it," Midnight Wolf said softly. "When your horse came to our village, it still had the saddlebag on it."

"So that's where my horse went," Sheleen said, sighing with relief that her horse had been found.

"He came to our village," Midnight Wolf said, gently placing a blanket on her.

"Thank you," she murmured, then looked quickly away from him. His handsomeness was affecting her so strangely!

Hearing a shuffling beside her, and thinking that Midnight Wolf had surely left her side, she slowly turned her head. Her eyes searched for him in the dimly lit interior.

He was resting beside his fire, his thoughts elsewhere, it seemed, as he gazed into the slowly burning flames.

She studied him again, finding so much in him that made her feel she had found the man she wanted to spend the rest of her life with.

But she wasn't absolutely sure that he was single. She had seen his attentiveness to both Gentle Bear and the child's mother. She had wondered if the child was his son and the child's mother, his wife.

Yet she reminded herself that she had seen no signs of a woman living in this lodge, nor a young brave.

Too tired and weak to concern herself about

these things right now, Sheleen closed her eyes. She smiled and opened them again as Midnight Wolf approached and gently placed Fluffy next to her in the bed.

She knew that Midnight Wolf had not left to go for the cat, so the cat must have searched her out.

"Thank you," she murmured, finding it hard not to use the Dakota word for "thank you," which she knew very well.

She did not want to give Midnight Wolf any reason to wonder why she should know his language. She had to guard her tongue to be certain she did not say anything in Dakota.

In reality, she knew his language as well as she knew the language of white people!

Suddenly Sheleen blurted out her name, for until now, she had not spoken it aloud while with the Dakota people. She had not even been asked to identify herself with a name.

Midnight Wolf was taken aback by her sudden decision to share her name with him. He gazed into her dark eyes, thinking her name was as beautiful and as mysterious as the woman herself.

"I am called Midnight Wolf," he quickly replied.

"I know," she said, smiling softly up at him. "I have heard you addressed that way by others."

"I must go, but instead of sending a woman to sit with you in my absence, I will send Gentle Bear," Midnight Wolf said. "The young brave owes you a debt. Even though he shot you by accident with his arrow, he was wrong to do it. He was not even supposed to be away from his village with his bow and arrows that day. I had forbidden him to leave the village because of the renewed unrest in the community over the loss of the white leader Abraham Lincoln. Gentle Bear will redeem himself, somewhat, by staying with you while no one else can."

Sheleen nodded, while wondering if the child was being asked to sit with her to redeem himself, or to make sure Sheleen didn't attempt an escape.

Midnight Wolf started to leave, then stopped and knelt beside her again. "Would you rather someone else sat with you?" he asked, searching her eyes.

Sheleen leaned up on elbow as Fluffy repositioned herself. "I am fine with his coming to stay with me," she said. "I understand that what he did was an accident. Everyone makes mistakes, don't they?"

Midnight Wolf wondered at the meaning behind her question, but he needed to meet in council with his warriors. He had no time left to ask her.

"Gentle Bear will arrive soon," he said, then left the tepee.

Sheleen stretched out again on the wondrously soft bed of blankets and furs. She watched the entrance flap for Gentle Bear, admitedly somewhat uneasy to be left alone with him.

But she reminded herself that he was only a child!

At that moment, the injury on her leg began throbbing, bringing to mind the damage this child had already done.

Sheleen inhaled a quick, shaky breath when Gentle Bear drew aside the entrance flap and stepped inside.

They stared into one another's eyes.

CHAPTER EIGHTEEN

A perfect woman, nobly planned,
To warm, to comfort, and command.
—*William Wordsworth*

There was a strain in the air as Gentle Bear sat by the lodge fire with Sheleen. She could tell that he still felt guilty for what he had done to her and she needed to find a way to make him relax with her. She wanted him to know that she realized what he had done was an accident.

She had seen how he had glanced often at Fluffy this evening as her cat sat contentedly purring on her lap.

She remembered now that Midnight Wolf had said Gentle Bear was caring for the cat until Sheleen was well.

"Would you like to hold Fluffy?" Sheleen asked, seeing how that offer lit up the child's eyes.

"Is that her name?" Gentle Bear asked, reaching for the cat as Sheleen handed her to him.

"*Ho,* that is her name," Sheleen said. She saw surprised puzzlement in the child's eyes. She had accidentally said a word in the Dakota language, not English.

Where did you learn the word 'yes' in my people's language?" Gentle Bear asked.

Sheleen knew that this was not the time to explain her history to him.

Most who knew of her and her father's connection to the Dakota people would think this alliance with them was the reason she knew their language. But it was a still deeper connection than that, and she was not ready to share the knowledge with anyone. Her father had taken that secret to his grave, leaving only Sheleen, and others she would never see again, aware of why she knew the Dakota language so well.

"I heard your chief and Shaman talking and made out the word *ho* to mean 'yes,'" Sheleen said, her explanation sounding true enough.

"You are a smart woman to learn so quickly," Gentle Bear said, stroking his hand through the cat's beautiful white fur. "I can see why you call your cat Fluffy."

"Yes, even when she was a tiny thing that I could hold in one hand, she was fluffy, so it seemed the right thing to call her," Sheleen murmured. "Do you have any pets?"

160

"My colt is all," Gentle Bear said, then smiled. "But that is enough. I am proud to have a colt of my own. Not all braves my age can say the same." A sadness swept through his eyes. "My *ahte*, my father, gave me this colt the day before he died. That makes the colt even more special." He smiled at Sheleen. "When I say *ahte*, I am saying the word father."

"Then your *ahte* couldn't have been dead for very long because the colt is still young, not yet grown up into a powerful steed," Sheleen said softly, bringing her own father's death again to mind. The pain she felt over her loss swept over her anew.

"No, he has not been dead for all that long," Gentle Bear said, but he did not say when his father had died.

He gazed intently into Sheleen's eyes. "You are alone in the world," he said. "Do you no longer have a mother and father? You do not have a husband? Did something happen to them?"

Sheleen's heart ached as she tried to answer the child. She was not yet ready to discuss her father's recent death with anyone. Nor the death of both of her mothers.

And there was no husband, but something told her that would change.

"I have never been married and I would rather not talk about my parents," Sheleen said, fighting back tears that burned at the corners of her eyes. "It hurts too much, but I will tell you that my parents are dead."

"I am sorry that I asked," Gentle Bear said. "I understand the hurt. I will not ask you again about them."

"When I first arrived at your village, I thought that Chief Midnight Wolf might be your *ahte* since he seems to treat you differently from the other children. You are special to him," Sheleen said, searching his eyes. "But I now know that he isn't, since only moments ago, you spoke of your father having died."

"My chief seems like a father because he has chosen me to be his special charge," Gentle Bear said, his bare shoulders squaring proudly. "I am so proud to be his charge."

She didn't ask what being a charge meant, for she already knew.

"Your chief could not have made a better choice," she said softly. "I have only known you for a short time, but it is time enough for me to see that you are a special young brave. You deserve this honor the chief has bestowed upon you."

"Even though I was the one who . . . shot . . . you with an arrow?" Gentle Bear asked, his voice breaking.

"Yes, even though you were the one who shot me," Sheleen murmured. "It was an accident. Even men the age of your chief make mistakes. Gentle Bear, I do see you as special, someone I would be proud to call my son."

162

She could see a blush on his copper cheeks and knew that she had embarrassed him. To change the subject, she quickly asked, "Do you know anything about the condition of the child who was bitten by the spider?"

"Pretty Wing?" he said, still stroking Fluffy, while the cat lay there purring. "She is very ill, but our people's shaman will make her well. She will play with the other children soon."

"I'm so glad, because the spider that bit her is very deadly," Sheleen said, sighing with relief.

"It was a black widow spider," Gentle Bear said, then looked eagerly into Sheleen's eyes. "Would you like to hear a story about spiders? One that is not bad, but good? But first would you like to hear other things about my people that I feel you should know?"

"Yes, I would enjoy hearing it all," Sheleen said.

She was glad that she and the child were becoming friends. She hoped he would be the first friend among many here.

She now knew without a doubt that she wanted to stay here with this band of Dakota.

This place was like the village where she had lived as a youth, where she learned to dream.

Gentle Bear smiled at Sheleen. "Stories of my people are journeys backward into the forgotten yesteryears," he said. "In talking to children, the old Dakota places a hand on the ground and explains

163

to those children who listen, that when we all, old or young alike, sit in the lap of our Mother, we know that one day we will all pass. But the place where we rest will last forever. From her, Mother Earth, we, and all other living things, come."

He smiled at Sheleen. "So we, the children, learn to sit or lie on the ground and become conscious of life about us in its multitude of forms," he continued. "Sometimes we boys will sit motionless and watch the swallows, the tiny ants, or perhaps some small animal at work, and ponder on its industry and ingenuity. Or we lie on our backs and look long at the sky, and when the stars come out, we point out to each other how they make shapes, in groups. The Milky Way is my favorite. My *ahte* told me the Milky Way is a path traveled by ghosts."

Sheleen nodded, acting as though she did not know about how the stories of the Dakota were journeys backward into the forgotten yesteryears.

But she did know.

She had heard many, many stories of the Dakota and how they had evolved into the people they were today.

"Stories about spiders are usually good, so how could a spider bite possibly kill my sweet friend?" he asked matter of factly. "*Ho.* She will be all right and will be listening with the other children to stories of our people's forgotten yesteryears."

Sheleen was becoming more impressed by this

young brave's intelligence and confidence. She saw in him the qualities that could make him a powerful leader . . . a leader such as Midnight Wolf.

She could most definitely see why he had been chosen to be his chief's "charge." He was a child of much imagination and knowledge. No doubt his chief enjoyed every moment he spent with him.

She could only imagine Midnight Wolf's disappointment over the shooting. Gentle Bear had not been behaving as a chief's charge that day when he had gone hunting for duck after being told not to.

"Please tell me more," she said softly.

"The stories about spiders are the most fascinating to me," Gentle Bear said. "I shall share some of them with you . . . ."

He stopped when his mother came into the lodge with a wooden tray of various foods, all of which could be eaten with the fingers.

Sheleen gazed hungrily at the platter and all that was there. There were strips of meat, and she recognized fat and juicy *cannakpa,* a mushroom that grew from the roots, stumps, and branches of box elder and elm trees.

She also saw *pangi,* called artichoke in the white world. It resembled a potato, and was pure white when peeled. It was eaten raw, or in soup. Today it would be eaten raw with delicious-looking corn cakes.

Sheleen wished she had maple syrup to eat with

the corn cakes as she had so often eaten them with her father. She was very skilled at making delicious corn cakes, herself!

"Thank you," Sheleen said, making certain that she didn't say the words in Dakota.

Rosy Dawn stroked her fingers through her son's hair. She smiled at him as he smiled up also at her. "I hope my son isn't talking too much," she murmured. "He is one who likes to talk a lot."

"He is telling me about your people," Sheleen said, smiling at Rosy Dawn. "I am enjoying it. May he continue?"

"*Ho*, he may continue," Rosy Dawn said, again tousling her son's hair with her fingers. "My chief told me that he had asked Gentle Bear to come and sit with you. Tomorrow I will sit with you."

Sheleen wanted to ask if they were sitting with her to keep her company, or to keep her from leaving. How surprised they would be to know that she didn't want to leave.

"You are being so kind to me," she murmured.

Rosy Dawn's smile faded as she gazed down at Sheleen's bandaged leg, then over at Gentle Bear. "If there is anything else I can do for you, please tell me," she murmured.

"You have already done so much," Sheleen said, gazing down at the lovely beaded dress she wore. She looked up at Rosy Dawn again. "I love the dress. Thank you."

"I will bring you another one later so that you will

have a change of clothes," Rosy Dawn said. She reached down and hugged her son, then turned and left.

"Now will you please tell me your spider story?" Sheleen asked, drawing a blanket up and around her shoulders, still enjoying the extra warmth after having been so cold and wet for so long.

She was starved, but since Gentle Bear showed no interest in eating, she would wait, herself, until later.

"One night a vision came to a Dakota warrior," Gentle Bear said, his eyes watching the rolling flames of the fire in the firepit. "In his vision came to him a human figure dressed all in black. The person in black handed to the brave a plant and said, 'Wrap this plant in a piece of buckskin and hang it in your tepee. It will keep you in good health always.'"

When the brave asked who was speaking to him, the figure answered. 'I can walk on the water and I can go beneath the water. I can walk on the earth and I can go into the earth. Also I can fly in the air. I am smaller than you, but I could kill you in a moment. I can do more work than any other creature, and my handiwork is everywhere, yet no one knows how I work. I am Spider. Go home and tell your people that the Spider has spoken to you.'"

When he was finished, Gentle Bear looked at Sheleen and smiled broadly. "Did you enjoy the story?" he asked. "Did it not intrigue you?"

167

"You are a good storyteller," Sheleen murmured, nodding. "I scarcely breathed as I listened to you. I shall never look at a spider in the same way again."

"I never have since my father told me that story a short while before he died," Gentle Bear said, his smile waning. "I wish he was here to tell me more stories."

"Just hug what he has told you to your heart and he will still be with you, forever," Sheleen said.

In her mind's eye, she saw her own father as he had sat beside the fireplace so many times telling her stories when she was a child. Her stepmother would be sitting close by, knitting, smiling at the fanciful nature of her father, who seemed to enjoy the stories more than his daughter, even though he had heard the same tales from his own parents so long ago!

"Gentle Bear, if I tell you something, will you keep it to yourself?" Sheleen asked. "It could be a secret just between the two of us."

She wanted to win this child as her ally, for she felt that she needed one in the village. She knew a look of resentment when she saw one, and knew that many of the people of this village did not want her in their midst.

"What do you want to tell me?" Gentle Bear asked anxiously.

"It has to be a secret between only the two of us, or I can't tell you," Sheleen said, seeing the anxiousness building in his eyes.

"I will not tell anyone, not even my mother," Gentle Bear promised. He scooted closer to Sheleen. "What is it? What will be the secret between us?"

"I oft times have dreams of wolves," Sheleen said, watching his eyes widen.

"You do?" he asked. "Are they good or bad dreams?"

"Always good," Sheleen said softly. "In my dreams they are usually running beside my horse, protecting me from harm."

"How many?"

"Too many to count."

"Are there any white wolves among them?" Gentle Bear asked. "White wolves are mystical. They carry many people's dreams with them."

"In my dreams the wolves are always white, and their eyes are so blue, it is as though the sky is reflected in them," Sheleen murmured.

"Are they always running beside your horse?" Gentle Bear prodded.

"Well, not always, but generally," Sheleen murmured. In her mind's eye she was recalling the most intriguing of her wolf dreams. It had been the night before her father had died. She now knew that this particular dream had been meant as an omen . . . warning her that after the next day, things would never be the same again for her.

There was a moment of silence, and then their eyes were both drawn to the entrance flap.

Midnight Wolf stepped into the tepee and smiled first at Gentle Bear and then at Sheleen.

"I shared the spider story with Sheleen," Gentle Bear said. He exchanged a glance with Sheleen, appearing to be thrilled that she had made him her confidante. They would now share many secrets between them.

He rose and gave Sheleen her cat, received a gentle hug from his chief, then left the lodge.

"He is a child of many words," Midnight Wolf said, sitting beside Sheleen. He eyed the food, and then her. "I asked Rosy Dawn to bring food for both you and me. Is there anything on the tray that pleases you?"

Sheleen was very aware of the time of night, that darkness had fallen some time ago and she would soon be sleeping in the tepee with Midnight Wolf.

She could not help wondering how either of them would have any privacy.

Although this tepee was much larger than any other in the village, still the space was not as much as what was to be found even in a smaller cabin.

It would be her first full night in Midnight Wolf's lodge with him!

That thought made her heart race, and not because she was afraid to be with him.

It was because she desired him so much and knew not how to act on such desires, or even how to rid herself of them. She had never even wanted a man before, much less someone as powerful and handsome as Midnight Wolf.

CHAPTER NINETEEN

Love is a circle that doth restless move,
In the same sweet eternity of love.
—*Robert Herrick*

"You have not answered me," Midnight Wolf said, holding the tray closer to her. "Choose what you would like and then I shall make my own choice."

Hoping that Midnight Wolf couldn't recognize how infatuated she was with him, Sheleen knew that taking food and eating it was the best way to hide her feelings from him.

She selected a piece of meat and as soon as she sank her teeth in it, she knew that it was duck meat.

She shot a questioning look at Midnight Wolf, remembering that she'd been about to kill her own supper of duck the moment she was shot by this chief's charge. And she knew that the young brave had been away from his village to bring home duck meat for his mother's cook pot.

She had to wonder if Midnight Wolf had gone for this duck. If so, had he shared some with Gentle Bear and his mother?

"I was delayed coming back to my lodge because I left the village long enough to hunt while it was still daylight," Midnight Wolf said, choosing a piece of duck meat himself. "I knew that Gentle Bear had wanted duck meat for his mother, and feathers for his shaman, so that Moon Eagle could make a fancy fan from them, so I left council early to hunt many ducks for many people. I made certain Rosy Dawn had plenty for her own cook pot."

He paused, then said, "And when I returned I joined the council again."

"Before you went into council, did you take the beautiful green feathers from the ducks to your shaman?" Sheleen asked, finding the duck meat tender, sweet, and delicious, as she bit into it.

"I took the feathers to Rosy Dawn and asked her to give them to her son, so that Gentle Bear, himself, could take them to Moon Eagle," Midnight Wolf said, now choosing a corn cake after finishing the piece of meat.

"You are so kind and generous," Sheleen said, blushing when he gave her a look that seemed to speak directly to her heart. He seemed to be saying that he felt the same for her as she felt for him.

"He is a special child who made a mistake," Midnight Wolf said quietly.

He explained then how it came to be that Gentle Bear was his charge, explaining the meaning of "charge" carefully and at length to Sheleen, obviously unaware that she already knew everything he was telling her.

When he was through, she felt uneasy, for she was becoming more and more excited by his presence.

"I was fascinated by the story about the spider that Gentle Bear told me," she blurted out. "But I imagine there are many more stories such as that, which are told around your people's evening fires."

"Many, many," Midnight Bear said, settling down beside the fire. He stretched out on his side and rested an elbow on the thick mats. "And there is much to say about the spider. According to legend, the spider made the flint points for my people's arrows and left them on the ground for the Dakota to find. They were, therefore, called spider arrowheads."

"How interesting," Sheleen said, even though she had known this legend for years. But she still couldn't share with him how much she knew about his people.

She fed a piece of meat to Fluffy. When the cat was finished, the little creature crawled on Sheleen's lap and was soon fast asleep, purring.

"Please tell me more?" Sheleen encouraged, but

not because she wanted to hear stories. It was Midnight Wolf's voice that she wanted to hear.

Oh, how it intrigued her. She could listen to him talk the whole night through.

"Legend says that one day long ago a party of warriors were traveling," Midnight Wolf said, glad that this woman of mystery showed such an interest in learning about his people.

His feelings for her were growing into something more powerful than anything he had ever felt for other women.

He hoped that in time he could confide as much to her. But for now, he continued to tell her the tales of his people.

"These travelers had made camp, and one of them led his horse to a creek for water," he went on. "There he heard a tapping noise, like someone close to the earth chipping on a stone. He listened, but the tall grass concealed whatever might be there, so, as the sound continued, the warrior called his companions to come. They, too, heard the noise. When they parted the tall grass, a spider jumped up quickly and ran away. Where the spider had been resting, there was a stone arrow point, and the warrior picked it up and saw that it fitted on the end of his arrow. Thereafter the Dakota found plenty of arrow points and have used them ever since to tip their arrows, finding them more effective than fire-hardened wood or bone tips."

The moon was splashing its white sheen down the smoke hole above the firepit. Owls were hooting from somewhere close by. But all else was quiet, for the Dakota people had retired to their lodges for the night. "It has been a long day," Midnight Wolf said. He eyed the platter of food, then Sheleen. "Do you or your cat want any more food?"

Sheleen laughed softly. "My cat seems perfectly content, and, no, I need nothing else," she murmured. "It does not take much food to please me."

Midnight Wolf gazed at her, his eyes slowly raking over her, again aware of her tininess.

He laughed, too. "I can see that you do not eat all that much," he said. When he noticed how that statement caused her to blush, he took the platter and set it just outside his entrance flap, leaving what was left for any tiny forest animal that might need it, then busied himself by tying the entrance flap closed.

Sheleen scarcely breathed as she watched him prepare the tepee for the night, wondering anew how they would sleep without brushing up against each other. If he even touched her at this moment, she would absolutely melt.

She was relieved when he came with a blanket and hung it between lodge poles, leaving him on one side, her the other.

"This will assure you the privacy you need for sleeping," Midnight Wolf said beyond the blanket.

"You will find rolled blankets behind you. There are enough to make a comfortable bed. I hope you have a good night."

"Thank you for everything," Sheleen murmured.

"You do not have to thank me for the things I do for you," Midnight Wolf said, settling down onto blankets and furs on the opposite side of the divider. "Know that it is done with gladness."

Sheleen smiled to herself. She no longer felt like a captive, but instead like a woman being pursued by a handsome chief! She wasn't quite sure how to behave now, while around him, for his mere presence made her feel like a young girl in love for the first time.

Needing to distract herself and hoping sleep would temporarily end her thoughts of Midnight Wolf, Sheleen gently put Fluffy aside.

She found the blankets, unrolled them, then stretched out with Fluffy snuggled against her.

But she found herself watching the blanket that hung on poles between herself and Midnight Wolf. She couldn't take her eyes off the dancing shadows that the fire was making on the opposite side.

Feeling as though the sight might hypnotize her, she shook her head, then found herself immersed in thoughts of Midnight Wolf again, thoughts that made her realize what it meant to need a man for the first time in her life.

Yes, she was going to have trouble going to sleep tonight, with him so close, and not because she didn't trust him. Her feelings for him were out of control.

He was such a magnificent specimen of a man.

To her, he was like no other man before him.

Having been kept so busy helping her father, Sheleen had never taken the time even to consider falling in love.

How could she? Her life had been complicated by those who had attacked the Dakota Indians in Minnesota, stealing their homes, or blatantly killing them.

But now, feeling so far from that life, and believing herself safe among these Dakota people, she was able to experience something she had never felt before.

She was feeling pangs of love!

Oh, but if Midnight Wolf could only feel something for her . . . could love her.

She had seen it in his eyes that he cared for her.

And his touch was always so gentle, as were his eyes when he looked at her.

Now that she was so close to him in his tepee, sleeping in this tiny space, she was drawn to him like a moth to the flame. She could not stay away from this handsome warrior, this chief!

Fluffy stirred, her green eyes opening only partially, as though Sheleen's cat was reminding her that she was there to sleep, not stew over things that she had no control over.

"I know, Fluffy," she whispered. "I know."

She snuggled even more closely with her cat, sighed heavily, then closed her eyes.

But when she heard Midnight Wolf stirring restlessly amid his blankets, and knew that he was having trouble sleeping, too, she hoped that it was because she was so near to him. She hoped that he could hear her heartbeats . . . beating for him!

She tried not to make any noise as she repositioned herself, attempting to find a more comfortable position, one that might help her fall asleep.

But no matter what she did, or how she moved this way or that, she just could not keep her eyes closed for long!

And then she heard the haunting song of a single loon, and a moment later, another loon responding in kind. Their calls echoed across the lake to each other, and Sheleen had the feeling that this place was a paradise, where the trees were tall, thick, and beautiful, and that the land, except for where the village had been established, was untouched by man.

Yes, this was a place made for lovers!

"Oh, what am I thinking?" Sheleen whispered to herself, finally finding a comfortable position. Fluffy had left her some time ago and was now sleeping close by.

Slowly her eyes closed, but even then she found no peace in sleep.

She dreamed of a lady riding beside a handsome warrior, their eyes speaking to each other what they no longer needed to say aloud.

In that dream, the warrior was Midnight Wolf and the lady was herself! She smiled contentedly in her sleep.

Midnight Wolf lay wide awake on the other side of the blanket. He had heard the stirring of the woman and knew that she had had trouble falling asleep. He was finding it hard, himself.

Until now, he had not allowed himself to fall in love. He could not bear to think of what might happen to his Wolf Band if they had a leader who was lax in his duties.

When his people were confronted by whites who with a passion hated red men and women, even their children, a chief's role was to concentrate only on the welfare of his people.

But now it seemed only right that he allow himself something else. He felt that he would be an even more powerful, better leader, if he had a woman at his side, one with whom he could share his dreams and doubts.

He had even begun hungering for a son. Gentle Bear was a daily reminder that a man should have a son to follow in his footsteps. As chief, it was his duty to find a successor, an heir who could take on his responsibilities one day when the son grew up to be strong and powerful in his own right.

But should Midnight Wolf even consider having that son with a white woman?

Did he not feel hatred for all *washechu* . . . ?

Yet Sheleen was different from the other whites

he had known. She was compassionate and oh, so much, much more.

She was everything that he would look for in a wife, were he to allow himself the luxury of marriage!

Tomorrow he would think more on it.

He would watch her.

He would talk with her.

He would discover even her hidden secrets.

Then he would truly be able to measure the worth of this woman.

CHAPTER TWENTY

Whene'er she speaks, my ravish'd ear
No other voice than hers can hear.
—*George Lyttelton*

Sheleen sat beside the fire in Midnight Wolf's tepee. She was astonished at how quickly things were changing between herself and this proud chief.

He was actually braiding her hair as she sat there trying to be nonchalant about it. Inside, her heart was racing, and she hoped he couldn't tell just how his nearness made her feel.

Again she was thinking about how she had heard that one could fall in love instantly. She now knew that was absolutely true, for she had not known Midnight Wolf for long, yet she most certainly was in love with him.

She had finally gotten a good night of sleep, and had been awakened by the sound of someone shoving a warm basin of water beneath the blanket that Midnight Wolf had hung between their beds.

Midnight Wolf had explained that the water was for her morning bath, and she would find a soft buckskin cloth in it.

She had brought her own bar of soap along with her, knowing that she might not be near any place where she could purchase any, so she hurriedly undressed and bathed herself. Before she had put the dress back on, a fresh one had been shoved beneath the blanket. Sheleen had guessed that it was another gift from Rosy Dawn.

She knew well how clothes were made by the Dakota women. Today's dress was sewn of a lightweight buckskin, as soft as those made from the unborn buffalo calfskins. She had worn dresses like this while staying with various bands of Dakota as she and her father helped them in any way they could.

Today's dress was trimmed with fringe, quillwork, and painted designs; it was so lovely she felt doubly blessed to have been given it.

After having bathed and dressed, she had poked her head around the edge of the blanket. Midnight Wolf had quickly taken it down in order to have more room in the tepee, and they had shared breakfast sitting beside the fire.

She knew that in the spring and summer the diet of the Dakota was varied with an abundance of fruit and vegetables. Today's breakfast was a dish made from wild onions and potatoes, eaten with the fat of the beaver's tail.

She knew that Midnight Wolf had watched her eat after telling her about the use of the beaver's tail in their morning meal, so she had made certain not to look as though she found the food at all distasteful.

He just did not know that she had learned long ago how to tolerate things that most white people wouldn't.

But now they had finished their morning meal and Sheleen continued to sit straight-backed while Midnight Wolf braided her hair. She knew that most husbands performed this chore for their wives . . . but she was nowhere near to being this chief's wife . . . !

He had told her that all of the women brushed and smoothed their long braids to keep them from breaking, and that they washed their hair often in *hupestola,* to keep their hair glossy.

She tried to continue focusing on other things to keep her heart from beating so wildly, even though she would love to spend a lifetime with Midnight Wolf. Sadly, she knew the chances were that soon she would be gone, and he would only be a memory.

She was sure that he was not going to keep her there as a captive. No chief treated a woman as he was treating her and thought of her as a captive.

She longed to be his wife, yet knew the chances

of that were slim. Her skin was white and she was seen as a *washechu* by his people.

How could there be any future between them when there was so much resentment among the Dakota for people of her skin color?

She gazed over at where his bow and quiver of arrows hung on a tripod just inside the entrance flap, so that they would be close at hand, if needed, both day and night.

She hoped that they wouldn't ever be necessary to defend the peaceful village against attackers.

"Again I am sorry that my charge shot you with one of his arrows," Midnight Wolf suddenly said, his fingers now twisting the other braid after having already readied one for her. "He had been forbidden to go on a hunt alone. Hoping his need to hunt might be satisfied, I took him hunting for rabbit the day before he shot you. Rabbit hunting is safe and great fun for young braves. I had thought that one hunt was enough. Obviously it wasn't."

"Truly, I hold no grudge against the young man," Sheleen said, glad to have something to talk about instead of just sitting there feeling more awkward by the minute.

She wished she could turn around and look at Midnight Wolf. She never got enough of gazing at his unique handsomeness. His dark eyes were so penetrating and beautiful, as they met hers.

She had never fallen in love before, but knew that she had now. Just his voice made her insides melt. When his fingers occasionally touched her shoulder, or the flesh of her neck, as he was braiding her hair, it was almost too much to bear without letting him know how she felt.

She had to be certain not to tremble from ecstasy as he did these things, for she knew that it was best if he never knew just how deeply he affected her. Soon she would be gone, and probably she would never see him again.

"It is hard for the young Dakota braves to understand the depths of hatred felt by the white community toward our people. It is hard for them to understand the true danger in not staying close to home," Midnight Wolf said, trying to focus on anything other than sitting there so close to Sheleen, actually touching her hair, and occasionally touching her flesh.

He could not deny how much she affected him.

Now he knew just how it felt to fall in love and want a woman past all reasoning.

He had to keep himself centered, and he knew that there were some things he could talk about that might do just that. Every time he was reminded of how much the *washechu* had taken from his people, he was reminded that Sheleen was of that world, not his.

"It is imperative that the young braves stay under close supervision of their families. They do not understand the extent of the deceit the white government is capable of," Midnight Wolf said tightly. "Too often Dakota chiefs touched the pen to treaties with whites but the papers held no true power, nor did the white man's spoken words. The wind carried the good words away as easily as the browned leaves of cottonwood trees in autumn."

"I am so sorry for what has been done to your people," Sheleen murmured. In her mind's eye she saw her father moving among the Dakota people, trying to reassure them that things would be all right, even though he knew, deep down inside himself, that it would never be all right again for them.

"I know about your people being restricted to a narrow strip of river land in Minnesota, and how severe a blow it was to your hunting traditions," she said. "And how your land decreased while white settlements rapidly increased. Nothing your people did pleased the white man, and nothing escaped the white man's transforming hand."

"Then you know that millions of acres of Dakota land were opened up for white settlement, and that some of our Dakota men even converted to become farmers alongside white people," he said.

"I know about it," Sheleen said, her voice drawn. "I understand that those who deserted their own Dakota people were called 'cut hairs' because they had to cut their long hair in order to live among the whites."

She swallowed hard, then continued, "I know their hair is the pride of the Dakota men and women. . . ."

Midnight Wolf tied the last string of painted buck-skin around her second braid, then placed his hands on Sheleen's shoulders and turned her slowly to face him.

"You know so much about my people, and I hear the caring in your voice," he said, searching her eyes. "Why is that? What is there about your past that perhaps I should know? Why do you care?"

Scarcely breathing, and stunned by the sudden-ness of his question, Sheleen gazed into his eyes. Now was the time to tell him about her father, who he was, and how he had had such a big role in helping the Dakota people of Minnesota.

Her father had deplored the white government's lack of pity for the red man's plight. It seemed Wash-ington never saw the injustice being done these proud people.

She started to speak, to finally tell Midnight Wolf everything about herself and her father, but just as she opened her mouth, she was startled by a sud-den loud wailing outside the tepee. The noise grew louder and more mournful by the minute.

In only a matter of moments, someone was out-side Midnight Wolf's lodge, speaking his name.

"That is Night Walker calling for me to come from my lodge," he said.

Midnight Wolf recognized the one who was loudly mourning, and feared that the young child who had been bitten by the spider had just lost her battle and had passed on to the other side.

Sheleen sat there as Midnight Wolf hurried to his feet and held the entrance flap aside so that Night Walker could enter.

Night Walker glanced at Sheleen, then gazed into his chief's eyes. "It is Pretty Wing," he said. "She lost her battle. She is gone."

Midnight Wolf placed a gentle hand on his best friend's shoulder, nodded, then dropped his hand to his side as Night Walker turned and left the tepee.

Midnight Wolf turned to Sheleen and saw tears in her eyes.

He was touched deeply by her caring. She truly had a place in her heart for the Dakota.

She had said enough to him that he was certain of that. He wished they could continue their conversation, but now was not the time to hear how she would answer his questions. He must give comfort where comfort was so badly needed.

Sheleen rose to her feet and started to walk toward Midnight Wolf, to tell him just how sad she felt about the child's death. But this was one of the first times she had tried to walk since her slow recovery, and she felt her knees weaken. She gasped and reached out for Midnight Wolf. He grabbed her in his arms as she was about to fall.

They stood gazing into one another's eyes as he held her around the waist.

"I am so sorry about the child," Sheleen sobbed. She could not tell him how guilty she felt over not having offered her father's medicines, even though she knew they wouldn't have been accepted. Most Indians did not believe in white people's medicines, except for those who knew her father and trusted him and those medicines he had used to help the Dakota.

Midnight Wolf could see that Sheleen was sincere. He was certain now that she had not been traveling near his village with any thought of harming his people.

Still, one day he did want to know why she had been traveling alone and especially why she had chosen to dress like a man.

For now, he just wanted to kiss her tears away, but he knew it was best not to. He must go to Singing Water and comfort her and help prepare her for the days and weeks ahead, when she would no longer have a daughter to love and care for.

His duties as chief were many, and comforting those who had lost a loved one was especially important.

It was up to him to keep a balance at his village, and death was one of the things that always upset the balance among his people.

Always, in the end, after the burial rites, things began to become normal again, although mourning continued for some time, but in private.

Now everyone mourned together.

That was just the way it was among the Dakota.

They were all as one with each other!

And he hoped that one day soon Sheleen would be counted as one among them also.

When he felt the time was right, he would explain to her just how he felt about her, and how lonesome he had been for a wife, and even children.

He was always comforting families. He ached now more than ever to have a family of his own!

"I must go," Midnight Wolf said, taking the time to brush some of her tears from her cheeks with the flesh of his thumbs.

"Yes, I know," Sheleen murmured, touched heart and soul that he had delayed leaving at all.

"Come. Let me help you back down on the blankets beside the fire," Midnight Wolf said.

He gently took her by an elbow and eased her down onto the blankets.

He knelt beside her, gazed deeply into her eyes, then rose and hurried from the tepee.

Overwhelmed by her feelings at this moment, Sheleen gazed deeply into the dancing flames of the fire.

"He does care," she whispered, smiling at Fluffy as her cat came and crawled onto her lap, purring. "Fluffy, he does care for me!"

Fluffy just closed her eyes and fell into one of her peaceful naps, but Sheleen was too agitated to relax.

With everyone lost in mourning over Pretty Wing, Sheleen was reminded all over again of her tiny sister's death.

She openly cried, for her own feelings of loss were sweeping over her once again. First her tiny sister had died, then her true mother, and then her second mother, whom she had grown to adore.

"And then Papa," she whispered, thrown back in time to the moment when she had first seen him hanging from that old oak tree.

It was something that had been imprinted on her brain, as a leaf's imprint can become fossilized into stone.

"Papa, oh, Papa, I miss you so much," she sobbed, holding her face in her hands as tears wetted her fingers. At this moment her losses seemed almost too much to bear.

She was filled with such a gnawing loneliness for her father, she wanted to wail, herself!

But she knew that she must get control of herself, for she had to make her way alone, now. And she was a strong person with a strong will. She knew that she could do it.

Yet. . . . there was that portion of her heart that spoke the name Midnight Wolf.

If only she could have him in her life! She would never have to be lonesome again!

But surely that longing was only what dreams were made of. How could such a powerful Dakota chief truly want her, a mere white woman?

Yet . . . if he truly knew all about her, wouldn't the truth make a difference? She wasn't sure if she could ever tell him her real history. He might think

191

she was making it all up so he would feel more comfortable around her.

No. She could not tell him. Not yet, anyhow.

She hoped there would come a time when she could open up to him. She just had to make certain that he already trusted her enough to actually believe her story!

She cringed when again she heard the horrible wails, now coming from the whole village. Together they were mourning the tiny, sweet child who had died far too young.

Suddenly her own losses seemed so small compared to what the family of the beautiful child was going through. The loss of a child was something no one could ever understand, or get over. She knew because she had never gotten over losing her beautiful, sweet sister!

CHAPTER TWENTY-ONE

Love? I will tell thee what it is to love!
It is to build with human thoughts a shrine,
Where Hope sits brooding like a beauteous dove.
—*Charles Swain*

It had been three long days since the beautiful child had died and Sheleen had spent most of that time alone while all of the Wolf Band immersed themselves in mourning and preparing for Pretty Wing's burial rites.

Even Midnight Wolf had spent a scarce amount of time in his lodge with Sheleen, coming only long enough to eat and sleep.

Since Sheleen had so much time on her hands, she had concentrated on exercising, taking many walks down to the lake and back. She had gotten most of her strength back, and had walked off the pain in her leg.

She had not gone farther than the lake, for she did not want anyone to think that she was trying to escape. In, truth she hoped never to leave Midnight Wolf.

She was amazed at how cleanly her wound was healing. Like her father, the shaman of this village was a skilled healer.

She knew that Moon Eagle had resented caring for her, but he had done it because his chief had asked him to, and because he felt a calling to make people well, even a person whose skin was white.

The sounds of mourning had begun anew and when the wailing seemed to be getting closer, Sheleen went to the entrance flap and slowly shoved it aside.

Tears flooded her eyes when she saw a procession of the Wolf Band's people walking slowly toward their burial grounds. Many raised their arms and hands heavenward, crying "*hownh, hownh,*" as they walked toward the spot where they would soon leave the child.

Sheleen gasped when she saw a deerskin doll tied to the top of the red blanket that wrapped the child. Her little body was being carried on a travois, pulled by a lovely white stallion.

Even the cradle board that had been Pretty Wing's when she was just a baby was tied to the red blanket, as well as other things loved by the child and the child's mother.

Sheleen knew that when they reached the scaffolding that had been prepared for the child's body, rattles of antelope hoofs strung on rawhide would hang from the scaffolding, as well as an animal's bladder with little stones inside, and also a painted willow hoop.

Everything dear to the child would be placed on the scaffold with her and left there so Pretty Wing would always have them with her.

All of these things reminded Sheleen all over again of her tiny sister's death.

It was as though she were reliving that day when her Dakota sister had been laid to rest with her own beloved doll and everything else that was dear to her.

Sheleen's Dakota heritage was so tangible to her. She could almost forget that she had lived the life of a white girl for so long. The deception had been necessary so that she could go to school to get an education. Her father had insisted on that, and he'd wanted to live in the white world so that he could practice his medicine after the death of his Indian wife, Sheleen's true mother.

It was not difficult for Sheleen to pass for a white girl, especially when her father married a white woman shortly after he and Sheleen moved to St. Paul. Sheleen had grown to adore her new mother, welcoming her love and care.

Yes, she carried the blood of both white- and red-skinned people and she was never ashamed of her heritage. But she knew that she would be safer living as white, for the white community seemed to abhore a mixed breed even more than a full-blooded Indian.

Only now did she understand how she had missed her life as a Dakota. She had been raised among her mother's people and considered the Indian blood running through her veins her true heritage.

She let the sorrow that had been locked in her heart sweep over her as she relived the day of her sister's burial.

The first preparation had been to paint her sister's face as if for a festive occasion, and then to dress her body in the finest of clothing.

A buffalo robe had been wrapped around her tiny sister's body, and lastly, the body had been placed in a buffalo rawhide and securely tied with a rawhide rope. Her body had been placed on a travois and taken into the lovely forests of Minnesota, where it had been fastened high in the branches of a tree.

Today's funeral was the same. No actual ceremony would be performed, and only the weeping and wailing of the sorrowing was heard.

No flowers were taken to be left with the dead. An offering would be made in the form of a prayer stick painted green at the lower end to symbolize earth, and yellow at the upper end to symbolize the sky. To it would be fastened an eagle feather and a breath plume, to carry unspoken prayers to "Those Above."

Knowing that the funeral procession would soon be over, and everyone would leave Pretty Wing and resume their daily activities, Sheleen went back and sat down beside the lodge fire. Midnight Wolf would be returning to his lodge, and she did not want him to realize that she had been mourning in her own way, for someone as dear as Pretty Wing had been to this band of Dakota.

She tried not to think any more about what had been. She must concentrate on the here and now. It was as though she had been purposely led to this Indian village, so that she could return to her true roots and be Dakota again, as she had been when she was a child. Her skin color might differ from the people around her, but her heart beat the same rhythm, saying with each beat that she was just as Dakota as they!

Suddenly, Sheleen realized that Midnight Wolf had come into the tepee. She looked quickly up at him and caught him gazing at her so curiously.

Needing to tell someone about all the feelings that had filled her heart today, she knew then that she must confide in Midnight Wolf. Feeling as she did about him, and feeling that he might care the same way for her, she got up and went to him. She knelt beside him, the pain in her leg suddenly forgotten, the pain in her heart all she was aware of right now.

For a moment, they just looked into each other's

eyes. Then, realizing just how puzzled Midnight Wolf must be over her strange behavior, Sheleen opened her mouth to begin her story of a past that she knew would surprise him. She hoped that eventually her revelation would make him even more comfortable with her since she was, in part, Dakota, herself.

Just then, a voice outside the lodge was heard, breaking the strained silence between her and Midnight Wolf.

It was Moon Eagle, a man who did not bother to hide his dislike for Sheleen, or his disapproval of her presence in his chief's lodge. Suddenly she realized that what she had almost revealed to Midnight Wolf could damage her future among his people.

Moon Eagle already disliked her because she was white. What would he say if he knew that she was a . . . "breed."

It was a word that all whites and red-skinned people despised. Maybe she should not be so open with Midnight Wolf, after all.

At least not now.

She wanted to secure her place among his people before she told Midnight Wolf the secrets that she had almost poured from her heart.

She didn't want to give the shaman any ammunition to use against her. She knew he would try to discourage his chief from loving her.

Sheleen went back to the other side of the fire as Midnight Wolf stood to go outside. Before leaving, he stopped for a moment to gaze into Sheleen's eyes.

"Is there something you want to tell me?" he asked, searching her eyes. "You seemed ready to speak before Moon Eagle called my name."

Sheleen lowered her eyes. "It was not important," she murmured.

She looked slowly up at him. "Please go on," she said softly. "Surely whatever Moon Eagle wants is important, or he would not be here asking for you."

Midnight Wolf gazed at her questioningly for a moment longer, then turned and left.

Sheleen could not help breaking into tears again, for she had so badly wanted to unburden her heart to Midnight Wolf.

CHAPTER TWENTY-TWO

> Ah! What is love? It is a pretty thing,
> As sweet unto a shepherd as a king,
> And sweeter, too.
> —*Robert Greene*

Raymond and Big Bear Moon stopped and dismounted. Big Bear Moon had spotted something on the ground as they were riding toward a lake to get water.

Big Bear Moon bent to his haunches and picked up two broken arrow shafts. He studied them, then gazed up at Raymond, who still only stood there, watching.

"It's a broken arrow," Raymond said, shrugging. "What about it?"

"When you find an arrow broken like this, it could mean that it has been taken from somebody's body," Big Bear Moon said. "But a child's arrow?"

"It was probably used on some damn animal," Raymond said, scoffing.

Big Bear Moon studied the ground around him. He saw signs that someone had been lying there, and even though it had recently rained, he saw signs of blood that had soaked into the ground.

"No, it was not an animal," Big Bear Moon said, standing up. "The tracks we followed were made by Sheleen's horse. The tracks led here."

"Do you think she was shot by that arrow?" Raymond asked, lifting an eyebrow.

"Perhaps," Big Bear Moon said. He looked into the distance. "I do sense that she is close, very close."

Raymond smiled wickedly. "Let's go on and find her," he said, chuckling.

"Not now," Big Bear Moon said, laying the broken arrow shafts aside. "We've gone as far as we're going today. But tomorrow is another day. It just might be the day we find her."

"Yep, tomorrow," Raymond said, his eyes narrowing angrily. "And then I'm going to make her pay for what she did to me."

Big Bear Moon shifted his gaze over to Raymond, glowered, then walked away from him and began gathering firewood. He did believe that he would be finding Sheleen soon, and when he did, he could hardly wait to see the surprise in Raymond's eyes when Big Bear Moon changed the ugly, cruel-hearted *washechu's* plans right before his eyes!

CHAPTER TWENTY-THREE

We parted in silence—our cheeks were wet
With the tears that were past controlling;
We vowed we would never—no, never forget,
And those vows at the time were consoling.
—*Mrs. Crawford*

The wind blew hard outside Midnight Wolf's tepee, rustling the closed entrance flap and occasionally causing it to fly open, then flutter closed again.

Sheleen gazed up through the smoke hole. The sky was a perfect blue today, except for a few white, puffy clouds that occasionally came into view as they scudded quickly away across the heavens and were soon lost from her view again.

Sheleen's gaze moved slowly down as she stared uneasily over the fire at Moon Eagle. He sat there stripping leaves from medicinal plants, then placing the leaves in a small buckskin bag with others he had prepared.

It was the day after Pretty Wing's burial and everything in the village was back to normal, so much so that Midnight Wolf had left only moments ago to go on a hunt with two of his warrior friends.

Before he had left, he had asked Gentle Bear's mother if the child could sit with Sheleen for a while, to help keep her company in Midnight Wolf's absence.

But Rosy Dawn had explained that Gentle Bear was not feeling well today; he had a stomachache. Midnight Wolf had gone to his shaman and asked if he would sit with Sheleen.

Sheleen had told Midnight Wolf that she didn't need anyone to sit with her; she would be all right by herself.

She especially didn't want Moon Eagle sitting with her. Although he was a holy man, a shaman, she still didn't trust him.

But Midnight Wolf had told her that he had left her alone too often these past days, and felt that one more day would be too much. He didn't want her to be lonely, but he did want to go on his hunt with his friends.

Many white-tailed deer had been spotted close by and the Dakota could not fail to take advantage of a hunt that came almost to their doorstep.

Rosy Dawn had left her ailing son long enough to bring Sheleen a bag of lovely beads, saying that it would please her if Sheleen would string them for her. She had added that one day soon she would teach Sheleen how to sew those beads onto buckskin.

Glad to have something to busy her hands with, and knowing that Rosy Dawn had only brought the beads to give her something to do, Sheleen had gladly taken them. Already she had more than one string filled.

Moon Eagle's presence unnerved her because she knew that he did not approve of her being there, especially in his chief's private lodge.

Now that she was well enough to mount a horse and ride, Moon Eagle seemed unhappy that his chief had not taken her away from their village. He probably believed she should go to a white man's fort.

As though he were able to read her thoughts, Moon Eagle laid aside his bag of plants and gazed intently at Sheleen. "Surely you are anxious to leave and be among those of your own kind," he blurted out, his eyes steady on hers.

He didn't wait for her to respond, but instead, leaned forward and smiled a strange sort of easy smile. "I will help you leave," he said.

"You will what?" Sheleen asked with a low gasp.

She was stunned at the shaman's boldness. How dare he do something so vastly different from what he knew his chief would want?

Sheleen knew that it was no secret now to the Wolf Band that their chief had special feelings for this white woman. He had not pretended otherwise while in the presence of his people!

Sheleen knew that he did care, deeply, for her, even though he had not yet admitted it to her.

Nor had she told him yet how she felt about him. But she had hoped to tell him tonight, when he returned from the hunt. It was too hard to hold her feelings inside any longer!

"You know that it was not meant for you to be here among my people for long. And it is not right for you to reside in our chief's lodge," Moon Eagle said resentfully. "It was understood when you were so ill. My people know well the goodness of our chief's heart. But now that you are able to travel, my people will begin doubting the intelligence of their chief if you stay in his lodge any longer."

He cleared his throat. "I have prepared already how you will leave," he said tightly.

He stood and held a hand out for her. "Come with me," he said, his jaw tight, his eyes narrowing. "Come with me now."

Sheleen didn't know what to do. She was certain that Midnight Wolf would not approve at all of what his shaman was doing. That was evident from the fact that Moon Eagle had chosen to act behind his back, taking advantage of his chief's absence!

Her eyes defying him, Sheleen didn't budge.

She laid the beading aside and angrily folded her arms across her chest. "I'm not going anywhere," she said, her eyes battling with the shaman's. "So you had just better go to your lodge. You . . . you . . . aren't needed here. You never were. I am capable of looking after myself."

Moon Eagle bent low and spoke into Sheleen's face. "You will leave today," he said tightly. "You know as well as I that it is not in my people's best interest that you stay among them. *Washechus* only bring trouble. When it is learned that you, a white woman, are living with our Wolf Band, other whites will come for you. They might not even stop to ask questions about your presence here. They might come with firearms, kill my people, then take you away to be among people of your own kind."

She wanted to insist that she was with people of her own kind, that more of her was Dakota than white.

But she knew he was not the one to tell such a secret to. He would not believe her. He would think she was just trying to manipulate him.

Also, she wanted to tell Midnight Wolf first about who she truly was. She didn't want him to find out from someone else.

She needed to explain to him why she had kept this secret to herself for so long. That was exactly why she had planned to tell him when he returned from today's hunt.

But now all of that had changed. The shaman's attitude toward her, which surely matched the feelings of many others, made it clear her dreams were never going to be realized.

She would never be able to tell Midnight Wolf how much she loved him. She would never be able to tell him who she truly was. He would never know of her role in helping the Dakota of Minnesota alongside her father.

Because too many of his people would see her as more white than Dakota, especially since their shaman openly held a grudge against her, Sheleen slowly got to her feet.

"All right, I will go," she said, her voice breaking. "But I am only doing this because I see that it is in the best interest of the Wolf Band. I would never want to be the cause of the white government sending soldiers into your village to search for me."

Feeling as though her heart was breaking at the thought of never seeing Midnight Wolf again, or being held in his powerful arms, Sheleen went to the back of the lodge where her two bags sat among Midnight Wolf's own belongings.

She stopped and turned quickly toward Moon Eagle. "My cat," she said, her voice breaking. "She's not here. I must find her."

"She is with Gentle Bear," Moon Eagle said, as he stood beside the entrance flap. "The child is very fond of the animal. It would be good if you left her in his care."

"My cat is all I have left of my family," Sheleen said, near tears.

She lowered her eyes as she thought of just how much the child loved Fluffy. She knew that no matter how much she would miss her cat, she could not take Fluffy away from this child who adored the animal with all his heart.

Except for his mother and Midnight Wolf, Gentle Bear was a child alone in this world. Sheleen understood the loneliness of a child who had no brother or sister. Although her parents had cherished and loved her so much, she had still ached sometimes for another sister, or a brother. But time had been her enemy. First her true mother died, and then her father's second wife.

Gentle Bear would never understand why she must leave, or why she was taking the cat from him. He had grown so very fond of Fluffy. Sheleen made a quick decision to leave her cat behind. She would not go and hold her cat one last time, or she might change her mind about leaving her.

She picked up her father's satchel, and then her own bag, and walked sorrowfully from the tepee with Moon Eagle.

Once outside, she didn't take the time to stop and look around. She didn't want to see the people staring at her, wondering where she was going, and why?

No. She would not do that. She would make a clean break. Once she was gone from the village, she would decide where she would go, and what she would do with the rest of her life now that she would never have the man she loved with her.

What would Midnight Wolf think when he found her gone?

And where *could* she go now that she was alone in the world?

When they reached Midnight Wolf's corral, Sheleen was stunned to see that Moon Eagle had obviously known all along that he would coerce her into leaving. He had already gone to the corral earlier and prepared her horse for travel, with her saddle in place and a sack of provisions tied to one side of it.

Dispiritedly, Sheleen loaded her own bags onto the horse, then stopped and looked past the shaman into the village. She found herself hoping that someone *had* seen her and would disagree with what the shaman was doing. She wished some-one would stop her from going.

But no one was paying her or Moon Eagle any heed. It was as though they were all in on the shaman's plan to rid themselves of a thorn in their sides!

Sheleen strained her neck to see Rosy Dawn's te-pee, hoping to catch one last glimpse of her cat. But all she saw was the closed entrance flap.

She could envision Fluffy lying trustingly on Gentle Bear's lap, not doubting that she would see her mistress again. Sheleen had looked after the cat since she had been born, the littlest in a litter of eight.

"I shall miss you," she whispered to herself.

"You should go now," Moon Eagle said, looking nervously over his shoulder toward the busiest part of the village, where men, women, and children were engaged in their daily activities.

Sheleen followed his gaze and saw that some warriors were busy developing their physical strength by doing various exercises, while others were practicing their hunting skills.

She looked again at the shaman. "Yes, I know, I must leave before someone sees what *you* are doing," Sheleen said bitterly, bringing Moon Eagle's eyes back to her.

When she placed her foot in the stirrup, she realized that her leg had not truly healed enough for riding.

But she wouldn't let the shaman see her pain. She settled herself into the saddle, looking past Moon Eagle as he moved aside the poles that kept the horses in the corral.

"Go in that direction," Moon Eagle said, pointing where he wanted her to ride. She noticed it was in the opposite direction from where his chief was hunting. "And do not look back. You are joining your world and leaving mine behind."

Their eyes met and held momentarily.

"This is best for everyone," Moon Eagle said, nodding for Sheleen to go. "Ride where I have told you to go, not elsewhere. You will not have to travel a full day before arriving at a fort, where whites will welcome you. From this moment onward, forget you ever knew of the Wolf Band of Dakota."

He glowered as he leaned closer to her. "Forget you knew my chief," he said tightly.

She glowered back at him, then sank her heels into the flanks of her horse and trotted from the corral.

Sheleen made a wide swing left in order to avoid coming anywhere close to the outer boundaries of the village.

Although her injured leg was throbbing with an almost unmerciful pain, Sheleen rode onward, traveling in the direction that Moon Eagle had pointed out to her.

But after she was only a short distance from the village, where the shaman could no longer see her, something told Sheleen to turn and go in the opposite direction.

Something about the way he had made these plans for her, down to the direction she should ride, made her uneasy. If his own chief couldn't trust the shaman any longer, why should Sheleen?

Glad to be able to defy the shaman, although he would never know it, she swung her horse around and started off again, but this time in the opposite direction from where she had just been traveling.

She rode for a while, putting more and more distance between herself and the Dakota village. Her heart ached anew at having left behind the only true love of her life.

Then her heart skipped a beat when she heard a horse approaching from somewhere behind her.

A cold, quick fear gripped her heart. Who in the world could it be?

Frightened, she made a sharp turn right, and ignoring the throbbing pain in her leg, she again sank her heels into the flanks of her steed and sent it into a hard gallop.

Her heart sank when she realized that she hadn't eluded the horseman, for she heard the horse advancing on her again.

She was afraid to turn and see who was riding after her!

Her heart racing, her leg aching, she continued at a hard gallop, but the other rider was gaining on her.

The pain in her leg was worsening, and she wasn't sure just how much longer she could go on.

She now knew that in a matter of moments, her pursuer would catch up with her!

Chapter Twenty-four

> Our love was free as the wind on the hill,
> There was no word said we need wish unspoke,
>   We have wrought no ill.
>   —*Ernest Dowson*

Her hair flying in the wind, her leg throbbing so much that she knew she couldn't go farther, Sheleen sobbed out Midnight Wolf's name. She felt a strange light-headedness when she suddenly heard his voice!

It was Midnight Wolf!

He . . . was . . . calling *her* name, as though he had heard her.

She didn't see how that was possible. How could she think of him one moment and hear his voice the next? She had had mystical dreams of beautiful wolves since she was small, and she felt things many people didn't feel, but this was different. How could she conjure up the man she loved from thin air?

When she heard Midnight Wolf shout her name again, she knew that she wasn't imagining it. She knew that he was there.

He was the one following her.

Midnight Wolf had somehow found her!

Sobbing harder, overwhelmed by her emotions, Sheleen drew rein and brought her horse to a sudden, plunging halt.

When she wheeled her steed around, Midnight Wolf was riding toward her on his black stallion. She sobbed his name and reached a hand out for him just before she slid from her saddle, the pain too unbearable to sit there any longer.

When Midnight Wolf saw her fall, his heart skipped a beat. When he'd first seen her riding on her horse, he had thought she was an apparition. Sheleen was supposed to be in his village. His shaman was supposed to be sitting with her, keeping her company until Midnight Wolf's return.

How was it possible that she was riding away from his village at breakneck speed, instead?

He now knew that his intuition had been right. Even before he shot that first deer while hunting with his friends, he had felt that Sheleen was in danger.

And he *was* right!

Here she was, now quite a distance from his home. But he was not certain just why she had fled.

Was it on her own initiative? Or had someone co-erced her into going?

No matter what, or who, or why she had left, the fact that he had found her before she had disap-peared forever was all that mattered.

Sheleen lay on the ground, her body wracked by heavy sobs as she watched Midnight Wolf draw closer to her.

She had been riding so hard, she had torn her wound apart, and the blood was even now seeping through her bandage, onto the lovely doeskin dress that Rosy Dawn had so sweetly and generously given her.

And now Sheleen had ruined it.

Just as she had probably ruined everything, espe-cially her relationship with Midnight Wolf.

How could she explain why she had fled him and his people without causing harm between him and his shaman?

Midnight Wolf came up beside her horse and quickly dismounted. With questioning and concern in his midnight-dark eyes, he knelt down before Sheleen.

He gazed at the blood on the skirt of her dress, and then looked deep into her eyes.

"Why were you on your horse?" he asked. "Why were you riding so hard and so far away from my village? Did you leave of your own choice, or from fear? Was I wrong to trust you? Had you come near my village because you were helping white men who would enjoy seeing me and my people dead? Did you leave my village to return to those men?"

Sheleen gasped and went pale at the accusation.

Yet she wasn't sure what to say to him, especially about why she had left him and his people. If she told him that his shaman had encouraged her to go, it could cause trouble.

But if she *didn't* tell him the truth, Midnight Wolf would continue to think the worst about her and she would die a slow death inside if that were so.

Yes, she must think of herself at this critical moment of decision. Her entire future depended on how she answered.

"No, I wasn't near your village to bring harm to your people," she blurted out. She reached up and wiped tears from her cheeks with the back of her hand. "And, no. I didn't leave your village of my own choosing. Your . . . shaman . . . Moon Eagle . . . *he* encouraged it. He made it very clear that I wasn't wanted among your people."

Midnight Wolf was so stunned by what she'd said, he found it hard to speak.

His shaman?

Moon Eagle?

How could his trusted shaman do such a thing knowing that his chief had powerful feelings for this woman?

It was proof of just how much Moon Eagle resented the woman—not only because her skin was white, but because she had stolen his chief's heart!

He tried not to reveal to Sheleen just how upset he was over what Moon Eagle had done.

"Do you want your freedom now that you have gotten a taste of it? Midnight Wolf asked, searching her eyes.

From the intense way he was looking at her, Sheleen no longer doubted the depth of this wonderful man's feelings for her.

She knew that if she didn't share her life with him, she would have no life at all.

"No, I didn't want to leave," she murmured. She lowered her eyes. "Truly, I didn't."

"Why then . . . did . . . you?" he asked, placing a finger beneath her chin, and lifting it so that their eyes would meet.

"Do you really need to ask?" she murmured, gazing as intensely into his eyes as he was looking into hers. "Midnight Wolf, I love you. I truly . . . love . . . you."

"I love you, too," he said. "I knew shortly after I brought you into my village that you were no threat to my people. Even though I questioned you again today, I knew the answer without hearing the words come from your mouth."

He reached up and gently brushed a fallen lock of hair back from her eyes. He smiled. "I have trusted you from the beginning," he said. "Had I not trusted you, I would not have taken you into my personal lodge, or allowed you to sleep there as I slept. My weapons were never far away. If you were a spy or an enemy, it would have been easy enough for you to take one of my knives and use it on me as I slept."

Even the thought of what he said made Sheleen gasp. "That is too horrible even to think about," she said softly. "I would never do anything to harm you. Never."

"I know that," Midnight Wolf said. "*Hecitu-yelo,* yes, that is true. I knew it then. I am not the sort who tempts fate."

Sheleen laughed softly. "Nor I," she murmured. Then her smile waned. "What are we to do?" she asked, her voice breaking. "Your shaman . . . Moon Eagle . . . hates me."

"Not you, but instead the color of your skin . . . your white heritage," Midnight Wolf said. "You know how we Dakota people have suffered at the hands of whites. My shaman cannot look past the fact that . . . you . . . are white."

"Not entirely," Sheleen said, looking into his eyes to gauge his reaction.

"What do you mean . . . not entirely?" Midnight Wolf asked.

"I want to tell you everything, but first I would like to see to my wound," Sheleen said. She winced when she again gazed at the blood on the dress. "I believe I've torn it open."

"I should get you back to my village so that my shaman can doctor it again," Midnight Wolf said.

He reached over to pick her up, but stopped when she placed a hand between them.

"No, I don't need your . . . shaman," Sheleen murmured. "In fact, I never needed him at all. I know how to treat a wound such as this."

"You know . . . ?" Midnight Wolf asked, his eyebrows rising in question. "What do you mean . . . ?"

"Let me doctor and rebandage it and then I will explain everything to you," Sheleen said, understanding the puzzlement in his eyes.

She nodded toward her father's bag, which hung at the right side of her horse. "The black bag?" she murmured. "Will you get it for me?"

Midnight Wolf studied her expression for a moment longer, then stood up and released the bag from where it had been tied to the saddle. He handed it to Sheleen. As she opened it, he knelt beside her.

He was amazed at what she carried in the bag.

He had seen medicinal items like these before when a white doctor had stopped at his village and cared for a small child long ago.

In fact, this could be the same bag, for Midnight Wolf had been only a small brave then and curiosity had caused him to go closer than the other children his age. He had taken a good look inside the bag, thinking it magical.

Even then Moon Eagle had been his people's shaman, although he was much younger at that time. Midnight Wolf remembered the resentment in the shaman's dark eyes as the white man did what Moon Eagle could not do.

The child had gotten well and walked again, whereas before the white doctor came, everyone thought the child would die!

No one thought any less of Moon Eagle's medicines, and Midnight Wolf's father, the chief at that time, did not choose another shaman over him.

But from then on Moon Eagle had resented all people with white skin, especially those who called themselves "physicians."

As Sheleen chose which medicine to apply to her throbbing wound, Midnight Wolf watched. He was in awe that this woman should know the same skills as that white physician of so long ago.

After cleaning the wound with a horribly burning alcohol medicine, Sheleen applied a cream that her father had, himself, concocted for such wounds as this. Already, her pain was lessening. She placed everything inside the bag again, then took out a roll of gauze and wrapped it around her leg, making sure the bandage was not too tight on her wound. Midnight Wolf had become quiet. She realized that he had studied her every movement as she had cared for her wound. And now his eyes were full of questions.

"You want to know how I learned so much about medicine," she murmured as she closed the bag and secured the latch, as she had seen her father do so often. Touching the latch, knowing how many times her father's fingers had done this, Sheleen felt suddenly close to him. She knew that as long as she had her father's bag with her, it would be like having a part of him.

She was thankful that Moon Eagle had thought to place the bag on her horse when he had prepared for her departure. He could just as easily have thrown it into the fire.

"Why . . . how . . . do you know so much about medicine?" Midnight Wolf asked as she set the closed bag aside.

"Did you ever hear of Harold Hicks, the white physician who helped the Dakota people whenever he could?" Sheleen asked, searching his eyes.

Midnight Wolf's eyes widened.

Sheleen had just spoken the name of the doctor he had been thinking about only moments ago.

How . . . could . . . that be possible?

CHAPTER TWENTY-FIVE

A little while in the shine of the sun,
We were twined together, joined lips, forgot
How the shadows fall when the day is done.
—*Ernest Dowson*

Midnight Wolf gazed at the bag again, then at Sheleen. "*Ho,* I knew of such a man," he said. "When I was only a young brave, aspiring to be a proud warrior, even a chief, a white man's shaman came into our village and cared for a child who was close to death. When our shaman, who was even then Moon Eagle, could not make her well, my chieftain father sent for this Doctor Hicks, who was known to go from village to village with his own type of magical medicines. My father knew that this white shaman was admired by all people with red skin. My father knew that he had a Dakota wife and a daughter who was of both the white and red world.

225

Her skin was white because of her white father, but her hair and eyes, and her heart, were Dakota."

He paused and gazed more intently into her eyes, again seeing how midnight black they were, like the eyes of his people.

He gazed at her long, flowing black hair, which had the same coarseness of his people.

Then he again looked deep into her eyes. "The last I heard of this white shaman, his Dakota wife had died and he had taken his daughter away to live in the white community," he said guardedly.

"Because Doctor Hicks wanted his daughter to be educated just as he had been. And this daughter wanted to know as much as possible in order to help her Dakota people once she returned to her true roots." Sheleen said.

"How do you know so much about what happened to this daughter . . . to this white shaman?" Midnight Wolf asked, his heart thumping inside his chest because he thought he already knew the answer without her saying it.

"Because I am that daughter and my father was that wonderful man, a physician, who eventually gave his all to the Dakota cause, even chancing being caught and hanged for his actions," Sheleen murmured. She could not stop the tears that filled her eyes.

"I imagine you never saw him again because when you became chief, you took your band far from the others in Minnesota. You were wise enough to see the fate of the Dakota people whose land was being grabbed by *washechus*," she said softly.

"Your *ahte* was that man?" Midnight Wolf asked, his eyes wide. He saw her tears and knew her answer before she even spoke it. "You were that daughter whom so many spoke of?"

"*Ho,* I am that daughter, and I am that woman who has never denied her Indian heritage to herself. I became my father's assistant as he traveled from one Dakota band to the other, helping them in their time of trouble," Sheleen murmured. "I did attend school to become a doctor. I am proud to say that I did follow in my father's footsteps and helped the Dakota whenever I could."

She swallowed hard, lowered her eyes, then gazed again into Midnight Wolf's eyes. "The reason I was found, alone, so far from my home, is because my father . . . my father . . . was found by an evil white man who knew of my father's love of the Dakota people," she said, her voice breaking.

Tears flooded her eyes.

"My father and I had fled into Wisconsin after the hangings three years ago because it was rumored that we were going to be hanged, too, for our role in helping the Dakota," Sheleen said. "Recently we heard that the Dakota people who had not fled far enough from Minnesota were being hunted down and hanged. We knew that if such hangings were taking place again, both my father and myself might be targets, as well.

We decided to move on, to find a new home, even though we had found peace in Wisconsin. I . . . I . . . left my father just long enough to get supplies before our departure. When . . . when . . . I returned . . ."

She almost choked on her sobs as she was overwhelmed by grief.

"When you returned?" Midnight Wolf asked, placing gentle hands on her cheeks, and directing her eyes ahead so that he could look into them.

"I found my father hanging from a tree," Sheleen choked out. "A white man had found our home. While I was gone, he killed my father and was waiting for me. He was in our cabin. But . . . but . . . I got the best of him. I shot him."

"You killed him?" Midnight Wolf asked, slowly lowering his hands away from her.

"No, but I wish that I had," Sheleen said, swallowing hard. "I . . . I . . . shot his rifle from his hand and while doing so I shot off his trigger finger."

Midnight Wolf was amazed by all that she had told him. Now that he knew how the wonderful white shaman had died, and how Sheleen had kept herself from being killed, too, he couldn't find the words to express how he felt.

He was so sad that the white shaman had met such a horrible end, but so proud that Sheleen had been able to protect herself from the same fate as her father.

He was also astonished that she was part

Dakota. He could only gaze at her, loving her even more now.

"There is so much more I want to tell you," Sheleen said, wiping tears from her eyes with the backs of her hands. "But mainly I want to say that with you I feel protected and loved again. You make me feel so much more than that. I love you so much."

She flung herself into his arms and clung to him as he held her close.

"In time you can tell me everything," he said huskily. "But the main thing I want you to know is that you are a part of my life now, no matter what my shaman says or does."

He leaned her slightly away from him. "You are, in part, Dakota, which should make it easier for my shaman to understand my feelings for you. But you are also. . . ." he began, but couldn't find a way to say that she was also part white.

"I am a breed," Sheleen said, saying what he would not. "But in my heart I am full-blood Dakota. My mother was Dakota. My sister? She was Dakota, too. She had the same father as I, but no signs that she had white blood mingled with red running through her veins. Had she lived, no one would have ever have called her a breed."

"Had she lived?" Midnight Wolf asked, framing her face between his hands. "Are you saying . . . ?"

"My father's medicines were not powerful

enough to save her," Sheleen gulped out. "She was only two. She died the same way Pretty Wing did, from a deadly spider bite. She did not live even as long as Pretty Wing."

"I am so sorry," Midnight Wolf, again gathering her into his arms. "I am so very, very sorry."

"It was not long after that that my Dakota mother passed on to the other side," Sheleen said, her voice breaking. "She could not get over the heartache of having lost her smaller daughter. One day she just did not wake up. Although I was only four winters of age at that time, I made a decision to follow in my father's footsteps. That is when I decided I must attend school in order to be as knowledgeable as he."

"You left the world of the Dakota and joined the white world," Midnight Wolf said.

"*Ho*, and my father found another wife, but this time, she was a white woman," Sheleen murmured. "At first I resented her, but I soon grew to know the goodness of this woman's heart. She became my mother and then . . . then . . . she had not been part of our lives for long before she also died."

"She also died?" Midnight Wolf asked, searching her eyes.

"Someone heard of my father's relationship with the Dakota and . . . and followed my mother one day as she left home to go shopping," Sheleen said.

She hated to relive that day. But she would tell Midnight Wolf all, and that would be the last time she would talk about it ever again, to anyone.

It was important that he knew everything about her, especially how her life had made her into the person she was today.

"That day Mama got only a short way from our home in her buggy before she was ambushed and killed," Sheleen said, lowering her eyes. "No one ever found the murderer. But everyone who knew of my father's alliances with the Dakota knew why she was killed. You see, many white people saw my father as a traitor for having helped Indians. I am lucky they did not look more closely at me, for they could have guessed that I was even more a part of that Dakota world than my father. If the white community knew that, I would have either been killed, or run off. My father probably would have been hanged much sooner."

"Were you finished with your schooling by then?" Midnight Wolf asked softly.

"Enough for me to know how to assist my father," Sheleen murmured. "We left our home and wandered around, helping the Dakota when we could. After a time, my father was afraid for my safety, so he bought a home on the outskirts of St. Paul to make it look as though we were a normal family. We lived there until the hangings three years ago."

"Had I not found you today, I would have lost you forever, and who is to say what might have become of you," Midnight Wolf said. "Those who resent people with red skin, find a way to kill those they see as enemies of the white world."

"How did you know where to find me today?" Sheleen asked, searching his eyes.

She looked over at his horse and saw no signs that Midnight Wolf had had a successful hunt.

"I could not concentrate on the hunt," Midnight Wolf explained. "Something seemed to be beckoning me away. *Mitawin*, my woman, that something was you. I left my friends to do their hunting without me and I followed my heart . . . then found you."

"Now that you have, what are we to do?" Sheleen asked softly. "It is so apparent how your shaman feels about me. What if your whole Wolf Band feels the same?"

"I will talk with them all in private, one family at a time, and explain how it is going to be," Midnight Wolf said. "I will take special care with my shaman. He must know the wrong he has done and he must apologize and be sincere in the apology. Otherwise I will have to find another shaman for my people . . . someone that I know I can fully trust."

"He will hate me even more and . . . and . . . I am afraid I won't feel safe," Sheleen murmured.

"You will be safe," Midnight Wolf said, smiling slowly. "Know that while you are in my care, you will never have to worry again about whether or not you are safe."

"Do we have to go right home?" Sheleen asked, again flinging herself into his arms. "All I want is to be with you. Please hold me tightly."

Midnight Wolf held her tenderly in his arms, then put her away from him and gazed intently into her eyes.

"No, we do not have to return home," he said hoarsely. "Not yet, anyhow. We will find a comfortable place, and then . . . then . . . *mitawin*, I want to prove to you just how much I do love you."

Sheleen blushed, for she knew without his saying it that they were going to make love. She had never been with a man like that before. She was perhaps the least skilled about such matters of any woman on this earth!

Until she had met Midnight Wolf, being in love, making love, had been the farthest things from her mind. Along with her father, she had mainly concentrated on surviving in a world that had seemed to have gone mad!

She had never known such peace as she had found while she was in Midnight Wolf's arms.

Surely making love would bring their two worlds together, as well as their hearts and souls.

"*Ho,* let us find that private place. I, too, want to prove my love for you," Sheleen said, seeing that her words made Midnight Wolf's eyes brighten.

He swept her into his arms.

He carried her away from their horses, to a spot where he knew there was a tiny stream with soft moss lining the banks.

He had been there before while stopping to water his horse after a long day's hunt.

He knew they would be alone, for his two friends, who were busy at the hunt, were far, far from this place. It was a peaceful hideaway with lovely flowers and willows that hung low over the embankment, which would give him and his woman the privacy they needed.

"Where are you taking me?" Sheleen asked, spotting shine of water up ahead, where branches of willows hung long and low beside the water.

"To a place that we both shall remember forever, because it will be there that you and I will make love for the first time," he said huskily. "I ache for you, Sheleen. I need you."

"As I need you," she murmured. Her words were stolen away as Midnight Wolf gave her a passionate kiss. He placed Sheleen on her feet beside the beautiful stream, where tiny minnows darted like flashes of light along the pebbles at the bottom.

Above them in the trees, a cardinal broke into song.

CHAPTER TWENTY-SIX

But the lark is so brimful of gladness and love,
The green fields below him, the blue sky above,
That he sings and he sings; and forever sings he—
"I love my Love, and my Love loves me."
—*Samuel Coleridge*

What was already an enchanted paradise, with the slowly meandering stream on one side and the green forest wilderness so lush and beautiful on the other, was now heaven on earth as Sheleen stood facing Midnight Wolf while he slowly undressed her.

Her heart was thumping wildly as her breasts were exposed to a man for the first time in her life. Moments later, she stood before him completely nude as the last of her garments fell away from her.

She could not help blushing bashfully as Midnight Wolf's eyes moved slowly over her.

When his eyes touched her, she felt a wild, exuberant passion sweep through her.

Never had she even dreamed of such a moment as this, for she had not given herself time to think about loving a man, especially not someone as wonderful as Midnight Wolf.

He was everything a man should be. He was kind, compassionate, caring, powerful, and oh, so loving.

The first time she had gazed into his eyes, something had whispered inside her heart that nothing would ever be the same again for her.

That quickly, she was caught up in the appeal of this man, this chief.

And now this was the fulfillment of what she had yearned for from the moment she'd realized that she was in love with him.

When he reached out and gently cupped her tiny breasts in his hands, a desire gripped Sheleen that she had never known possible.

She closed her eyes, sighing as his lips found one breast, his tongue sweeping around the nipple. Then his hot and hungry mouth closed over the nipple, suckling.

Midnight Wolf was awakened today in ways he had never been awakened before. He had never wanted a woman as he wanted Sheleen. Her shy, quick breaths, the smell of sweet grass on her skin, made his insides tremble with a building passion.

His entire being was in tune with his needs, his

love for this woman. He wanted to fulfill her every longing. To do so would be to fulfill his own.

Her destiny was his destiny!

Sheleen felt a tremor from deep within her as his tongue made a hot trail from her breasts, down across her flat belly, to touch her with a flick of his tongue that made her eyes open wildly in question.

She saw that he was no longer standing, but instead kneeling before her, his eyes now gazing up at her, a sort of questioning wonder in their dark depths.

"You are beautiful everywhere, even here," Midnight Wolf said, placing a hand over the small patch of black hair at the juncture of her thighs.

He gently pressed his palm against her there, making a blaze of urgency rush through Sheleen so that her knees almost buckled.

"What you are doing to me . . . ?" Sheleen murmured, questioning him with her eyes. "My body is responding to everything you are doing. I . . . did . . . not know such feelings existed."

Midnight Wolf slowly stood, then took one of her hands and brought it to where she could feel how she was affecting him.

He smiled as her blush deepened when he pressed her hand more tightly against his swollen manhood, then moved her hand slowly over him.

"And now you know how you are affecting me," he said huskily. "You are feeling the strength of my need for you."

He drew her hand away.

He placed his fingers in the band of his breech-clout, and as she watched, wide-eyed, he lowered his clothing, his manhood soon visible and ready for her.

Sheleen saw just how endowed he was there, and wondered if he could even fit inside her?

Suddenly she was afraid.

But she was more needy than afraid, and as he reached for her and lowered her onto the soft green moss, so that he was now above her, blanketing her with his body, she moaned with ecstasy.

His lips came to hers in a stormy kiss. One of his hands ran from her thigh, to her hip, then to a breast, while she sought out the contours of his muscled, sleek back.

"I will be gentle," he whispered against her lips as she felt him probe gently where she was wet and ready for him.

With a knee, he parted her legs, making her more accessible to him, then pressed himself inside her, holding her close when he had reached that thin membrane that proved she had never been with a man before.

With a husky groan he pushed through it. He gave her meltingly hot kisses as he thrust rhythmically into her.

Slowly, he pressed into her, over and over again.

Feelings such as Sheleen had never known possible overwhelmed her.

She was so taken by a drugged passion, she had not felt any pain at all when he had entered her.

Instead, she felt blissful and gave herself up to the rapture.

She spread her hands across his muscular male buttocks, pressing her fingers against him and straining her hips upward as he came to her. He thrust deeply, continuing his rhythmic movements, while kissing her passionately, heatedly, wonderfully!

"Oh, my love," she whispered against his lips when he moved them a little away from hers.

He gazed at her through passion-heated eyes. "This is how it should be," he said huskily. "There is only now. There is only you and me. I want you, Sheleen, forever and ever. I want you for my *mitawica*, my wife."

Those words were magical to Sheleen. She smiled as she gazed at him through her lashes. "I want you for my husband," she said, oh, so happy that they had found one another again.

Had she continued her flight from his village, her entire universe would have been torn asunder!

"We will marry soon," Midnight Wolf said. He reached for and brushed locks of hair back from her brow.

He kissed the spot where her hair had just been, and then again swept his arms around her and held her tightly. His lips bore down on hers, his body moving, the sexual excitement building ever higher.

"I am feeling something . . . so different," Sheleen said in a whisper against his lips. "I feel as though I am floating. The feeling. It is spreading. Oh, Lord, it is so delicious a feeling."

With a sob she clung to him, then she shuddered, arched and cried out, as those feelings totally overwhelmed her, and she realized that his body was reacting the same as hers!

Afterward they clung to one another.

"It was so beautiful," Sheleen said. She gazed into his midnight-black eyes as he looked into hers. "What we just experienced is something I . . . I . . . cannot even describe. Will it always happen that way when . . . when . . . we make love?"

"Always," Midnight Wolf said, chuckling as he rolled away from her and lay on his back.

The sun was still high in the sky but he expected a red sunset tonight, as dazzling to the eye as the white of midday.

"In the evening, the sunset is always watched, for it holds the secret of the next day's weather," he said, looking over at her.

"I know," Sheleen said softly. "My Dakota mother taught me that and so many other things."

"She was a good mother," Midnight Wolf said. He reached over and pinched off a spray of mint that grew by the edge of the stream. He rolled over and

240

floated the mint on the surface of the water, sipping the cool liquid through it.

"Draw the water into your mouth through the leaves of mint," he said. "It will be refreshing."

She knew this, too, but didn't brag that she did, for she didn't want to make him think that she was boasting too much about her Dakota knowledge.

In time, he would know that before she had entered the world of the white community, she had been taught many, many things Dakota by her mother, even some that were secretive!

She drew the sweet water into her mouth, enjoying how refreshing and tasty it was, then moved over and snuggled against Midnight Wolf. "I wish we didn't have to leave, but I know that we must," she murmured. "None of your people know where you are. We must not worry them."

"When I arrive with you, there will be mixed feelings, but when they learn the truth about your heritage, no one will question your right to be among us any longer," Midnight Wolf said.

He slowly moved his hand over her bare flesh, hating to have to hide her beauty beneath clothes.

"I will never do anything to disappoint you, or them," Sheleen said, sitting up and reaching for her dress.

She noticed the blood spots on her dress, only then reminded of her wound. She smiled as she gazed down at her bandaged leg.

While making love, she had totally forgotten the soreness of her leg.

The scar that would stay with her forever would be a reminder of how she had met Midnight Wolf.

Ah, she was so glad that Gentle Bear had been there that day to stop her flight. If he had not, at this moment she would be far, far from this place where she had found such wonder in the arms of this powerful Dakota chief.

After they were both dressed, they mounted their horses and turned back in the direction of the village. "Remember this, my woman, you will never have to fear anything or anyone again. I will always be there to protect you from all harm," Midnight Wolf said.

In this world, where white men took up arms against the red man so quickly, he knew that no matter what he did, there might be times when he could not be there to protect his woman. He would have to go hunting with his warriors, and leave the village for council with other chiefs.

At those times, he knew he would have to leave her alone, vulnerable to the evils of the white man. But he hoped she would be safe with the Wolf Band.

CHAPTER TWENTY-SEVEN

It is not while beauty and youth are thine own,
And thy cheeks unprofaned by a tear,
That the fervor and faith of a soul may be known.
—*Thomas Moore*

Gentle Bear stood just outside his tepee, his eyes searching again for Fluffy.

Moon Eagle had only moments ago come to him and told him that the nice white woman had decided to leave their village, and that it had been her decision to leave Fluffy with Gentle Bear.

At first all Gentle Bear could wonder was why the woman would suddenly decide to leave?

And why hadn't Sheleen told him that she was going?

People who shared special secrets were friends for life. He would never forget the secret about her dreams of wolves.

And now she was gone?

Somehow it didn't seem right. He just couldn't believe she wanted to leave.

But why, then, had she?

She had become attached not only to Gentle Bear, but also to Gentle Bear's chief!

Gentle Bear had watched other people who were in love, and knew how differently they acted while with that particular person. He had concluded from his observations that Sheleen and Midnight Wolf had very special feelings for one another.

Gentle Bear had even thought that they would become man and wife!

But Moon Eagle had explained her departure to Gentle Bear, saying that her place was not with the Dakota people, and that she just could not live among them any longer.

Moon Eagle had said that Sheleen was well enough to ride her horse now, and she was anxious to join the white community again.

Gentle Bear had found that somewhat peculiar, for he knew she had fled the white world, where her father had been murdered by a white man.

Although Sheleen had not told Gentle Bear her future plans, he did know that she was afraid the man who killed her father might eventually find her and kill her. She had actually told Gentle Bear that she felt safe among his people.

She had not spoken once to him about wanting to leave!

But for now, all he was concerned about was Fluffy. Sheleen had left the cat in his care, and he was afraid he was not doing a very good job of it. In fact, he had not seen the cat since yesterday, and until now, he had thought nothing of it because he had assumed Fluffy was with Sheleen.

Where could Fluffy be?

Gentle Bear was too restless and worried to just stand there wondering. He needed to find Fluffy and bring her home with him, to prove that he was worthy of such a lovely gift.

He gazed down at the lake, where his mother was bent over, washing clothes. He knew that would take a while.

He would have time to go and make a broad search for the cat. Apparently Fluffy had gone beyond the perimeters of the village, for she was nowhere to be seen.

If so, the cat could find herself in mortal danger, for there were predators in the dark forest.

The thought of Fluffy becoming some creature's dinner caused a sick feeling in the pit of his stomach.

He gave his mother one last look, then spun around and hurried into his tepee.

Soon his quiver of arrows was secured at his back and his bow was clasped in a hand. He went to the entrance flap and slowly drew it aside. He knew his mother would not approve of what he was about to do.

And his chief! Midnight Wolf had warned Gentle

Bear about leaving the village. How could he disobey his chief twice?

He did hate to disappoint the two most special people in his life, but surely they would understand! He had been given the duty. He must see to his responsibility, and face what might be said to him later.

Surely both his mother and his chief would see what he was doing as an admirable thing. He was trying to look after the welfare of a beautiful, defenseless animal . . . an animal that now belonged solely to him. He truly felt that both his mother and his chief would see him as a *wicasa okinihan,* an honorable and respected individual who was going to save a cat's life.

He turned and gazed at the oak box, where the medicine bag that his chief had given him rested among his other treasures. His chief had told him to carry it when he left the safety of his village.

It would keep him safe!

But he doubted that his chief would want him to carry it with him today, for Gentle Bear was again going against his chief's orders. He was leaving the village without permission.

That surely meant the bag would not work its magic for Gentle Bear. His chief would not even want the bag to be a part of Gentle Bear's flight.

Breathing hard, his pulse racing, Gentle Bear ran quickly from the tepee and hurried around to the back where no one would see him.

He stood there for a moment longer to gather his

courage. Then he broke into a hard run, his moccasined feet taking him into the dark shadows of the hardwood forest.

His eyes moved steadily from side to side, then forward, watching for any sign of the cat. But no matter how far he ran, or how much he looked, he still could not find Fluffy.

"I must be going in the wrong direction," he whispered to himself, stopping for several deep breaths. He turned and ran in a different direction, not even conscious of just how far he had already gone. All he could think about was Sheleen's gift to him, and that he had to prove himself worthy of such a gift.

Suddenly fear grabbed Gentle Bear in the pit of his stomach when he saw two men a short distance away, through a break in the trees.

They were bending over a stream, drinking from it.

He knew that those men wouldn't be so close to his village for any good reason.

He had no choice but to stop them, for he was the only one who was aware of their presence!

To him, they were on holy ground of the Dakota, where no white man should tread. It was dangerous for any white man to know where his people had made their home after having fled Minnesota land!

He looked back in the direction of his village.

He knew that even if he ran there at top speed to alert the warriors about these men, it might take too long. By the time the warriors returned, these white men might already have joined others, with the intention of invading the Dakota village!

He looked guardedly around him.

He saw no one else. Yet might not others be close at hand?

Studying the two men again, as they sat on the banks of the stream, discussing something, he saw that one of them was red-skinned!

Hate filled his heart for any red man who aligned himself with a white man, and a white man who looked so grizzly and mean!

Yet he knew that some red men had gone against their own kind and joined the white man's cavalry, as their scouts, or interpreters.

Surely this red man was one of those.

If so, he deserved no better fate than his white companion.

Gentle Bear reached for an arrow and notched it to his bowstring.

Just as he started to make his presence known, he noticed something about the white man. His right hand was bandaged.

He would not be able to use a firearm against Gentle Bear, even if he were given the chance. That realization gave Gentle Bear still more confidence to proceed with his plan.

He would take them captive.

Although he knew that he shouldn't have left the village again, his chief would surely not be angry at him if he took two captives who might have planned evil against their people.

He would prove himself to be a proud, courageous brave, who looked fear in the eye and was not bothered by it.

His mother and his chief would be proud of him!

Gentle Bear circled around, and when he was directly behind the men, he called out to them. "You men! Stand up and hold your hands in the air, or you both will be shot," Gentle Bear warned. "Now! Stand!"

He saw how the red man started for his firearm as he stood and gazed at Gentle Bear.

"Do not be foolish," Gentle Bear warned. "I might be only a small brave, but I am very skilled with my bow and arrows. I can sink an arrow in your chest before you can pull your trigger."

He shifted his gaze to the white man, who held his bandaged hand in the other one, a glower on his whiskered face as he rose slowly to his feet beside the red man.

"Look at you," Raymond said, snickering as he gazed sourly at Gentle Bear. "You are just a boy in a man's moccasins. Do you really think you can best two grown men? Never!"

"I already have," Gentle Bear said, slowly smiling. "Who is holding who captive?"

When the red man started for his pistol again, and Gentle Bear saw what he was doing, a fear he had never felt before siezed his gut. He found himself incapable of releasing the arrow from its bowstring!

The white man was right to call Gentle Bear a child, for he was behaving like a child.

Suddenly a voice spoke up behind Gentle Bear, coming from the dark shadows of the forest. "Red man traitor, do not draw your firearm, for I have a rifle aimed directly at your heart," the woman's voice warned. "Although I am a woman, I am not too afraid to shoot both of you. Do you feel big now, facing down a brave my son's age?"

Gentle Bear was stunned speechless at the realization that his mother had found him in such a predicament. Now she knew that he had betrayed both her and his chief by leaving the village when he had been told more than once not to.

His mother had caught him in another act of defiance, and she had also seen his cowardly side. He hadn't even been able to successfully defend himself!

Rosy Dawn stepped out into the open, a rifle leveled at Big Bear Moon's belly, for he was the one who was about to threaten her son with his firearm.

A feeling of revulsion swept through her at the knowledge that a red man would align himself with the white man in such a way, that he would even shoot an innocent child.

"Gentle Bear, hurry home," Rosy Dawn said tightly, still holding the rifle steady. "Now!"

"Mother, I should stay and defend you," Gentle Bear said, again aware of his notched bowstring.

While fear had him in its grip, he had forgotten that he had a weapon that could kill both men if he were brave enough to shoot his arrows from the bowstring.

"Home, Gentle Bear," Rosy Dawn said tightly. "Now!"

Sobbing, Gentle Bear took his arrow from his bowstring, thrust it inside his quiver, then with his bow clutched tightly in one hand, he ran off, his head lowered in shame.

Disappointed in her son, who just could not understand right from wrong, yet also seeing Gentle Bear's father in the courage he'd displayed, Rosy Dawn stared at the men.

"Why are you here?" she demanded, looking slowly at first one man, and then the other. "What brought you this close to my Dakota village?"

Big Bear Moon was the first to speak. "We just happened along," he said, with what Rosy Dawn thought was honesty in his eyes and voice. "We had no intention of going anywhere near your village. It was an accident. We stopped for a drink and would have then traveled onward except that we were confronted by your son. We are headed for Fort Destiny. We are going to work there, I as a scout, the white man as an interpreter. Trust me when I say that our intentions are good."

"But you would shoot my son, a child?" Rosy Dawn said, her eyes narrowing as she gazed at the pistol in the red man's holster. "I saw you. You were ready to draw on my son. Had I not come, would you have shot him, or shot a warning into the air? Would you shoot me even now if you had the chance?"

"My skin is the same color as yours, and I was raised with the same ideals as you, but when my family died in an ambush and I was the only survivor at age eight winters, I was taken to live among whites. I could not help becoming as one with them," Big Bear Moon said, lying through his teeth in order to be able to travel onward.

He was traveling with this white man for only one reason. To find Sheleen.

When that deed was done, his job would be over and he would go on with his life.

"It was when I grew into adulthood that I was appointed scout, for even though I was not raised to adulthood among my own people, I had already learned the art of tracking from my father," he said. "Tracking is what makes a good scout. So that is what I have been paid to do."

"And who are you tracking now?" Rosy Dawn asked guardedly.

"I am not tracking anyone," Big Bear Moon said, again lying. "Like I have already told you, we are on our way to Fort Destiny."

"And you, white man, I see that you are wounded," Rosy Dawn said, having noticed the bandaged hand. "How were you injured? And who injured you?"

Raymond's eyes narrowed. "No one did this to me," he said flatly. "I did it to myself. My knife slipped. I happened to cut off a finger. That is why I am riding with someone, not alone. I can no longer protect myself."

All of the explanations seemed plausible, so Rosy Dawn nodded at them. "Move onward," she said, still holding her rifle on them. "Get as far as you can from this place as fast as you can, or I will send many armed warriors to find and kill you."

"You're lettin' us go?" Raymond asked, his eyes widening. "You are not taking us captive?"

"No, I am not taking you captive," Rosy Dawn said softly. "But hear me well when I warn you not to bring pony soldiers to my village. My chief has done nothing to cause such action. The wrong was done by a mere child who hungers to be the man of his house since he no longer has a father. Go. Now. Do not turn your eyes or your horses back in this direction, or you will pay."

They both nodded, hurried to their horses, and rode off on them.

For a while, Rosy Dawn continued to stand there with the rifle aimed in the direction of the two men who had fled from her.

As long as she could hear the steady gallop of the horses, she knew they were still running from her. And when she could not hear the horses, she would know they were far enough away for her to hurry back to her village.

Should she tell Midnight Wolf? If she did, he would see her son as the reason their people had been put in danger. Gentle Bear would never be given the chance to be the warrior he aspired to be.

He would no longer be his chief's proud charge!

No. She could not chance telling Midnight Wolf what Gentle Bear had done today, for it would turn Midnight Wolf away from both herself and her son.

They would be castoffs . . . banished.

Surely those two men were there by accident and would heed her words . . . her warnings.

No one would ever know!

Plagued by guilt, she hurried home.

She found Gentle Bear crying beside the lodge fire.

Slowly he looked up at her and saw the disappointment in her eyes.

"I am sorry, Mother," he said, his voice breaking. "So very, very sorry. I went into the woods to search for Fluffy. Sheleen left her in my care, but the cat is lost."

Rosy Dawn set her rifle aside, then sat down beside Gentle Bear.

She gently took his hands in hers and gazed into his tear-swollen eyes. "I do not yet forgive you for what you did today, but listen to what I say, and this time you must obey me," she murmured. "If you do not, all will be lost for both of us."

She gazed intently into his eyes. "Do you understand?" she asked, her voice drawn.

All Gentle Bear could do was nod.

She told him her plan as he gazed incredulously into her eyes.

"Now that you have heard how I feel about what you did, you know that you must never tell anyone what happened today," Rosy Dawn murmured. "You are never to speak of seeing those men, and you are never to leave the village again, alone, no matter the reason, unless I, or Midnight Wolf, say it is all right." She framed his face between her hands. "It will be a secret. Ours. Only ours."

"A secret?" Gentle Bear repeated, remembering the secret Sheleen had shared with him. "Ours? Only . . . ours . . . ?"

"Yes, only ours," she murmured as she slowly lowered her hands from his face.

He was stunned that his mother was willing to do this for him, to actually hide something from her chief.

Gentle Bear flung himself into his mother's arms. "I promise never to bring disgrace to you or my people again," he said, sobbing once more.

Rosy Dawn held him tightly, for she was terribly frightened that Midnight Wolf would discover the truth about what had happened today. And she was also afraid of what the two strangers might do.

She would pray that she had made the right choice.

Hearing a "meow" just outside the entrance flap, Gentle Bear scurried from his mother's arms. He lifted the flap and Fluffy pranced in as though she had never been gone.

Gentle Bear turned to his mother. "May I?" he asked.

"The cat is yours, so pick her up and love her," Rosy Dawn said, then rose to her feet. "I must return to the river and finish what I was doing when I saw you slip into the forest. I was delayed only because I returned to our tepee to get a rifle. But all is well. You are safely home."

"And so is Fluffy," Gentle Bear said, hugging Fluffy to him. "Fluffy, my cat."

He was so proud to be able to call the cat his, yet sad that he would never see Sheleen again.

CHAPTER TWENTY-EIGHT

Speak now, lest at some future day
My whole life wither and decay.
—*Adelaide Anne Procter*

Just as Sheleen and Midnight Wolf rode into the village, they saw Moon Eagle give them a startled look, then hurry inside his tepee.

They both knew why.

Sheleen noticed that their arrival had disturbed some of the older children's activities. Some were running races, while others played games such as tossing arrows through willow hoops, or throwing back and forth balls stuffed tight with deer hair.

She saw some girls sitting in a circle, playing the plum-pit game, tossing the baskets and then laughing as they counted the string of beads and brass rings and ribbons piled in the center of where they sat.

As they rode onward through the village toward

Midnight Wolf's tepee, Sheleen saw groups of small children sitting around a heap of bone chips that had been placed on a clean rawhide mat by their mothers, after the women had broken bones up for marrow.

The bone chips were used to help keep their children' teeth and gums healthy. The bone chips also whitened the childrens' teeth.

Sheleen knew these things, for her own Indian mother had made Sheleen do this. She was so glad of it, for her teeth were even now white and strong.

At a later date, when she was familiar with the ways of the white world, including dentists, she had laughed oft times about the Dakotas' bone chips, which seemed to keep teeth healthier than the white people's dentists.

She smiled even now, knowing that most Indians kept their teeth to the grave, while so many white people had none left!

Sheleen and Midnight Wolf rode past many tepees where people stepped outside and stared at them.

Even the children were now stopping what they were doing to gaze at their chief and the woman they'd thought had left them forever.

Sheleen could see disappointment in many of their eyes, and happiness in others.

She surmised that those who seemed glad she had returned were Gentle Bear's special friends, for they all knew how Gentle Bear felt about her.

She looked more carefully at a group of children

who were standing in a cluster. She was looking for Gentle Bear, but he wasn't to be seen anywhere, and that surprised and disappointed her.

Did that mean he was not happy about her return?

He was one of the reasons she had regretted having to leave. She truly had thought they had a special friendship, a bond even.

She had even left her precious cat there for him to have as his own.

But most of all, he held the secret of her dreams of wolves inside his heart! She had not shared that with anyone but Gentle Bear. Had she chosen the wrong one to receive her secret?

She looked past the children, searching for Rosy Dawn. Surely Gentle Bear's mother was glad that Sheleen had returned, for she had become a good friend . . . an ally.

But Rosy Dawn wasn't anywhere to be seen, either. That made Sheleen wonder if something was wrong.

Had the shaman talked with them and told them it was best she was gone? Had he turned mother and child against her?

She glanced over at Midnight Wolf.

She saw that his interest was focused on the shaman, for Midnight Wolf had not moved his eyes away from Moon Eagle's lodge after seeing him hurry inside like a scared puppy.

Sheleen was anxious to arrive at Midnight Wolf's tepee. She needed a brief retreat from those who openly resented her.

But what about later?

When they all discovered her true reason for returning, that she was going to marry their chief, oh, what would their reaction be?

Would some of them gather together and plot against her?

Was her stay at the village to be short-lived?

If enough of his people showed their chief that they did not approve of her, would he change his mind about marrying her?

Preoccupied by these worrisome thoughts, Sheleen was hardly aware of arriving at the corral, dismounting, and handing her reins to a young brave.

She was scarcely aware of Midnight Wolf carrying her bags inside his tepee as she walked beside him, for she was truly afraid that she would eventually be told to leave.

But surely this powerful, wonderful man could not be persuaded to do anything that his heart told him not to do.

"Sheleen?"

Midnight Wolf's voice broke through her troubled thoughts. She turned quickly and faced him just as he set her bags on the floor of the lodge.

He reached out for her and placed gentle hands at her waist, drawing her against him.

"Have my people made you feel uneasy? You seem not to remember where you are, or who you are with," he said, searching her eyes. "*Mitawin*, you are welcome at my village because I say it is so. You are going to be my *mitawicu*, my wife, because we both say it will be so. My people will adjust to this change in their lives as they have adjusted to many changes through the years."

"By changes, aren't you speaking of hardships and unhappiness?" Sheleen blurted out, now returning his serious gaze. "My darling Midnight Wolf, I know so much about the hurts the white man has inflicted on your people, and your people still see me as white. I truly can understand why they do not approve of my coming here again. Do you think that marriage between us will really work? Especially when your shaman despises me?"

She lowered her eyes, then looked into his again. "Even Rosy Dawn and Gentle Bear seem to have changed their minds about me, for they did not welcome me back to your village," she said, her voice breaking. "Did you not also notice that they did not come out of their lodge to greet us?"

"I saw mainly that my shaman quickly hid away from us," Midnight Wolf said. "He is my main concern. We will worry about Rosy Dawn and Gentle Bear later. It is my shaman that must be dealt with, and now, not later."

"I doubt that you can make him accept me, ever," Sheleen murmured. "And if he doesn't, won't that mean . . ."

Midnight Wolf placed a gentle hand over her mouth so that she would not say words he did not want to hear. "I will go and talk with him now," he said tightly.

He slid his hand away and gently kissed her, then embraced her. "I will not be gone for long," he promised softly.

"Midnight Wolf, please do not be hard on him," Sheleen said, gently easing herself from his arms. She gazed into his eyes. "He was only thinking about his people when he urged me to leave. He sees me as a threat. He believes that if I remain here among your people, and any white people see me, they will think I am a captive and come in force to take me away from you."

She lowered her eyes. "I am afraid that perhaps Moon Eagle is right," she murmured. "My being here could even bring the cavalry to your village, and that would mean the end of your people's peaceful existence here in Wisconsin."

She lifted her head quickly. "No one has disturbed you here," she said softly. "Not until I came into your lives."

"You have not disturbed my people's peaceful existence," Midnight Wolf said tightly. "The disturbance is only in the eyes of my shaman. I will correct that impression now. Stay here. I will not be long."

"What are you going to say . . . do?" Sheleen asked.

"I am going to talk with Moon Eagle, and then bring him back here so that you can tell him, yourself, about who you truly are, and that you are more Dakota than white," Midnight Wolf said. "After you tell him, I will watch closely for his reaction. Then I will decide what is to be done about his actions."

"What do you mean?" Sheleen asked, almost afraid to hear his answer.

Sheleen knew that she could not dissuade him from confronting Moon Eagle. His shaman had done something that he had known his chief would not approve. That action could not be allowed to stand.

Midnight Wolf just gave her a look, then said, "I will return soon, my love."

He snaked an arm around her waist and drew her against his hard body. "And we will marry soon," he said huskily. "That is my promise to you, my woman. And I never break my promises."

She clung to him, their hearts beating as one. Their embrace lasted a moment longer, and then Sheleen watched Midnight Wolf leave the tepee.

His absence left a strange void behind in the lodge.

Sheleen looked slowly around her, oh, so familiar now with where her beloved lived, and oh, so anxious to be a permanent fixture in that lodge!

"I so badly want to marry you," she murmured. Just the thought of being his wife and awakening every morning in his arms caused a sensual tremor across her flesh.

She went to the entrance flap and slowly drew it aside, just far enough for her to see the shaman's lodge.

Midnight Wolf was there, even now speaking to his shaman.

Sheleen wondered if Midnight Wolf was going to shame Moon Eagle for the wrong he had done, or just talk reason to him?

Would Moon Eagle respond in the right way, or protest his chief's decision so much that he would be banished from their village?

Sheleen began to pace back and forth as she waited.

But when time passed and Midnight Wolf still had not returned, she stopped pacing and busied herself by taking her bags to the back of the lodge.

Although she knew that Moon Eagle was a possible obstacle in the way of her happiness, she was filled with joy at the knowledge of just how much Midnight Wolf loved her.

Finally her life amounted to something again. She had a true purpose for living!

When she heard footsteps outside the tepee, Sheleen turned on a heel and watched the entrance flap.

Her heart pounded, for she knew that those approaching were Midnight Wolf and Moon Eagle.

What if Moon Eagle still stubbornly disapproved

of her relationship with Midnight Wolf after hearing her explanation about everything? She would hate to be the one who interfered in the two men's respect for one another!

And it might be even worse than that. If Moon Eagle did not see reason, there was a good chance that he would be forced to give up his title of shaman, and be banished from the Wolf Band.

That thought made Sheleen's insides turn cold. If Moon Eagle were banished, would Midnight Wolf ever really feel free to love her?

Would he not always think of his banished shaman when he looked at Sheleen?

She clasped her hands nervously behind her as she waited for the entrance flap to be shoved aside.

But when it didn't open and the footsteps continued onward outside, she felt as though she had had a reprieve for now.

She sat down beside the fire and watched the entrance flap, wishing it would open soon. As time kept slipping by, and Midnight Wolf still had not returned to his lodge with Moon Eagle, she began to feel more afraid, than hopeful.

She could never forget how Moon Eagle had tricked her into leaving!

Chapter Twenty-nine

The night wind whispers in my ear,
The moon shines in my face;
A burden still of chilling fear
I find in every place.
—*John Clare*

After riding a good distance from the place where they had been surprised by first the young brave, and then his mother, Raymond Hauser and Big Bear Moon stopped to rest, and to eat.

After eating a rabbit they had shot and cooked, finishing the meal off with big, fat, ripe grapes, Raymond and Big Bear Moon stretched out beside a creek to rest for a while longer before resuming their journey.

They had lost track of Sheleen's horse's hoofprints long ago, so they were now traveling blind in the hope of accidentally running into her as she stopped to rest, eat, or sleep.

They knew that being a lady, she could not go far each day without stopping. It was just not in a lady's makeup to be as strong as a man when it came to riding long spells on horses!

"Haven't you had enough?" Big Bear Moon blurted out as he tossed pebbles into the water, watching minnows streak away just beneath the surface.

He looked slowly over at Raymond. "Are you ready to return to St. Paul and forget the vengeance you are seeking against this . . . white woman?" he asked, his eyes narrowing.

Big Bear Moon hoped that Raymond hadn't noticed how Big Bear Moon had paused momentarily before he described Sheleen as a "white" woman.

It had been a slipup and he had to make certain it didn't happen again.

He did not want Raymond to figure out just exactly why Big Bear Moon had accepted the job of hunting down this woman, or Big Bear Moon might get a knife in his gut while he slept!

"What do you mean?" Raymond growled, plucking a piece of grass and sticking it in the corner of his mouth to chew on. "Do you think I'd ever give up on findin' the one who shot off my trigger finger? Never, Big Bear Moon. Never."

"I don't see why you'd waste time on a mere woman," Big Bear Moon growled. His eyes narrowed angrily. "As far as I'm concerned, she isn't

SAVAGE INTRIGUE

worth the aggravation." He shrugged. "Anyway, surely she has been found and taken captive by Indians. Let them deal with her."

Raymond scooted closer to Big Bear Moon and thrust his hand up close to the scout's face. "Do you see this?" he growled. He had removed the bandage a short time ago, revealing a ghastly-looking scar where the finger had been. "Now if this was you with a worthless hand, and all because of a female, would you give up on findin' that damnable wench? No, I don't think so. She got away with besting Raymond Hauser once, but not twice. As I see it, she is a dead woman walking."

Big Bear Moon's dark eyes flared with a hidden anger.

He slapped the four-fingered hand away and got up to go kneel beside the water.

He leaned over it and looked at his reflection.

He was not certain how long he could keep up this charade with a man he loathed, a man he could kill so easily, and never think twice about it.

But he would wait a while longer, then make his move.

He first had something to prove to the heartless bastard of a man who was so prejudiced against people of Big Bear Moon's own skin color.

Ho, soon the grizzly-faced man would pay for his crimes against the Dakota!

CHAPTER THIRTY

Prithee, why so pale?
Will, when looking well can't move her,
Looking ill prevail?
Pr'y thee, why so pale?
—*John Suckling*

Midnight Wolf stepped just inside Moon Eagle's tepee. He silently stood there, gazing at his shaman,
who was quietly praying beside his lodge fire.

And then Moon Eagle's head slowly lifted. He
looked squarely into Midnight Wolf's eyes, but still
said nothing, yet he was pale, oh, so very, very pale!

Still, Midnight Wolf did not see a trace of guilt on
his shaman's face, or in his eyes, which puzzled Midnight Wolf. Moon Eagle had to know that Midnight
Wolf was there because of what he had forced
Sheleen to do.

271

He knew Moon Eagle was aware that Sheleen had returned. The shaman had seen her with Midnight Wolf just before he escaped into his tepee.

Midnight Wolf did not want to be put in the position of choosing between his shaman and Sheleen. The shaman was an important figure in the village, second only to his chief in the love he received from his people.

Midnight Wolf had also felt love and respect for Moon Eagle until a woman had entered his life and heart!

It was his shaman's open resentment of Sheleen that made Midnight Wolf's feelings for him wane, for Moon Eagle was a man who should show no prejudice.

He was a man revered by his people because of his goodness!

But of late, Moon Eagle had not shown that good side of himself very often. His behavior toward Sheleen had not been good at all.

Midnight Wolf stepped closer to Moon Eagle and then stopped, his eyes battling with his shaman's.

Still not saying anything, Moon Eagle rose slowly to his feet and walked past Midnight Wolf. He stopped and held the entrance flap aside and again looked directly into his chief's eyes.

Midnight Wolf stepped past Moon Eagle, who soon joined him as they both walked silently toward Midnight Wolf's tepee.

It was apparent to Midnight Wolf that Moon Eagle

understood, without having been told, where his chief wanted him to go, and why.

They walked past laughing children, then past elderly warriors who were sitting peacefully in small groups, and talking and sharing smokes on their feathered, long-stemmed pipes.

The children seemed oblivious to what was happening, or was about to happen, but the older men's eyes seemed to say that they knew their chief had lost some respect for their shaman.

They, the elders, being so atuned to their chief, seemed to know without being told that Midnight Wolf wanted to regain the respect for his shaman.

Midnight Wolf gazed silently at Moon Eagle, whose eyes remained directed straight ahead, with no emotion whatsoever in their depths.

So much depended now on how his shaman reacted to what Sheleen was going to tell him about who she truly was.

How Moon Eagle responded to Sheleen was what Midnight Wolf was eager to hear. If the shaman still treated Sheleen as though she were a nonperson, Midnight Wolf knew that he would have no choice but to send Moon Eagle away and bring someone new into the shaman's lodge, to be their people's holy man.

That was the last thing Midnight Wolf wanted. Moon Eagle had been their people's shaman ever since Midnight Wolf was a young brave aspiring to be a strong leader like his father.

When his father was ambushed with his wife, and murdered by renegades that no one ever found, Moon Eagle had become both mother and father to Midnight Wolf.

He had taken Midnight Wolf under his wing and taught him what was required of him as chief, since Midnight Wolf had stepped immediately into that role upon the death of his father.

It would be doubly hard for Midnight Wolf to have to make a choice now between his shaman and the woman he loved. But he knew that there had to be peace between them, or one of them would have to go.

He knew that it would not be Sheleen, for she was everything to Midnight Wolf.

Although Moon Eagle was very important to Midnight Wolf, too, it was the woman who had been betrayed. The one who had betrayed her must either make amends, or leave the village and those he loved.

So much depended on what Moon Eagle said to Sheleen. If everything turned out the way Midnight Wolf wanted it to, his shaman would show respect for Sheleen, and even welcome her into the lives of his people, and his chief. In that case, he had something to tell his shaman. He would tell him that he had asked Sheleen to marry him. That would be the true test of his shaman's loyalty.

When they reached Midnight Wolf's tepee, he

stepped ahead of Moon Eagle and held the entrance flap aside for him.

As Moon Eagle entered the tepee, Sheleen's eyes met the shaman's. Sheleen felt goose bumps break out along the flesh of her arms, for she saw no friendliness in Moon Eagle's dark eyes.

She truly was afraid of the upcoming moments . . . moments that could decide her future.

Would it be one of happiness and joy? Or would it be one of despair? Would she lose another loved one, this time not by death, but because of a stubborn shaman?

Would Midnight Wolf finally decide that Sheleen could not be totally accepted into his people's lives if his shaman could not do it, himself? Sheleen was afraid that in the end, Midnight Wolf would choose his shaman over the woman he loved!

Midnight Wolf led Moon Eagle gently by an elbow to plush pelts opposite the fire from where Sheleen was sitting.

Midnight Wolf then went and sat beside Sheleen, not his shaman, which caused a shocked, injured look on Moon Eagle's face.

"Sheleen, please tell Moon Eagle what you told me . . . that you had a Dakota mother, and everything else that brought you eventually into my people's world," Midnight Wolf said, ignoring Moon Eagle's gasp.

Sheleen questioned Midnight Wolf with her eyes.

He nodded. "Tell it all to him," he said, nodding toward Moon Eagle. "He needs to know."

Sheleen nodded, then turned her gaze to Moon Eagle, who sat stiffly beside the fire, his legs crossed, his hands resting tightly on his knees.

She started from the beginning, revealing who her true mother was, how Sheleen had been raised for a while among the Dakota with her white father, up to the moment she had been found injured in the forest.

As she revealed everything to the shaman, Sheleen's voice broke more than once with emotion.

Midnight Wolf knew that Moon Eagle must be able to hear the emotion in her tone. His shaman, who was so caring toward others, surely would not be unmoved by this tale.

When she had finished speaking, Sheleen and Midnight Wolf exchanged questioning glances, then they both turned to look at Moon Eagle.

They both saw a softening in his expression. Then he rose and went to Sheleen and held his arms out for her.

Sheleen was near to tears as she stood and moved into Moon Eagle's warm embrace.

"You have suffered enough inhumanity at the hands of the *washechu*," he said. "You are safe now. You can be a part of this Wolf Band's lives. You will become one of us."

Admiring his shaman's goodness of heart, Midnight Wolf got to his feet and embraced both Sheleen and Moon Eagle at the same time.

"I am so happy that you have accepted Sheleen into our lives," he said. "For Sheleen is going to be my wife."

Moon Eagle gasped and stepped stiffly away from Midnight Wolf and Sheleen.

He looked with wavering eyes into his chief's face. "Marriage?" he breathed out. "You would marry her? Her skin is white. She is a "breed." If you marry this woman, she will bring much heartache into our people's lives."

Midnight Wolf stiffened. "Did you not hear a word that Sheleen said?" he asked, trying to keep control of his temper. His heart was pounding so hard he felt as though it might leap from inside his chest! "She is Dakota! No matter the color of the skin she was born with, her heart has always been Dakota! She only lived among whites because her white father took her there. And he did this for a good purpose. Sheleen needed the white man's education in order to be able to cope with the changes the white people have brought into the Dakota people's lives. Because both Sheleen and her father were educated in the white world, they were better able to help the Dakota, and they did help them, until things got out of hand in the white community and the hangings began. Her father was on the list of those who were to be hanged. I'm sure she was on the list, as well."

He turned to Sheleen, taking her hands in his. "No matter how my shaman feels, *mitawin*, we will become man and wife," he said firmly. "We were meant to be together. It was fate . . . destiny . . . that brought us together."

Seeing the strife her marriage would bring to the Wolf Band, Sheleen was uncertain what to do.

Oh, Lord, she did love Midnight Wolf with every fiber of her being. She too believed that fate had brought them together.

From her very first breath, destiny had been leading her to this man . . . the man she would love forever.

But she could not be the one responsible for destroying the love and respect between Midnight Wolf and his shaman.

She knew that Moon Eagle had become both father and mother to Midnight Wolf when Midnight Wolf's parents were ambushed and killed.

No. She would not be the one to tear this special bond apart.

Sobbing, she fled the tepee.

She ran to the lake and crumpled to the ground. Her body was wracked with deep sobs.

No sooner had she found true happiness again, than it was going to be denied her.

Suddenly she felt a gentle hand on her shoulder. She looked up and into the dark eyes of the man she would love forever.

"*Hiyupo*, come. Come with me," he said.

Sheleen looked past him and saw Moon Eagle standing outside Midnight Wolf's lodge, staring at her.

She looked up at Midnight Wolf. "No," she murmured. "I must leave, Midnight Wolf. I can't bring such disharmony into your life."

Midnight Wolf straightened up abruptly, but he still gazed down at her.

He reached a hand out for her. "*Hiyupo,* come," he said again, his eyes begging her.

She realized now that he was not going to change his mind. He was determined that she would go with him.

She took his hand and rose slowly to her feet.

He held onto this hand and led her to a beached canoe, then lifted her into his arms and placed her inside the canoe.

He shoved the canoe out into the water, waded there, knee-deep, then boarded the canoe himself.

He paddled away from the village, into deeper water, while Moon Eagle still stood, watching. . . .

CHAPTER THIRTY-ONE

> Do you ask what the birds say?
> The sparrow, the dove,
> The linnet and thrush say,
> "I love, I love."
> —*Samuel Coleridge*

The village was now far behind them, and they rode in the canoe in silence. Sheleen didn't know what to think. She had just been swept up by Midnight Wolf and carried to the canoe with no explanation.

She would never forget Moon Eagle's reaction to the announcement that she and Midnight Wolf were to be married. His look was actually one of horror!

Sheleen felt that he saw her as some sort of "demon," although moments before he had been sweet and forgiving.

He had even hugged her! But she knew now that

CASSIE EDWARDS

was only because he had not understood the extent of Midnight Wolf's feelings for her. As he hugged Sheleen he had surely thought she would just blend in with his people, as one with them, but nothing more.

Perhaps he had even seen her as a positive addition to his Wolf Band, for after her wound was completely healed, she could work in the garden, she could help make lodge coverings, and participate in all the work that the women did from day to day.

Of course, she did plan to do all of those things while living among Midnight Wolf's people, but as his wife!

She glanced back at Midnight Wolf as he rhythmically drew the paddle through the water. He had not given her even one glance, but had kept his attention on steering the canoe.

She thought he must be deep in thought, trying to come up with the right thing to say to her in order to take away the sting of his shaman's harsh words.

She doubted, herself, that she could ever forget those moments when Moon Eagle had realized just what she meant to his chief. The look in the shaman's eyes was imprinted on her mind.

"Midnight Wolf, where are we going?" Sheleen asked, finally breaking the silence. "And . . . why?"

He paused, drawing the paddle up and resting it on the floor of the canoe.

He gazed at Sheleen for the first time since they had got in the canoe.

She saw that his jaw was tight, and that his eyes were even darker than usual, as black as the darkest midnight.

She began to fear his answer, and wished now that she had not pushed him into telling her what his plans were for her, himself, and his shaman.

He was a powerful chief with many people counting on him to make the right decisions for their well-being.

Had he decided that it was not in his best interest to take a white wife after all? If so, she would be devastated.

But she had learned to overcome the many hurts in her life, and the challenges.

This hurt, however, might be more than she could bear.

She felt defeated, and oh, so sad, to think she would soon be sent away by Midnight Wolf, the very man she would never stop loving.

He might feel now that he had no other choice but to send her away.

"I have no set destination in mind," Midnight Wolf said. "I have taken you from my village in order to give my shaman time alone to think about what you have revealed to him. I want him to consider the true person you are, and the fact that you are, in part, Dakota. My shaman needs time to sort through his feelings, whether or not he can accept this truth about you, and the idea that his chief is going to marry you. For I am going to marry you, my *mitawin*. I will not let you leave my village, or my life. My future would be too empty without you. Losing you would take away my strong will to be the best chief I can be for my people. They would suffer. I would suffer. So it is my decision not to allow one man to stand in the way of my happiness, yours, and the well-being of my Wolf Band as a whole."

Relief, so wonderful and sweet, swept through Sheleen. This man, this wonderful leader, loved her so much that he would not allow anyone to stand in the way of his taking her as his wife, not even a shaman who had much power, himself, among the Wolf Band.

"I was so afraid that you would have no choice but to send me away after seeing Moon Eagle's reaction to your plans," Sheleen said. She wiped happy tears from her eyes. "Oh, my darling, thank you for loving me so much."

She paused, then said, "But what about Moon Eagle?"

"We shall see," Midnight Wolf said. He sighed deeply. "We shall see. I truly do not want to lose him. He is revered by so many. He is loved dearly by me. But there is a line that should not be crossed by anyone, not even a shaman."

Sheleen could not help but feel sadness for Moon Eagle. He was an old man with his own set ideas. His decisions had probably never been questioned by anyone, especially not his chief.

Deep inside herself she hoped that Moon Eagle would be able to accept her position in his chief's life. If he didn't, yet he remained among his people, whether or not as their shaman, Sheleen might never be able to truly relax in his presence.

And she longed for a life of peace and joy. For so long she had awakened every morning wondering if she and her father would still be safe, or hunted down and made to pay for their alliance with the Dakota people.

She wanted a life now where she knew that she was safe. She wanted to wake up every morning in Midnight Wolf's arms, and go to bed each night sleeping with him at her side.

It would be paradise to live with the man she loved!

Midnight Wolf reached a hand to Sheleen's cheek, placed it gently there, smiled, then leaned away from her and took up his paddle.

Again they glided through the water in silence, but this time Sheleen was enjoying the ride with a happy heart. The words he had spoken made her heart sing!

Soon she would be his wife!

It was more than she had ever dreamed possible. Her plans had never included a husband. After her little sister died, and then her Dakota mother, her life had been altered forever.

She had wanted nothing more than to learn

everything her father knew about helping the sick and the injured. She wanted nothing more than to go from village to village, taking with her not only medicine to cure the ills of the Dakota, but taking also love and caring.

And she had done all of that as long as she could.

Utterly relaxed now, and able to enjoy the beauty of nature that was all around her, she soaked it all in as she looked from one wondrous sight to another.

She saw marsh hawks sweeping in a wide circle overhead.

She heard, then saw, a redheaded woodpecker perched on the side of a rough-barked elm tree. It was pecking away, the sound echoing across the water, and through the forest.

Although it was daylight, she saw many short-eared owls perched in one tree.

As the canoe glided through the water, the white gravel that lay at the bottom of the lake was visible. They traveled onward, past boulders. At first the lake was wide, deep, and smooth, a mirror image of the sky. The sun scattered diamonds across the surface.

Suddenly there was a splash and they both saw a young bull moose wading into the lake about fifty yards away. The moose stopped suddenly and looked at them, then turned and went crashing into the underbrush.

They traveled onward through this paradise, and

far from where they had seen the moose, they now saw whooping cranes by the hundreds on the other far bank.

"These special birds come here every spring to breed," Midnight Wolf explained to Sheleen, breaking the silence. "They are never killed. They are allowed to breed so that the offspring will return the next year."

"They are so gorgeous," Sheleen murmured. "There are so many it seems as though they are one huge body of white as I look at them. I think it's wonderful that you allow them to come here each year without any threat of being killed."

"All animals and birds have rights . . . the right of man's protection, the right to live, the right to multiply, the right to freedom," Midnight Wolf replied. "In recognition of these rights, the Dakota never enslave animals, and spare any life that is not needed for food or clothing."

"That is so beautiful," Sheleen said. She had never heard the Dakota philosophy explained like that.

"This concept of life gives to the Dakota an abiding love for all creatures," Midnight Wolf said. "It fills his being with the joy and mystery of living. It gives him reverence for all life. It makes a place for all things in the scheme of existence with equal importance to all."

He paused, then continued, "The Dakota could despise no creature, for all are of one blood, made by the same hand, and filled with the essence of the Great Mystery. In spirit, the Dakota are humble and meek."

Sheleen remembered a verse in the Bible that said, "Blessed are the meek, for they shall inherit the earth."

That was true for the Dakota, and from the earth they inherited secrets long since forgotten by other people.

"Sheleen, as you know, the Dakota is a lover of nature," Midnight Wolf went on. "He loves the earth and all things of the earth, his attachment growing with age. The old people come, literally, to love the soil, and they sit or recline on the ground, with a feeling of being close to a mothering power. It is good for the skin to touch the earth, and the old people like to remove their moccasins and walk with bare feet on the 'sacred' earth. The earth is the final abiding place of all things that live and grow."

"As a child, I was taught much that you are saying today," Sheleen murmured. "It is all so beautiful. And I have never seen such a lovely lake as this. Even the lakes in Minnesota do not compare."

"There are many such sights as the white whooping cranes, and all sorts of animals living around this lake. We were fortunate to have discovered it during our flight from our homeland," Midnight Wolf said. He suddenly turned the nose of the canoe landward. "And it is still secret from anyone but my people."

Sheleen knew how things happened in this world, where so many new settlers were flocking to land such as this. She feared the day would come when they would interfere with the peaceful lives of Midnight Wolf's people.

But until that day came, what his people had would be enjoyed to the fullest!

As they drew closer to the embankment, kingfishers streaked past them, and eagles and osprey soared overhead.

Sheleen saw a deer nervously step out into the water to drink. It lifted its head, gazed with dark, round eyes directly at Sheleen, then made a quick turn and bounded away into the thick brush.

When they drew near the bank, Midnight Wolf paddled more slowly, hugging the shore. He seemed to be looking for the perfect place to beach the canoe, looking for a private spot where they could spend time together before heading back in the direction of the village.

Suddenly a lone osprey took an interest in them. As Midnight Wolf continued to paddle onward, the majestic bird followed, gliding from treetop to treetop.

Then as suddenly as it had appeared, it was gone.

Sheleen soon saw why.

A pair of bald eagles glided into view. One of the eagles swept downward and skimmed along the lake, driving its talons beneath the surface to snare a fish.

And then it flew away, the other one beside it. Both were soon out of sight among the thick trees on the other side of the lake.

"This seems the perfect place," Midnight Wolf said, beaching the canoe on the graveled shore.

He stepped from the canoe, then bent low and swept Sheleen into his arms.

He stopped before taking her onward and gazed intently into her eyes.

"My *mitawin*, my woman," he said huskily, then gave her an all-consuming kiss that melted Sheleen's heart. She clung to him, knowing then that nothing would come between them, ever.

The proof was in the way Midnight Wolf held her so close in his arms and kissed her with such emotion.

Sheleen knew she had nothing to worry about, and that she *would* be married soon to this man who ruled her heart, her soul, her everything!

CHAPTER THIRTY-TWO

O' who but can recall the eve they met,
To breathe, in some green walk,
Their first young vow.
—*Charles Swain*

Midnight Wolf drew his lips from Sheleen's and carried her away from the rocky shore. Once he reached the mossy floor of the forest, he put her on her feet, yet continued to hold her.

"I want to hold you like this forever," he said hoarsely. "I want to be alone with you like this forever."

"My darling, no matter how many people are with us, we are still together, alone, you and I, in our hearts," Sheleen murmured. "There is nobody else. Just you and I."

"When I saw you fleeing on your horse, my heart stood still inside my chest, for I could not understand why you were there instead of in my tepee waiting for me," Midnight Wolf said. "I could not believe you were leaving me, not after realizing just how much we loved one another."

"I was wrong," Sheleen said, her voice breaking with emotion. "I should have listened to my heart, not . . . not Moon Eagle. My heart was telling me not to go, but at the moment, I thought I didn't have a choice. Your shaman can be very persuasive, you know."

"There is a time and place for his persuasiveness," Midnight Wolf said, frowning. "I believe he understands that now."

"I hope he does," Sheleen said as Midnight Wolf stepped away from her, his eyes scanning everything around them. Sheleen looked, too, and saw bushes covered with blueberries.

She saw many kinds of mushrooms growing on the damp forest floor a short distance from the soft emerald moss she knew she would soon be sharing with Midnight Wolf. That thought made her heart pound inside her chest.

Surely in a matter of moments they would be making love!

Except for the birds and forest animals, they had the privacy to do as they wished.

Sheleen realized that while she was taking all of this in with her eyes, Midnight Wolf had gone back to the canoe.

He returned, carrying a blanket which he spread on the springy, soft moss.

And still without saying anything to her, he gathered several types of mushrooms that were edible and not dangerous, as well as several handfuls of blueberries.

All of these he brought and placed in the center of the blanket, then gestured with a hand for Sheleen to sit down.

He sat down beside her.

He picked up a bright crimson russula mushroom and placed it at Sheleen's lips. She smiled at him as she bit into it and found it very peppery, yet tasty.

Midnight Wolf picked up another type of mushroom, known to her as a yellow boletus. When she bit into it, she found it surprisingly sweet.

"Watch this," Midnight Wolf said as he picked up another boletus mushroom. "See how its porous undersurface bruises blue when I press my thumb into it?"

"Yes, I know," Sheleen said, smiling. "When I was a small child, gathering mushrooms in the forest with my father, I enjoyed playing with this particular mushroom just because of how it changed color."

They ate some more, then Midnight Wolf picked up a blueberry and held it out to Sheleen. "Sweetness to wash away the peppery taste of the mushrooms," he said as she opened her mouth and plucked it from his fingers with her teeth.

She giggled as she chewed on it. She had startled

him by taking the blueberry from his fingers with her teeth.

"You had better watch out, I am quite lethal with my teeth," she said as he ate some blueberries himself, chuckling at her mischievous behavior.

Midnight Wolf brushed the remainder of the uneaten mushrooms and blueberries from the blanket, then reached out for Sheleen and slowly removed her dress and moccasins.

As she watched, her pulse racing, he took off his breechclout and moccasins, then reached for her and spread her out beneath him.

As the clear, liquid fluting of a hermit thrush pierced the air, they made slow and delicious love. The bird's song added to the sweetness of the moment with its exquisite purity.

Sheleen's thoughts were hazy with pleasure as their bodies strained together hungrily, Midnight Wolf's mouth hot, sensuous, demanding.

Their bodies moved and slid together, their groans of pleasure intermingling as though they were of one voice, one undying ecstasy!

He plunged into her, withdrew and plunged again. Her body responded in kind, as she placed her legs around his waist, drawing him even more deeply into her.

"Love me, oh, love me," Sheleen whispered against his lips.

She drew a ragged breath when he stopped and

crept downward, his lips now touching the spot where she throbbed almost unmercifully.

He loved her in that way for long minutes, as she wove her hands into his thick, flowing hair.

He again blanketed her with his body and kissed her with a fierce, possessive heat as he slammed into her, her gasps proving that she welcomed the wonders of the pleasure he was giving her.

She only hoped that he was receiving the same pleasure, but she knew he was by the way he breathed, and by the way he was kissing her again so possessively.

Waves of liquid heat pulsed through Midnight Wolf's body as he took from Sheleen what she so eagerly gave him, their bodies rocking together while he kept up his steady rhythm inside her.

He cupped a breast in his hand and gently squeezed it.

He cradled her in one arm, leaned down and swept his tongue around one of her nipples.

His body was growing feverish, almost out of control, his pleasure was so deeply felt.

Suddenly his mind splintered with an ecstasy that overwhelmed him as he pressed endlessly deeper within her, finding that point of fulfilment he had been striving for.

He held her as though in a vise as her body began trembling, her own pleasure sought and found.

They groaned in whispers against each other's lips as their bodies quaked and rocked, and then fell silent, their mutual climax enjoyed to the fullest.

Midnight Wolf's tongue brushed her lips lightly. "*Techila*, I love you," he whispered.

Filled with a flood of emotions, Sheleen whispered to him of her undying love for him, of her need always to give him the same pleasure that he had just given her.

He chuckled as he leaned partially away from her, their eyes meeting and holding. "My love, you need not worry about how much pleasure you did or did not give me. It was more than any man could ask for," he said huskily.

"Then you felt the same intense delight that I felt?" she asked, searching his eyes.

When he reached a hand between them and filled it with her soft breast, the nipple hard against his palm, he saw a glaze of pleasure sweep over her eyes.

"Did you not just feel the delight that my touching you brought you?" he asked huskily, his eyes twinkling.

"I never knew that there were such intense feelings in my breasts," she said, giggling and blushing at the same time as he now rolled her nipple with his tongue.

She closed her eyes and enjoyed the pleasure that he was again giving her.

"Never stop," she murmured. "Oh, please, please never stop."

Feeling renewed strength in his manhood, and the tingling of want as he pressed it against her woman's center, he did not hesitate to plunge it inside her again.

Her gasp of pleasure proved that she was as ready as he.

They made maddening love, over and over again, until a slanting shaft of sunlight coming through the leaves of the trees proved that evening was drawing close. They should be back at the village and out of the canoe before darkness fell over the land.

Midnight Wolf sat up and away from her. "We must return home," he said, pulling on his breechclout.

"I don't want to leave," Sheleen complained in a tone she was not proud of, but she did want to stay much longer.

They had found their own private paradise, where no one would interrupt them, and there was no shaman to cause tension between them.

Midnight Wolf leaned over close to her and brushed kisses across her lips. "I would rather stay, too, and make love over and over again, but I do not want to worry my people," he said. "We must return home before it gets dark."

"Oh, all right," Sheleen said, again not proud of the grudging tone that was new to her.

But all of this was new to her.

She was not even sure how to act now that she had become this woman she had never known was hidden inside herself.

She pulled on her dress and slid into her moccasins. Then as Midnight Wolf gathered up the blanket, she went and stood at the water's edge, sighing when once again she caught sight of an osprey flying gracefully overhead.

"We'll soon be gone from your safe haven," Sheleen said to the bird. "But we will return now and then."

Yes, after discovering the peace and wonder of lovemaking in this very private paradise, she knew that she would want to return, often.

But now it was time to leave.

She watched Midnight Wolf place the blanket inside the canoe. Then he carried her to it and kissed her before placing her on the seat at the far end, opposite where he would be sitting.

"We will come back here, won't we?" Sheleen asked before Midnight Wolf released her from his arms.

"We will come back," Midnight Wolf promised, smiling into her eyes. "It is our private place, is it not?"

"Yes, ours," Sheleen said, beaming as he climbed into the canoe himself, and soon had it moving softly through the water toward home.

CHAPTER THIRTY-THREE

Quit, quit, for shame! This will not move;
This cannot take her.
—*John Suckling*

Take a look at that!" Raymond said, inching his horse closer to Big Bear Moon's as they both watched the canoe slide noiselessly through the water.

"Finally, I've found the wench," Raymond gloated, not taking his eyes off Sheleen, who sat so quietly and beautifully in the canoe. "I didn't think I'd be this lucky, but there she is, in the flesh, ready for the taking."

Big Bear Moon said nothing to Raymond, but could not help glaring at him as Raymond continued boasting about having found the woman.

Big Bear Moon could hardly hold himself back, but knew this was not the time to stop Raymond at his game of hide and seek with Sheleen. The right time was later, when Raymond would least expect it!

"Yep, now I will finally have my vengeance," Raymond said watching the canoe move through the water. "I will enjoy killing both the powerful Indian chief and the white woman who made the wrong choice in life by allying herself with Injuns."

They suddenly lost sight of the canoe when it rounded a bend. No matter. Now that Raymond had found Sheleen, he didn't mind waiting a while longer to have his fun with her and the chief.

Now that he knew they were living in the nearby village, he would know exactly where to go to find them.

He rode beside Big Bear Moon for a short distance, then realized the canoe would soon be in view again as the horses found a shortcut through the trees.

Maybe he wouldn't have to wait, after all.

He would prefer not to go anywhere near that village of Injuns if he could help it.

When Sheleen and Midnight Wolf came into sight again, closer to the side of the lake that Raymond was on, because the lake narrowed there, he made up his mind.

"Get your rifle ready," Raymond said, glaring over at Big Bear Moon. "We're about to catch us two weasels!"

He cursed the day he had lost his trigger finger, for he hated having to depend on someone else to do his dirty work for him. But he had not had the time to practice shooting with his other hand yet. His eagerness to find Sheleen had taken precedence over learning how to use his left hand.

It truly didn't matter who did the shooting, just as long as he saw the wench dead!

CHAPTER THIRTY-FOUR

All night upon mine heart
I felt her warm heart beat,
Night-long within my arms
In love and sleep she lay.
—*Ernest Dowson*

Rosy Dawn stood at the entranceway of her tepee. She was holding back the entrance flap, still looking toward the lake, where Sheleen and Midnight Wolf had departed in a canoe.

She glanced then at Moon Eagle's lodge, seeing that he also stood at his entrance flap, looking in the same direction.

Rosy Dawn felt sure that Moon Eagle was the cause of Midnight Wolf and Sheleen's flight. She had overheard Moon Eagle's reaction to Midnight Wolf's plans to marry Sheleen.

Rosy Dawn had gone to Midnight Wolf's tepee

with food, but decided not to go inside after all when she heard alarming words between her chief and his shaman. She had returned to her tepee with the tray of food untouched.

"Mother, what is the matter?"

Gentle Bear's voice behind her startled Rosy Dawn back to the present.

She dropped the flap and turned to see that Gentle Bear had awakened from a nap and was gazing at her curiously.

"Mother, you are so quiet," Gentle Bear said as he came and took one of her hands. "What is wrong? I see much concern in your eyes. Is it our chief? Has something happened to our chief?"

Rosy Dawn drew her son into a gentle embrace. "I did not mean to alarm you by my solemn behavior," she murmured. "I did not know that you had awakened."

"When I did and I saw you standing there, so quiet, as you gazed from our tepee, I sensed that something is wrong," Gentle Bear said.

He stepped away from his mother and gazed into her dark eyes. "I still feel it, Mother," he said. "What is the matter?"

Unsure yet of what she should do or say, Rosy Dawn knelt down beside the lodge fire and slid a log into the flames. Then she sat down and stared into the fire, again oblivious to her surroundings.

After seeing Midnight Wolf and Sheleen set off on the lake, she had suddenly thought of the white man and the red man that she had held at bay with her rifle.

She wondered if those men might still be in the area.

Had she been too lenient with them? Should she have made them come with her to her village and let her chief decide what their fate should be?

She wished that she had at least told Midnight Wolf about the men. Then he would have been more cautious while he was away from the village.

Now he and his woman had left the safety of the village. Were they not more vulnerable in a canoe on the lake, where they might be the targets of anyone who saw them?

"Mother," Gentle Bear insisted as he knelt down beside her. "Tell me what is wrong."

Rosy Dawn slid a slow gaze over her son, then reached out and gently touched his cheek. "My son, I believe I have done everything wrong," she said, her voice breaking. "Do you remember the two men in the forest?"

"How could I ever forget them?" Gentle Bear said, visibly shivering from the fear he had felt when he suddenly realized that he was not able to release the arrow from his bowstring.

"While you slept, our chief and his woman left in a canoe," Rosy Dawn blurted out. "They were not accompanied by any of our warriors. They are traveling alone on the lake, vulnerable as they float along in a canoe. Those two men we saw close to our village might not have traveled as far away as we hoped. They might still be in the area. They might see our chief and his woman. Those men might have planned all along to find a way to ambush our chief. Would not that give them much attention in the white world?"

"Mother, do you truly believe this is possible?" Gentle Bear asked, his eyes wide. "Do you truly believe those men might have been near our village with plans to kill our chief?"

"We will never know . . . unless it actually happens," Rosy Dawn said, despair in her voice.

"What can we do to help our chief and Sheleen?" Gentle Bear said, his heart thumping. "We cannot let those men harm either one of them. We cannot allow them to take our chief captive, or . . . or . . . possibly hang him like so many of our people."

"No, we certainly can not allow that to happen. There must be something we can do to stop it," Rosy Dawn said.

She hurried to her feet, but then paused, uncertain what to do next.

If she went to the warriors and told them what she feared, then she would also have to tell them about having confronted two strangers near their village.

All of the wrongs that she and her son had done were coming back to haunt her.

If she told everyone about how they had kept se-

306

crets from their chief, no one would trust her or her son.

"Mother, we must forget that telling the truth now might cause us to be banished from our village. We must report what we saw to the warriors. They will go and warn our chief of the possible danger of his being ambushed by those two strangers," Gentle Bear said. "Mother, what we have already done is wrong, but to keep silent about what might happen to our chief and Sheleen is far worse."

Rosy Dawn stopped pacing and gazed at Gentle Bear.

She suddenly saw him as more adult than child. How clearly he saw what must be done.

"You are right," she said, her voice drawn. She drew him into her embrace. "You stay behind. I shall go and reveal what we did to our warriors, and what must be done in order to save our chief and his woman."

Gentle Bear yanked himself free of her arms. He gazed fearlessly up at her. "No," he said tightly. "I will not stay hidden like a frightened puppy. And I cannot allow you to take the blame for what I, myself, set in motion. I must help, mother. Surely you see that."

"I do," Rosy Dawn said. Feeling so proud of her son now, she was able to forgive any wrong that he had done.

She bent to her knees before Gentle Bear. She took his hands and gazed proudly into his eyes. "My son, we must do this very quietly," she murmured. "And not because I am ashamed and want to keep what we have done as quiet as possible. There is no reason to bring alarm into the hearts of the women and children. We must go quietly to the warriors and tell them our concerns."

"How can we do this?" Gentle Bear asked, searching his mother's eyes. "Surely the women will see us talking to the warriors. That will cause questions to be asked."

"And so be it, for it is certain they will eventually know what is happening, but there is no need to go outside and shout out our alarm," Rosy Dawn said. "Go quietly, my son, as shall I. We must be discreet in how we draw the warriors to the council house to hear our concerns."

"What shall I say?" Gentle Bear asked as Rosy Dawn got up.

"Tell them that there is someone in the council house who wishes to speak with them," Rosy Dawn said tightly. "When they ask who, tell them. Tell them that your mother needs to speak with them."

Gentle Bear nodded.

He and his mother left the tepee together, and after a while they went to the council house and awaited the arrival of the warriors.

When all were finally there, Rosy Dawn confessed what she and her son were guilty of, and told of her fear for their chief.

"I am so afraid that the two strangers will cause

our chief trouble if they catch him alone with Sheleen, a white woman," Rosy Dawn said in closing. "They might kill Midnight Wolf, perhaps even hang him, since it seems white men take such pleasure in seeing a red man hanging from the end of a rope. They might then rape Sheleen before they kill . . . possibly even hang her."

The warriors gathered together in a tight circle and discussed what had been told them, then turned to Rosy Dawn.

Night Walker, who was Midnight Wolf's most favored warrior and friend, stepped up to Rosy Dawn and Gentle Bear.

He placed a hand on Gentle Bear's shoulder and gazed kindly into his eyes. "What you have just done takes much courage," he said, smiling. "By telling the truth, you have proved that you are worthy of being your chief's charge. Thank you for alerting us to what must be done to protect our chief."

"I hope that what my mother and I are worried about does not happen," Gentle Bear said, his voice breaking. "And *pilamaye*, thank you, for being so kind to me. I feel that I do not deserve it."

"When our chief discovers what you have done, he will thank you himself," Night Walker said. He leaned down closer to Gentle Bear's face. "But I do not recommend you go against your chief's commands another time, or it could be one time too many. Do not tempt fate, young brave. Any more disobedience might prove to be disastrous."

"I know," Gentle Bear said, gulping hard. "I do know."

Night Walker turned to Rosy Dawn. He took her hands in his. "And thank you for having given our people such a courageous, brave son, who thinks more of others than himself," he said. "I know how hard it has been for you to be both mother and father to Gentle Bear since the death of your husband. I know that our chief has become a second father to your son, but it is you who have the full responsibility for his behavior. He is growing up to be a fine man."

"Go now, please go," Rosy Dawn said, tears spilling from her eyes. "Please see to our chief's safety . . . and to Sheleen's. I am afraid that too much time has been wasted while I was trying to gather the courage to tell what had to be told."

Night Walker nodded, then turned to the waiting warriors. "Split into two groups," he said tightly. "One group go by water in canoes to search for our chief. The other group go on horses. I will join those who travel by horse."

Rosy Dawn went outside and pointed the way, showing the direction that Midnight Wolf had headed in his canoe.

Several women and children came running up to Rosy Dawn and Gentle Bear as the warriors on horseback rode away, and the other warriors slid their canoes into the lake.

Rosy Dawn saw that the women were worried;

they had not yet been told where their husbands were going.

She told them all that she could, trying not to distress them too much. There were only two enemies out there, and many, many warriors headed their way to stop them!

"All will be right," Rosy Dawn reassured the women. "Go and busy yourselves with chores. Surely everyone will return soon, unharmed."

Gentle Bear joined the children, who stood in a wide circle around him.

As he told them his role in what had happened, Rosy Dawn went to the shaman's lodge and stepped inside.

"Moon Eagle, did you hear?" Rosy Dawn asked, wiping tears from her eyes.

"I know enough," Moon Eagle said. He rose and met her as she stepped toward him. He gestured with a hand. "*Hohahe*, welcome to my tepee. *Hiyupo*, come forward."

When she did, he placed his arms around her. "You did the right thing by revealing what had happened between yourself, Gentle Bear, and the two strangers," he said gently. "And I understand why you did not reveal any of this earlier. You saw your son's future threatened."

"When our chief knows . . ." Rosy Dawn stopped, unable to finish telling how she feared for her son's future.

"Our chief is a forgiving man," Moon Eagle said, hoping that he, himself, would soon be forgiven, too, for having upset his chief and his chief's woman.

His chief's woman, Moon Eagle thought to himself. He had now accepted that his chief did love a woman with white skin. He knew now that although her skin was white, her heart beat the same as the Dakota!

Moon Eagle believed that his chief would forgive him for his moments of weakness. In his behavior toward Sheleen, Moon Eagle had not acted like the shaman he was supposed to be.

"All will be right for us," Moon Eagle said, stepping away from Rosy Dawn. He gestured toward the thick pallet of furs beside his lodge fire. "Sit with me. We will wait for our chief's return together."

Rosy Dawn wiped the tears from her eyes and sat down on the furs opposite Moon Eagle. "I will sit for a while," she murmured. "I just hope that I spoke the truth soon enough."

"Our chief's *mitawin* is exquisitely lovely," Moon Eagle said, his old eyes suddenly twinkling.

Rosy Dawn gave him a look of wonder.

"*Ho*, she is very lovely," she murmured, smiling softly.

CHAPTER THIRTY-FIVE

> If our two loves be one, or, thou and I
> Love so alike, that none do slacken,
> None can die.
> —*John Donne*

Feeling as though she were floating on clouds instead of riding in a canoe, Sheleen smiled as she gazed toward shore.

She was surprised to see a rustling of the tall, thick bushes that stood along the embankment, heavy with ripe and delicious-looking blackberries.

She gasped when several white wolves appeared there, running along the embankment, their blue eyes following Sheleen as the canoe glided through the water.

She was too stunned to speak. Never had she actually seen the wolves! They had only appeared in her dreams! And they had appeared as a warning that something bad that was about to happen. That had to mean . . .

Her heart pounding, she looked back at Midnight Wolf as he drew the paddle through the water.

"Midnight Wolf, did you see . . . ?" she blurted out.

He, too, was looking at the embankment where she had seen the wolves.

"*Ho*, I see," he said, hearing the alarm in her voice. "It is surely only the wind causing the bushes to rustle."

"Wind?" she said, then looked toward shore again, gasping when she no longer saw the wolves.

She now only saw what Midnight Wolf was seeing . . . the rustling of bushes.

"*Ho*, the wind," Midnight Wolf said nonchalantly.

"But if it is the wind, why aren't the leaves of the trees disturbed by it? As you see, they are perfectly still," Sheleen said. "I meant . . . did you not see . . ."

She didn't finish what she was about to say. It was apparent that Midnight Wolf hadn't seen the wolves. What she had seen was an apparition . . . a figment of her imagination.

Yet . . . the wolves had seemed so real . . . so white . . . so large and beautiful.

But she now realized that she hadn't actually seen them. Yet surely they had appeared to her in such a way for the same reason they seemed to have always appeared in her dreams.

As a warning!

She gazed quickly down at the rifle that rested on

the floor of the canoe. Then she looked back at the movement in the bushes. "I still think something is there," she said, swallowing hard. "Should I get the rifle? Or should I wait?"

He didn't have to answer her, for her answer came in the form of a deer that meandered from behind the bushes, its mouth stained black from having been feasting on the plump, juicy blackberries.

"A deer," she said, sighing heavily. "It is only a deer."

She stared at the beautiful white-tailed deer as it stood there gazing back at her and Midnight Wolf with its big brown eyes.

Then its ears suddenly lifted.

It turned its head quickly to one side, as if it had heard something behind it, then bounded quickly away into the dark shadows of the forest.

"Midnight Wolf, did you see how the deer seemed to sense something?" Sheleen said, again feeling as apprehensive as moments ago. "I truly believe something frightened it away."

Midnight Wolf said nothing, only looked guardedly along the shore, for he, too, seemed to realize that the deer had sensed something.

Farther to the left, behind where the deer had been standing, there was again more movement in the bushes.

He didn't look at all comfortable about any of this.

Without explaining why he was doing it, he pointed the nose of the canoe toward a thick patch of willow branches that hung low over the water. There, hid among the branches, he beached the canoe.

Sheleen had not asked him why he was doing any of this, for she knew that things were not as they should be.

And she didn't want to speak, to allow her voice to travel to whomever might be lurking at the very edge of the forest, hidden in its shadows. She was certain that something besides a deer was there.

She fought off the fear that was building inside her, glad that at least they were no longer sitting ducks in the canoe on the lake.

At least they could find a safe haven amid the trees and then search for whomever might be there.

Communicating only with his eyes, Midnight Wolf helped Sheleen from the canoe, then reached for the rifle and started toward the forest. He stopped abruptly when two men stepped from the dark shadows.

One man was white, and Sheleen saw to her horror that it was the very man who had hanged her father, the man Sheleen had shot.

The other man was red-skinned, and it was he who held them at bay, his rifle aimed straight at Midnight Wolf's belly.

Sheleen was shocked to see the man she had shot—she had thought he would probably die from blood loss that night. How had he survived? And how had he tracked her to this wilderness?

But she was even more astonished to see who the other man was, so surprised she was momentarily rendered speechless.

"Cousin?" she suddenly blurted out as Big Bear Moon gazed back at her with eyes that were as dark as her own and Midnight Wolf's.

Her jaw tightened and she placed her fists on her hips. "And so, cousin, this is the life you chose when you left our band of Dakota? We were as close as brother and sister. It was such a surprise when I awakened one day and you were no longer there. You disappeared from our people's lives so suddenly. Now I see why. And now you are surely hunted by both white- and red-skinned people alike, for it is obvious that you lead a life of crime."

She glared at Raymond, then gazed into her cousin's eyes again. "Cousin, how could you ally yourself with the likes of this . . . this . . . snake of a man?" she demanded, her voice breaking. "Big Bear Moon, he viciously murdered my father. He would have done the same to me, but I was too fast for him. I am responsible for shooting off his trigger finger. I am responsible for his not being able to use that hand to kill any more of our people."

She paused.

Her eyes narrowed angrily. "Now, cousin, tell me what you have done for the good of our people since I last saw you?" she said, her voice drawn. "Or should I even want to know? Here you are, ready to kill one of the most peace-loving Dakota chiefs that one could ever know. Would you also kill me, your blood kin? Your cousin?"

Midnight Wolf was absolutely stunned by what was happening. The man who was about to kill him was blood kin to Sheleen!

And it seemed that he had not only abandoned his people, but even made it a practice to murder them!

Midnight Wolf had never before met a Dakota warrior who had turned his back on his people, his heritage as a whole. Midnight Wolf could only feel a bitter loathing for him.

He watched for any opportunity to catch the man off guard. If he saw one, Midnight Wolf would not hesitate to rid the earth of such a coward!

But, for the moment, the man named Big Bear Moon had the upper hand . . . !

Big Bear Moon smiled wryly as both Raymond and Midnight Wolf absorbed what Sheleen had said. Raymond seemed even more shocked than Midnight Wolf as he gaped openly at Big Bear Moon.

Then Raymond grew pale when Big Bear Moon turned his rifle on him.

"What the hell?" Raymond gasped, gazing incredulously at the rifle, and then into Big Bear Moon's dark eyes. "What do you think you're doing? Point that damn thing where it belongs. We're here to take care of . . ."

"Quiet! Do not say anything that will make me hate you even more," Big Bear Moon said. "The game I have been playing with you is now over. I have succeeded at acting a role only to find Sheleen. That was the real reason I came with you. Word reached me about the death of Sheleen's father and I became concerned over her welfare. Until recently, I was able to keep up on where my cousin lived, and made certain that she was all right, or I would have searched for her sooner. When you said you would pay top dollar to anyone who would help you find Sheleen, I saw this as the right time to find my cousin and make certain she was safe. I was going to make absolutely certain that the likes of you would not end my cousin's life. You had already done enough harm by killing her father."

"You filthy, double-crossing swine," Raymond hissed, his hand a tight fist at his side. "I should've taken hints when you talked down to me as though you were better'n me, when you are, in truth, only a savage."

"*Ho*, I almost said too much at times," Big Bear Moon said, laughing softly. "But I played the game of deceit to the end, and you were too stupid to see right through my sly, even insulting, remarks about you."

"How could I have let you double-cross me like this?" Raymond whined. "I thought I was smarter than that."

Big Bear Moon laughed and said, "*Ho*, I've been known to double-cross many a paleface, taking out all I could on my scouting ventures with them. I traveled with them only to kill them before they had the chance to kill any more of my people. That was my way to help the future of the Dakota, and I succeeded."

"Is that true?" Sheleen asked, stunned by what her cousin was telling Raymond. "Did you do these things to help our people? You never actually killed any of our people while you worked as a scout with the cavalry?"

"I have never killed anyone of our skin color," Big Bear Moon asserted. "I managed to dupe the white people who hired me. I always managed to kill those evil men before they even got near the redskins who were being hunted."

"How could I have been duped by the likes of you?" Raymond screamed, snatching the rifle from Big Bear Moon with his good hand.

He was awkward, but he did finally manage to maneuver the rifle so that he could place the trigger finger of his left hand on the trigger. He turned the barrel toward Sheleen. "I came after you, and by damn, even if I have to die while trying, I'm going to kill you," he said.

But he didn't get the chance to try his luck. One blast from Midnight Wolf's rifle was all that it took to down the evil man.

Just as Raymond's rifle hit the ground, it fired a bullet from its chamber.

Sheleen gasped when she saw Big Bear Moon

SAVAGE INTRIGUE

grab at his chest, then saw blood seeping through his fingers.

It was then that she knew Raymond had succeeded in shooting someone of red skin today, after all.

His bullet had entered Big Bear Moon's chest just to the right of his heart!

"Oh, no!" Sheleen cried as she knelt down beside Big Bear Moon, who was now lying on the ground, still clutching at his chest.

"Cousin, oh, cousin," Sheleen sobbed as she placed a gentle hand on his cheek. "Please don't die. Oh, please don't leave me after we just found each other again."

"Just know, Sheleen, that everything I said was true," he gasped out. "Everything I did after I left our people was all done *for* our people. Sheleen . . . all . . . for our people."

She was stricken by hard sobs as Big Bear Moon's eyes closed.

Midnight Wolf dropped his rifle and hurried to them. He knelt beside Big Bear Moon, placing a hand close to his mouth. When he felt breath against his palm, he turned and gave Sheleen a relieved smile.

"He is still alive," he said. "But we need to get him home quickly for Moon Eagle to see to his wound."

"He . . . is . . . not dead?" Sheleen asked weakly.

Raymond's voice made both Sheleen and Mid-

321

night Wolf look quickly at him. He lay in a pool of his own blood, yet his eyes were still open, and he was managing a proud smile. "I killed the sonofagun," he said. He laughed through sudden tears. "At least I did that."

Midnight Wolf went to stand over the fallen, gasping man, while Sheleen stayed with Big Bear Moon.

Raymond tried to reach for his rifle, which lay not far from his hand. "Give me one more chance to kill the woman, damn it," he struggled to say through gasps of pain. "I want her dead. I want her . . ."

His body lurched and his hand went limp only an inch from his rifle. His eyes were locked in a death stare.

"Is he finally, truly, dead?" Sheleen cried.

"*Ho*, very dead," Midnight Wolf replied.

Sheleen rushed to Midnight Wolf and flung herself into his arms. "How could anyone hate someone as much as he hated me?" she sobbed.

"That man had no love for anyone except himself," Midnight Wolf said as he held her close.

At that moment, several warriors suddenly appeared on horseback, drawn by the sounds of gunfire.

Those warriors who had set out in canoes, searching for Sheleen and Midnight Wolf, suddenly appeared around a bend in the lake.

"We must get Big Bear Moon to our village," Midnight Wolf said without taking the time to explain everything to his warriors. "Traveling by canoe is faster and will be much more comfortable."

Midnight Wolf lifted Big Bear Moon up into his arms.

Sheleen grabbed up Midnight Wolf's rifle.

They hurried to the canoe, where Sheleen positioned herself on the floor of the canoe, with Big Bear Moon placed so that his head would rest on her lap. He had regained consciousness.

As they headed out to the center of the lake, those in the other canoes followed, while those on horseback followed along the bank.

"Sheleen, please believe me when I say that I was only with Raymond to help find you and save you from that madman's plan to kill you," Big Bear Moon said as he looked up at her through pain-filled eyes.

"How can you think for one moment that I don't believe you?" she asked as she stroked his brow. "We were so close as children. Your mother was my mother's sister, and we were together so often, I felt as though you were more my brother than my cousin."

"When my mother was killed in cold blood by whites when I was but a young brave, I decided on a plan to help kill evil whites. I went and spied on them. I studied how scouts did their jobs, by watching when no one saw me. Then I became one, myself. I used my knowledge well, but only for the sake of our Dakota people."

"I know," Sheleen murmured. "I know."

She was terribly concerned about the blood he had lost, but fortunately the bleeding seemed to have stopped now.

She watched as he drifted into a restless sleep and held him until they finally reached the village.

Sheleen smiled weakly at Midnight Wolf as he beached the canoe and took Big Bear Moon from it. She was truly afraid that too much time had passed for her cousin to be saved.

She ran alongside Midnight Wolf to Moon Eagle's tepee. The recent confrontation between her and the shaman was forgotten as she knelt nearby while he cared for her cousin's wound.

"Please, oh, please, Moon Eagle, do all you can to see that Big Bear Moon lives, for he is my cousin," Sheleen sobbed out.

Moon Eagle paused long enough to give Sheleen a puzzled look.

"*Ho*, Moon Eagle, this full-blood Dakota is my cousin," she murmured. "My mother and his mother were sisters. Can you not now see, truly see, that it matters not that my skin is white? Can you not see that I am much more Dakota than white?"

Sudden tears filled Moon Eagle's old eyes. He nodded at Sheleen. "Please know that I welcome you among our people, to be the wife of our chief.

But please bring children into this world whose skin matches your Dakota ancestry."

At those words, Sheleen knew she had finally won part of the battle with the shaman. But the battle was not over. She realized now just how important it was that she give Midnight Wolf copper-skinned children!

Although no one but Moon Eagle would be so open in expressing their feelings about the color of their chief's children's skin, she knew that all would wish for the same as Moon Eagle!

But for now it was enough to know that Moon Eagle had finally accepted her!

She was free to marry the man she loved without always worrying about Moon Eagle's interference.

CHAPTER THIRTY-SIX

> My face turned pale as deadly pale,
> My legs refused to walk away,
> And when she looked, what could I ail?
> My life and all seemed turned to clay.
> —*John Clare*

Rosy Dawn stood back from the others as the people of the village waited outside Moon Eagle's tepee for Midnight Wolf and Sheleen to emerge.

Gentle Bear snuggled up more closely to his mother as he, too, waited. Surely by now Midnight Wolf knew why the warriors had gone for him and Sheleen.

Gentle Bear had been relieved to see that Midnight Wolf and Sheleen were all right, but the solemnness of his chief's face made him afraid to know what his chief thought of what he and his mother had done.

Rosy Dawn was filled with apprehension over what her chief might say to her when he left the shaman's tepee. She had seen no smile on his face earlier when he looked at her, and then Gentle Bear.

"Mother, I am afraid," Gentle Bear said, visibly shivering. "If Midnight Wolf does not forgive this newest error of mine, we might be banished even before the sun sets beneath the horizon today!"

"Come with me," Rosy Dawn said softly, placing a hand on his bare shoulder. "We will sit by our fire and wait for our chief, for you do know that he will seek us out as soon as he takes care of business in his shaman's lodge."

Gentle Bear walked forlornly beside his mother into their tepee, fighting back tears.

He tried to believe that his chief would forgive him this last transgression, for surely it was this transgression that had saved his and his woman's life!

Fluffy entered the lodge suddenly, causing Gentle Bear's eyes to widen. It was because of the cat that all of this had happened to him and his mother, because Fluffy had been away from their lodge so long that Gentle Bear had to look for her.

But he could never blame the cat. The animal had no sense of reason, and just went on its way enjoying itself.

"Where have you been?" Gentle Bear said, just as Fluffy crawled onto his lap.

He hugged the cat against his bare chest. "Shame

on you," he said. "If you only knew the trouble you have caused."

"Son, it was a blessing that Fluffy lured you away from your home," Rosy Dawn said, picking up a dress that she had finished except for the bead-work. Her hands trembled as she began sewing a bead on the bodice. "Had you not gone to search for Fluffy, you would never have seen the two men. And had you not seen them, neither you nor I would have known to send the warriors out to pro-tect our chief and his woman. My son, although you did wrong, as did I, the good that came from it is much greater."

She nodded as she sewed another bead on the dress. "*Ho,* after thinking it over, I do not see our chief scolding either one of us," she murmured. "He is a wise man, who thinks before he speaks. He will have thought through all of this before coming to our tepee to talk with us."

"Mother, I hope you are right," Gentle Bear sighed, as he stroked his fingers through Fluffy's thick fur. "I . . . hope . . . you are right."

He swallowed hard. "But do you think he will still want me as his charge?" he blurted out.

"*Ho,* he will still want you as his charge," Rosy Dawn said, nodding. "You are a fine young brave who is not afraid to act on his beliefs, even if he sometimes acts impulsively. That is a compliment, my son. It proves you care enough to try to right the wrongs you see."

Sheleen stood back from Midnight Wolf and Moon Eagle as Moon Eagle tore away Big Bear Moon's bloody shirt.

She felt dizzy when she saw the wound in her cousin's chest, but she had seen such wounds before and seen wounded patients survive.

She prayed her cousin would be one of those lucky ones.

She thought about her father's medical supplies in his satchel and longed to go for them and offer her assistance to the shaman. But she knew Moon Eagle would not appreciate her interference, so she stood there and watched him work his own magic.

After a few minutes, however, she could no longer keep quiet. She knelt down beside Midnight Wolf. "Will he live?" she asked softly.

She hated to think that she might lose her cousin after having been so recently reunited with him.

She thought about what he had done for her. He had accompanied the whiskered, four-fingered man on the hunt in order to keep the evil man from killing her. *Ho,* he had helped lead the man to her, but for his own reasons. After being parted from her for so long, he had found her and he had helped make sure that the evil man had not harmed her.

She gasped softly when the sound of her voice seemed to have brought Big Bear Moon out of his deep sleep.

His eyes fluttered open, and when he saw her

kneeling there so close, he smiled slowly and reached a shaky hand out for her.

Moon Eagle continued seeing to the wound as Big Bear Moon's hand clasped Sheleen's.

"Cousin, do not look so pale and afraid," Big Bear Moon said hoarsely. "Do you not know that I will not allow myself to leave you again after I have just found you? Sheleen, I will be fine."

"I have missed you so much," Sheleen sobbed out. "I always believed you were dead."

"As you see," he said softly, "I survived."

"And you will survive even this," Sheleen replied.

"I need to go and talk with Rosy Dawn and Gentle Bear," Midnight Wolf said, glancing over at Sheleen.

"Please go easy on them," Sheleen murmured, still holding her cousin's hand as though she was afraid to let it go.

"What they did was wrong, but it took courage to warn my warriors of the danger facing us," Midnight Wolf said.

"The woman is a woman of much courage," Big Bear Moon said, drawing Midnight Wolf and Sheleen's eyes to him. He winced when a sharp pain shot through his wound as Moon Eagle bandaged it. "As is the child. When I am well, I want to see them both and thank them for their part in stopping the evil white man."

Midnight Wolf and Sheleen gazed at each other in wonder at what Big Bear Moon had said, then smiled and nodded.

CASSIE EDWARDS

"*Ho*, what your cousin says is true," Midnight Wolf agreed. "It did take courage, much courage, for Rosy Dawn to hold the two men at bay with her rifle."

"So what will you say to her and Gentle Bear?" Sheleen asked, searching Midnight Wolf's eyes.

"The right thing," Midnight Wolf said, rising. He smiled at Sheleen and then at Big Bear Moon, and left.

After leaving the tepee, he found many of his people standing outside with questioning in his eyes.

He quickly explained the situation, then went on to Rosy Dawn's tepee.

As he stepped inside, he found Rosy Dawn and Gentle Bear beside the fire, with troubled looks on their faces.

He went and knelt beside them. "I understand what has happened, and why. Do not fret, either one of you, over what you did," Midnight Wolf said. He reached out and patted Gentle Bear on the shoulder. "You are still my charge."

Rosy Dawn burst into tears.

Gentle Bear set Fluffy aside, then crawled into Midnight Wolf's arms and clung to him, but he would not allow himself to cry. He just reveled in his chief's love as Midnight Wolf wrapped his arms around him.

"I am sorry," Gentle Bear said, even though he had already been forgiven.

"You have learned new lessons, and learning is good," Midnight Wolf said, stroking the child's bare back. "And I believe you have learned that this is the last time your chief will forgive you. Do you understand?"

Gentle Bear leaned away from his chief and looked him squarely in the eye. "I truly understand this time and I will not forget," he said, his jaw tight. "*Pilamaye*, thank you, my chief."

"I thank both you and your mother for sending warriors to protect me and my woman," Midnight Wolf said. "It took courage to reveal what you'd done. You put your chief and his woman ahead of concerns for yourself. It takes true bravery to put one's self in danger while saving others."

Sheleen came into the tepee and stood there for a moment, watching and listening.

Then she went and joined the group by the fire. "My cousin is going to be all right," she murmured.

"Your cousin?" Rosy Dawn said, her eyes widening.

"The scout who was with the white man is my cousin," Sheleen murmured. She then explained her relationship with Big Bear Moon, and what he had done in order to help save her.

"It has all worked out for the good," she said in closing.

She smiled as Fluffy came and crawled onto her lap. "And, Fluffy, what do you think about all of this?" she asked, stroking the cat's back.

Fluffy gazed up at her with her green eyes and meowed softly, then curled up on Sheleen's lap.

"And so everyone has come out of this situation all right, even my cat," Sheleen said, smiling at Midnight Wolf. "Now shall we tell them?"

Midnight Wolf smiled broadly. "*Ho*, they will be happy to hear that we are going to be married, as soon as possible," he said proudly. He looked from Gentle Bear to Rosy Dawn. "Sheleen is going to be my *mitawicu*."

Rosy Dawn rose quickly and hugged Sheleen; then she hugged her chief. "I am so happy," she murmured. She eased from her chief's arms and turned to Sheleen. "I shall make you the most beautiful wedding dress!"

"No, *we* shall make it," Sheleen said, laughing softly. "It is time for me to learn more than how to slide beads on a string."

They all laughed, the tepee filled with a soft, sweet happiness.

CHAPTER THIRTY-SEVEN

> Thou art my own,
> My darling and my wife;
> And when we pass into another life,
> Still art thou mine.
> —*Arthur Joseph Munby*

Several years later—November, The Moon of Falling Leaves

Sheleen stood at the entranceway of her tepee, gazing outside at the loveliness of the forest. Leaves of many colors still hung on the trees that stood near her people's village. Warm weather had lingered longer than usual, the evenings only now becoming frosty.

Ho, it was the best fall in a long time for the Dakota people.

And the hunt had been good, as well. There was

plenty of meat, which had been prepared to last them the long winter. Also there were parfleches of dried plums, fox grapes, buffalo berries, and turnips in every tepee.

And many sacks hung from the lodge poles, filled with the sacred herbs the women used for hurts and pains when illnesses were not severe enough to be treated by Moon Eagle.

Sheleen always enjoyed going away from the village for short spells with the other women. They gathered colored earth, yellow and brown dust of the puff balls, and other things of the forest that were used for paints.

She could not have ever had such a friend as Rosy Dawn had become. Gentle Bear's mother was now her cousin by marriage since Rosy Dawn and Big Bear Moon had wed. Their tepee stood right beside Sheleen and Midnight Bear's.

It was wonderful how they all enjoyed each other so much, especially now that both families had children, who were all as close to each other as brothers and sisters would be.

Gentle Bear carried a man's bow now and joined the warriors on their hunts. Alongside Big Bear Moon, he brought home much meat for Rosy Dawn's cook pot.

Midnight Wolf was away even now with his warrior friends, Gentle Bear and Big Bear Moon among them. They were hunting for fresh meat that would be used in today's and tomorrow's dinners.

Pride swelled inside Sheleen's heart as she watched her two sons, White Wolf and Yellow Hawk, playing with Big Bear Moon and Rosy Dawn's son. He was the same age as White Wolf, Midnight Wolf and Sheleen's first born, who was now six. A camaraderie such as she had never seen before had formed between these two children, and never had a brother been as proud as Gentle Bear was of his brother Gray Hawk.

Oft times, when Sheleen thought of Gentle Bear, she thought of the secret they shared . . . that of her dreams of wolves. Because she had told him that it was their secret only, she had not shared it even with her husband.

And it did not seem necessary to discuss the dreams now with anyone, for ever since her marriage she had had no more dreams of wolves. Her life was filled with contentment, and thus far there was no need of dreams to warn her of some upcoming tragedy. Secret Lake had remained that . . . secret, with no whites since Raymond Hauser coming anywhere close by to cause harm.

She hoped it would remain that way for many more years, yet deep inside herself she knew there would come a time when the white settlements would expand in Wisconsin to include land on which her loved ones now lived.

But until then, she would enjoy her happiness, and especially her family. She could never love a man any more dearly than she loved Midnight Wolf.

No, she had not shared her dreams of wolves with anyone but Gentle Bear. When he asked her one day if she had, she had told him that he was the only one who knew, because she had promised him that was the way it would be.

He had smiled, opened his medicine bag, and pretended to drop something inside with the other sacred things he carried with him on the hunt. He had said that what he was placing there was their secret; it would remain there forever.

Smiling, Sheleen closed the entrance flap and sat down beside the warmth of the fire. She picked up a doeskin dress that she had recently made and was now decorating with beadwork. She smiled as she thought of what the night would bring her . . . long hours of lovemaking with her husband after their children were asleep. She was hoping for another pregnancy . . . so that she could have a daughter to add to their family. And when she did, she would name her Whispering Waters, as her Dakota mother had been called.

That would complete her world of happiness!

Dear Reader,

I hope you enjoyed *Savage Intrigue*. The next book in my *Savage* series, which I am writing exclusively for Leisure Books, is *Savage Skies*, about the Assiniboine Indians. The book is filled with much passion, intrigue, and adventure.

Those of you who are collecting my Indian romance novels, and want to hear more about them and my entire backlist of books, can send for my latest newsletter, autographed bookmark, and fan club information, by writing to:

Cassie Edwards
6709 North Country Club Road
Mattoon, IL 61938

For an assured response, please include a stamped, self-addressed, legal-sized envelope with your letter. And you can visit my Web site at www.cassieedwards.com.

Thank you for supporting my Indian series. I love researching and writing about our beloved Native Americans, our country's true first people.

Always,
Cassie Edwards

Don't miss Victoria Morrow's sweeping saga of passion and revenge, set amid the blood, sweat and tears of linking East and West with the transcontinental railway.

Coming in September,

THE EAGLE

AND THE DOVE

CHAPTER ONE

Sangre de Cristo Mountain Range,
May 1851

He had been born in the dark of a November night twenty-four years before near the Canadian border. He was a Celt. The stark Highlands of his ancestry were apparent in his pale skin, which contrasted sharply with his dark eyes and hair. He towered over most men and spoke Gaelic fluently, the language his father spoke to him, as well as a curious mixture of French, English and Pigeon Blackfoot. He was a white man raised in a red world and comfortable in his skin.

He came from the high country where Old Man Winter still had a stranglehold on the land and the world was blinding white and his traps were full. He had ridden hard for nearly a week, pushing his big, dun-colored stallion until its powerful body was bathed in lather and its once nimble legs shook from exhaustion.

He slept little and ate less. Pulling a piece of deer jerky from his pack every now and then, he would suck on it until it softened and the smoky juices ran down his parched throat. He was going toward the dunes at the base of the ridge, a mountain man covered in buck-skins and fur with a shock of wild, midnight hair blowing in the wind and piercing, black eyes locked onto the horizon. He wasn't alone.

Above him in the zinc-colored sky, an elegant falcon-hawk circled lazily, easily keeping pace with his relentless speed; traveling beside him loped a lean slant-eyed wolf. The three were companions, a trinity of primitive power; beating wings, talons, fangs, sinew and cunning, bound together by the knowledge that they were of the same clan: predators. Yet, though all were formidable, the mountain man was, by far, the most dangerous of the three. Cresting a bald ridge of rock, he pulled back on the soaking reins, stopping abruptly in a shower of powder-red dust and fragments of nail-thin shale.

"Ease up, horse," he growled as he absently wiped the sweat from his upper lip. "'Tis the blighted camp of the Philistines."

His voice, though companionably soft, was filled with such unmistakable menace that his horse's ears came to attention and began to dance as nervously as its feet. Narrowing his eyes, the man studied the scene below.

Hatred, there was hatred in every breath he took, in every shuddering beat of his heart. And he didn't turn away from it—instead he touched it, breathed it in, owned it until he became it.

Other men might have walked away, trusting God or a badge to fight their battles for them. But not him. His blessing and his curse was the nobility of his soul. He knew right from wrong and took responsibility for every thought, action or deed his mouth uttered or hand performed, expecting others to do the same.

God might show mercy, but Jesse McCallum wouldn't.

Beneath him, nestled as contentedly near the root of the Sangre de Cristo Mountains as an infant to its mother's teat, was a small, crudely built cabin. Massive dunes of rolling sand surrounded it on three sides while on the fourth, a vertical wall of granite effectively sealed the basin from the rest of the range. No one could approach from across the dunes without being seen for miles.

Jesse knew the odds and weighed his options carefully. He knew it was certain suicide for anyone to attempt to approach the cabin on foot or by horse, especially in daylight. Yet he knew that even if he had to go through the front door with his guns blazing, he would do whatever it took to bring his father's killers to justice.

Calmly he noted that behind the house stood a makeshift pen fashioned with posts of thorny mesquite and rails of frayed hemp, spliced now and then with bits of knotted rags that still hinted at some nearly forgotten color. Every few feet, empty cans that were once filled with succulent peaches, tangy stewed tomatoes and other such citified delicacies, were tied to the uppermost rope, clanking noisily like a poor-man's chimes with each passing gust of wind. The "gate"— and it was charity to call it that—was nothing more than the mummified remains of a buckboard, bleached nearly white and laid on its side. Decorating its sagging top were stiff gray blankets, mile-worn saddles, tangled leather traces and rusty bits, one for each of the dozen horses and the odd assortment of New Mexico mules, mingling without prejudice, in the little pen. Just outside the corral and within mere spitting distance from the front door of the house was a pyramid of packs filled to overflowing with stolen booty.

All of this Jesse noted without a hint of surprise, as though he had beheld the scene many times before in the misty landscape of his mind. Yet he knew the picture wasn't complete, so he continued to search, scanning the grounds until he found the missing pieces to the puzzle he had come so far to solve.

"There you are!" he said.

His voice sounded strange. His words were whispered, barely more than a phantom of sound, spoken so gently they seemed less than a sigh. But what a frightful expression colored his eyes! They gleamed like black opals filled with infernal fire, hellish in intensity and intent.

Cursed.

It was as if the tortured soul imprisoned within the massive tower of flesh was slowly dying. A once proud soul ravaged so savagely by the cold hand of guilt that it believed itself lost forever. Beyond hope. Beyond forgiveness. Dead to everything except pain.

He suffered in silence, and he suffered alone.

"And here I am," he said at last.

He announced his arrival in a voice so heartbreakingly soft, so filled with sorrow and regret that the fickle wind seemed to moan in sympathy as it passed.

His journey was over; the circle was about to close....

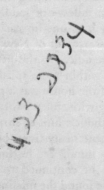